DISCLAIMER

Whisper of Fate is a dark paranormal romance that contains explicit content, graphic violence, profanity, and topics that may be sensitive to some readers.

Trigger warnings:

Graphic gore/death, torture, threats of sexual assault, drug use, historic child abuse (not on page) and sexually explicit scenes.

This book is written in British English, including spelling and grammar.

WHISPER OF FATE

CURSE OF THE GUARDIANS BOOK THREE

TAYLOR ASTON WHITE

DARK WOLF
PUBLISHING

Edited by Alexander Small
Cover by MiblArt

www.taylorastonwhite.com
Official Taylor Aston White Newsletter

Author Note

Sam's happy ever after has been a long time coming, and for everyone who's loved him since the first Alice Skye book, I hope I've done you proud.

To my professional gay, Aaron, whom was my knight in shining armour when writing certain *cough* scenes. You're amazing, and without your knowledge of male appendages, I would've had to resort to terrible 80's porn.

Lastly, for the homophobes who thought it was appropriate to leave rude reviews or comments because Sam settled for another guy, fuck you!

Much love,
   Tay

SUMMARY

He's tried everything to make the pain go away... *except* **him.**

Sam refuses to let his traumatising past dictate his future, so embraces life to the fullest. Stable, independent and attracted to a Guardian who's off limits, Sam couldn't be happier... until his father comes back from the dead.

Facing memories he's suppressed from childhood, and a new threat he never saw coming, Sam struggles to keep the life he's built from crumbling.

Cursed as a child and scarred from addiction, **Axel** never thought his life could get much worse. Until the poison that helps relieve his pain starts to affect his work, the sole reason for his existence.

With nothing else to lose, he finally gives into his desire that he's suppressed for so long, breaking his celibacy with the one man he's always wanted. But he quickly figures out there's something dark lurking in the shadows, ready to test his control.

As everything unfolds Axel must decide what's more important, Sam's life, or his own.

BREED INDEX

Celestrial - Also known as 'angels.' Can lose their powers and wings, known as 'falling'

Magic class - Unknown

Origin realm - Unknown

Other - Once a celestrial has fallen, they're rumoured to be as weak as humans, but none have openly confirmed (See Fallen Angel)

Daemon - Druids who choose to ascend into black magic. In return for more power, they sacrifice their bodies and sanity

Magic class - Black

Origin realm - The Nether (also known as Hell)

Other - Once imprisoned in The Nether, they now freely move between realms

Druid - Born male, druid genes are inherited from the fathers.

Magic class - Natural/Arcane. Can be strengthened with Ley Lines

Origin realm - Earth Side

Other - Breed governed by the Archdruid. When they come of age they must tattoo a siphon, known as a glyph, around their wrists to better control their arcane

Guardian - Druids who were cursed to share their soul with a 'beast.' Their bodies, including their 'beast' form, are designed to battle Daemons, with increased strength, agility and ability to survive severe damage

Magic class - Natural/Arcane. Can be strengthened with Ley Lines and glyphs

Origin realm - Earth Side

Beast - Unknown

Other - The Archdruid made the deal with Hadriel, the Fallen Angel who powers The Nether, creating the curse in return for soldiers

Fae - Umbrella term for anyone from Far Side. Includes faeries, selkies, pixies etc. Split into two castes, light (Seelie) and dark (Unseelie)

Magic class - Wild Magic

Origin realm - Asherah of Far (also known as Far Side)

Other - Never say thank you, and be wary of gifts (Fae stuff seem to have a mind of their own)

Fallen Angels - Celestrials that have 'fallen'

Magic class - Unknown

Origin realm - Unknown, but now reside on Earth Side

Other - Hide themselves amongst humans, always trying to regain their wings

Ghoul - Name for a failed vampire transition. Primal instincts only

Magic class - N/A
Origin realm - Earth Side
Other - Killed on sight

Human - Class themselves as the 'original' species on Earth Side. They have no access to their chi
Magic class - N/A
Origin realm - Earth Side
Other - Make over 60% of the population

Shifter - Born with a animal spirit, able to transform into said animal
Magic class - N/A
Origin realm - Earth Side
Other - Are not infectious, despite rumours. Usually live in groups/packs with a strict hierarchy

Witch - Humans who were gifted the ability to access their chi. Magic originated from the four elements, diluting through generations
Magic class - Arcane (balls of concentrated chi), Natural (plants) and Black (blood/death)
Origin realm - Earth Side
Other - Rumoured that it was Fae royalty who originally gifted humans magic

Vampire - Humans who've been infected by the Vampira virus
Magic class - N/A
Origin realm - Earth Side
Other - Low success rate, resulting in death and/or Ghouls. If turn is successful they must feed from a live source, surviving on proteins found in fresh blood

SHADOW-VEYN INDEX

Shadow-Veyn are wild creatures easily influenced by Daemons. They hide themselves from the general populace with glamour, but lower class cannot hide their shadows (hence their name)

Magic class - N/A

Origin realm - The Nether (Hell)

Other - Along with Daemons, they're no longer imprisoned in The Nether. Feed upon flesh, and as of yet, no evidence that they breed

Classifications -

A - Small. Weak. Used as scouts.

B - Venomous. Covered in black fur.

C - Can heal using dark vapour.

D - Scales as strong as armour, as well as fur.

E - Defined by sheer size, and extra bones along spine.

WHISPER OF FATE

CURSE OF THE GUARDIANS
BOOK THREE

TAYLOR ASTON WHITE

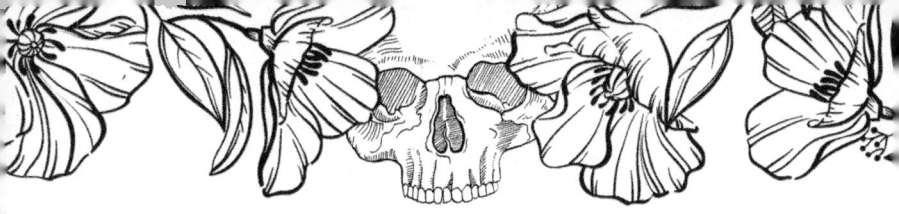

CHAPTER 1

SAM

S am smiled, listening to the woman who had just ordered a large Martini excitedly spill her day's gossip in one, long drunken slur.

Working behind a bar was, honestly, the fucking best.

The drama.

The love.

The heartbreak.

The sheer fucking chaos that followed anywhere alcohol was served. He watched it all from his position, flair-tending bottles and making cocktails as if it were an art, all while dancing and listening to countless stories.

"Axel's been in the bathroom for a long time," Payne said when Sam's customer finally took a breath in her story, flipping a bottle over her shoulder to the enthusiastic crowd watching by the bar. She turned to the person who'd ordered the drink, pouring the concoction into a glass.

"He drinks like a fish, what do you expect?" Sam replied, winking at a particularly beautiful woman who had just ordered one of their signature blood cocktails. Blood wasn't exactly a common ingredient found in your regular alcoholic drinks, but it added a little extra for those that preferred some iron with their vodka. Blood Bar had been one of the first establishments in the area to offer the option, the license alone costing a small fortune.

"You know exactly what I'm talking about." Payne took the money, quickly adding it into the register before moving on to the next customer. She was a dark shadow in both appearance and personality, the perfect juxtaposition to Sam's bright and friendly approach. But they worked well together, and he genuinely enjoyed teasing her until she smiled. Which was as often as the full moon.

"Enlighten me."

"Don't deny that you're interested." Payne pursed her lips, rolling her eyes when Sam sniggered. "I can smell a lie, you know."

"Aye, sure you can. And I'm the King of England."

"Titus asked me to keep a watch on him, and if you don't deal with it, I'll have to." Payne's copper eyes glistened. "We both know how he would prefer if it was *you* who checked on him."

Sam swallowed his hiss. "He's not interested in me like that, we're friends." He was more than aware that Axel watched him work, but so did everyone else in the bar. He put on a show, making sure to smile and flirt with everyone who waited in his section.

Besides, Axel was one of the Guardians, and they were off limits.

Which was a fucking shame.

"He's not into guys." Not that Sam really knew what Axel was into, the man never took up any offers from the bar, regardless of gender or Breed.

"Well, I disagree. He's into you and you're just too pussy to take it further. Pun intended."

Sam slammed down the glass harder than he intended. "You're a bitch, you know that right?"

Payne's lips were pressed tight, suppressing a smile as she turned her back, gesturing for the next customer to give her their order.

Sam shook his head. It was mid-week, yet Blood Bar seemed to be consistently busy, regardless of the time or day. Sam wasn't sure whether it was because of the location, quality of the cocktails or because one of the hottest bachelors in the city owned the place. Well, *had* been one of the hottest bachelors.

Riley Storm was no longer a bachelor considering he had soulbound to Alice, Sam's best friend and platonic soul mate. But the fact Riley was no longer single didn't seem to stop the gossip magazines from sprouting their usual bull-shit. Good thing Alice wasn't the jealous type, because no way would Sam put up with that crap. When he mated, he would make sure every fucker knew. Not that mating was really ever an option.

Why have one person for the rest of your life when you could have multiple? At once.

"Look, I caught him a few weeks ago snorting some powder," Payne said over her shoulder. "What if he's moved onto some harder stuff?"

"You caught him what?" Sam slammed down the glass harder than needed. "You got it from here?"

Payne dismissed him with a wave of her hand, the gold she had painted up her arm complimenting the matching beads in her black waist-length box braids. Sam jumped over the bar, moving his way through the crowd towards the men's bathroom.

It was late, but the horde still hadn't thinned, sweaty bodies dancing to the music. He made sure to smile and wave at whoever was close, wary of the attention. Usually he enjoyed the casual touch, a gentle stroke down his arm or a relaxed hug. He was a shifter after all, and his Breed thrived on the physical connection. But right then he didn't want to be touched, not when tension vibrated beneath his skin.

According to Alice, he was the image of a pretty-boy surfer, with long, white blonde hair, a warm tan, and a carefree attitude. But just because he looked harmless didn't mean he was. Yet again, he had met many a Breed and human alike who were stupid enough to initiate intimate skin privileges without permission. Those who didn't follow basic etiquette were quick to see his claws, unless they were hot. Then maybe he could be a little more forgiving.

Luckily, everyone kept to themselves as he entered the men's room, the stalls all empty bar one.

"Axel?" he called, closing the bathroom door behind him, quieting the music and voices of the crowd. "You in here?"

There was a grunt, glass shattering. "Fuck."

Placing an open hand on the stall door, Sam pressed it open slowly. Axel was sat with his back against the white tiles beside the toilet, his knees pressed against the opposite stall wall, and just like every bloody time, Sam felt an instant jerk in his stomach. Axel was one of the most devastatingly handsome men he had even seen. He usually kept his dark brown hair shaved close to his skull, but Sam was grateful that he'd allowed it to grow out, the strands having a slight curl he dreamed about brushing his fingers through. Axel's eyes were a deep hazel that shifted between green and brown with flecks of gold, and he had a jaw that looked chiselled from marble. All his hard lines were emphasised by the stubble that should have made him look homeless, but instead gave him a dishevelled, sexy vibe.

Then there were his lips, thicker than usual for a man, but somehow only added to the sheer masculinity that radiated from him in waves.

"Hey there, kitty cat," Axel said, his words slower than usual, and that was when Sam scented the sharp acidic liquid that had leaked from the broken vial by his heavy boot. It had been hot, cracking the tile on the floor.

Axel shifted to the side, drawing attention to the tourniquet tied around his thick bicep, his sleeve pulled up to reveal skin covered in tattooed glyphs.

"What the fuck, man?" Sam stepped inside, careful to not step on the shards. He knelt, grabbing Axel's wrist and pulling it closer. A hypodermic needle was still sticking out from inside his arm, empty. "What did you take?"

Axel only smiled, and Sam suppressed a growl when his eyes steadied on him, the pupils blown wide.

Grabbing for the needle he ignored Axel's frown, carefully placing it on the top of the toilet basin in clear view. His skin had healed immediately, not even a pearl of blood left as Sam pulled the tourniquet off next, shoving it into the back of his jeans' pocket.

Reaching down, he gripped Axel's jaw. "What. Did. You. Take?" He tried to emphasise every word as Axel smiled lazily.

"You're so fucking beautiful," he whispered, hand slowly stretching up to touch the ends of Sam's hair. It had fallen over his shoulder, and Sam quickly flicked it back and out of his reach. "Hey," Axel growled. "Mine."

Sam ignored the way his heart was beating against his ribcage. "Come on big guy, concentrate." Panic edged his tone. "What did you take?"

Axel frowned. "I didn't take anything."

Sam allowed his chest to vibrate, an internal growl as he pulled Axel's arm over his shoulder, hauling him to his feet.

Something crashed to the floor, and before Sam could see what it was, a ring echoed. "Bloody hell." Releasing

Axel, who swayed slightly but stayed upright, he reached for the phone, the screen slightly cracked.

"Hey, we need a pickup..."

"Yeah, I don't think he's able to drive," Sam replied firmly, watching Axel warily.

"Sam? Why do you have Axel's phone? Fuck, how bad is he?"

"Just get here before he does something even fucking stupider," Sam growled down the line. "And be fast." Before he could add any more the phone died, and Sam dropped it beside the needle, wiping his hand down his black work t-shirt. It had been covered in the acidic smelling liquid, not to mention whatever else was on the bathroom floor.

Axel pushed past, and before Sam could catch him, he was already out through the emergency exit and into the alley directly behind. He steadied himself on the brick wall, hands flat and shoulders hunched as he let out a slow, unsteady breath.

Sam waited, the noise from the bar a gentle vibration beneath his feet, the music muffled through the door. He couldn't leave, not until one of Axel's brothers collected him. What if he choked? Or overdosed?

"What the fuck, Axel?" Sam said between gritted teeth, anger and frustration darkening his tone. "At Blood Bar, really?"

Axel remained silent, the only evidence he heard was the slight contraction of his shoulders.

"I've seen you high a few times, but a fucking needle? What's wrong with you? Why would you do that to yourself?" Sam felt the presence of his leopard, deciding he needed his animal's strength to stop from punching Axel square in his beautiful fucking face.

"You make everything go away," Axel said, his voice so

soft as he turned that Sam strained to hear. "So fucking quiet."

"Well, I'm not being fucking quiet right now!" Sam seethed, even more so at Axel's smirk, his eyes hooded.

"You don't make it hurt." Axel continued, stepping forward until his breath was a warmth against the cooler wind. They were almost level, his height only an inch or two taller. Axel took another step, forcing Sam to back away until he felt the heavy door pressed against his back.

Sam stilled, Axel's attention dropping to his lips as he planted both palms against the wood, trapping Sam between them.

Tension thrummed, confusing his leopard's instincts. He was being pushed by someone bigger, stronger, and yet rather than attack he wanted to see what Axel would do. It wasn't like he was a stranger, not considering Sam had been working at that particular bar on and off for years and would even call Axel a friend. He was one of the brothers of his boss, after all.

The air burned between them, static as Axel dropped his head, his lips so close that Sam instinctively opened his. It was wrong, he knew that as they stood bathed in the shadows. And yet his pulse raced, blood a roar in his ears that drowned out his conscience to leave nothing but a strained promise.

"What are you doing?" he whispered, and Axel seemed to tremble at his voice, all sin and threat wrapped tightly in leather. Fighting clothes. Why was Axel in fighting clothes?

Axel's breathing hitched, and Sam froze as one of his hands moved to grip his hip. "I don't know."

"Axel you're high, you don't want –" Sam's words were swallowed, and he all but groaned at the first touch, pressing against Axel, who kissed him like a man starved. Sam wanted to purr, embrace the force at which Axel pushed him, pinning him to the wall as his other hand wrapped tightly in his hair.

Axel tasted like fucking heaven, his tongue sweeping across Sam's lips in a dominant swipe. In any other situation he would have embraced it, would have even gone to his knees right there in the alley because that was what he did, what he was good at. Sex was a language Sam was fluent in, but as he pulled back for a breath, he realised Axel's eyes were open, vacant. Sam could have been anyone, and while that usually worked fine with all his other lovers, right then it pissed him off.

Sam bit Axel's lip when he went in for another kiss, drawing blood. "Get the –" A sharp pain along his scalp, and then suddenly Axel was a few steps away, breathing heavily with Sam's hair tie and a few blonde strands wrapped in a tight fist.

His smile was crooked, his eyes hazy. "Here kitty, kitty," he chuckled, but the sound was hollow. "You know you want to come play."

Sam released a hiss, stepping forward to shove against Axel's hard chest. "Aye, if you carry on, I'll happily sharpen my claws on your bones."

A pause, Axel's voice deepening. "Is that a promise?"

Sam's jeans tightened, but his anger was stronger, hotter than the desire that clenched his stomach and had him wanting to stroke his naked body against the man who literally looked like a sex god.

Off limits, he reminded himself, opening his mouth to reply. The retort caught on his tongue just as the door to the bar opened.

"What's he taken?" Kace asked as he appeared.

Axel tilted his head towards his brother, a fake smile curving his lips. "Hey there K, you joining the party?"

Sam scowled, knowing his leopard prowled behind his

eyes. He shared the same colour iris as his animal, a bright amber that glowed slightly when he called on the instincts of his leopard. It was rare, and Sam always lied about the reason his eyes were that of a predator.

No one but his best friend knew the truth, and even then, he never went into detail, and she had never asked.

"I don't know," Sam said as he dragged a hand through his hair, tugging the loose strands behind his ears. "I found him slumped in the fucking toilets." He felt Axel's attention, his gaze a brand that Sam refused to meet. "He's high as a fucking kite. He won't tell me what he took, but I found a needle."

"Sam, can you give us a minute?" Kace was rigid, his temper barely controlled.

Axel tensed, but Sam simply nodded, his own anger an acidic taste on his tongue. "I've never seen him like this."

Kace clenched his fist. "I'll deal with it."

Sam didn't look back at Axel, not when his lips were still sensitive from their kiss.

The music and dancing hadn't slowed down, and Payne waved at him from across the room as Sam parted the crowd. This time he didn't return the flirtatious smiles, the attention like oil on his fur, unwanted and hard to get off. He held up his finger, asking for a moment as he made his way back to the bathroom and to the same stall where he found Axel. Closing himself inside he crouched, pressing the palms of his hands into his eyes.

It wasn't the first time he had caught Axel sneaking pills, powders and alcohol. But it was the first finding him on the hard stuff. Brimstone, he guessed, from the acidic scent that still polluted the small space.

Sam understood the need for a release, an escape, but drugs were never a vice he could lose himself in. So instead, he fucked like it was a catharsis, not caring who he was with as long as he felt good, and for those few moments he was nothing but pleasure. It wasn't exactly an approved method of therapy, but it worked. His nightmares were all but gone, and he lived life to the fullest.

His past was his past, and he refused to let it dictate his future.

Drugs would take away his control, and he would never put himself into a position where someone could take advantage.

No. Never again.

"Fuck's sake," he whispered, glancing up at the needle. He grabbed it, wrapping it in tissue paper before he took it with him behind the bar to discard safely later. He took the phone too, placing it in the lost and found box for Axel to deal with when he sobered up.

Payne frowned at his expression when he returned, but knew not to push. "Did you see those creeps dressed as skeletons outside?" she said, trying to lighten to mood. "It's like they don't realise Samhain isn't for another five months."

Sam didn't bother with an answer, instead turning to the next customer, who was a woman barely five foot, and who blushed when he smiled. She pulled back her shoulders, presenting her breasts while she asked for a drink. She would be easy enough to talk into his bed, and he could lose himself in her gorgeous body while thinking about the one Guardian that he had no business desiring.

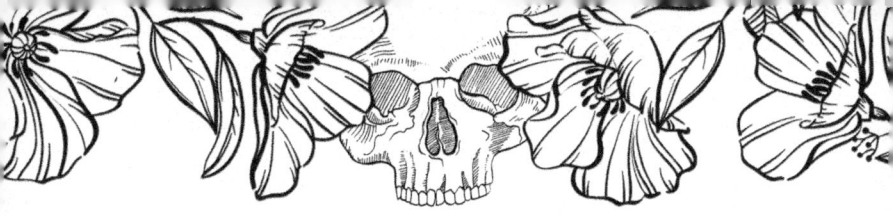

CHAPTER 2
AXEL

FOUR WEEKS LATER

A xel had smoked so much he wasn't sure whether he could feel his face, never mind the serrated knife that had just sliced through his abs like fucking butter.

"Fuck, you okay?" Titus asked as he shot the Shadow-Veyn that raced towards them between its eyes. A classification A scavenger who was eating the remains of some poor bastard. Not that much remained of the body, which meant they didn't need to call and deal with clean-up. Silver linings.

Sythe let out a grunt, swinging his sword at the possessed human who had just tried to re-decorate Axel's insides. Hunting for Shadow-Veyn and Daemons had become a full-time job, the activity skyrocketing in the last few months to the point there were constant sightings.

People were going missing, creatures made from night-mares were being found lurking in the dark and not to mention the sheer number of fucking possessions. Daemons were clearly lazy bastards, using a conduit to run their errands rather than doing it themselves. Luckily, in a city as populated as London, one or two people a week acting out of character, eating their pets, or drawing dark runes on their kitchen floor wasn't going to be noticed.

At least not yet.

Sythe swung his sword again, cutting across the man's chest in one clean cut. There was no blood, just a black sludge that seeped into his shirt. It was a nice shirt, white with delicate little blue flowers. Except now it was ruined. His trousers were well made, black slacks that looked expensive apart from the dirt and mud that caked the hem. His shoes too. Loafers, which weren't the obvious choice for a murder spree.

Or maybe they were, Axel couldn't exactly judge his attire when he lived in t-shirts, leather, and boots.

"You're not supposed to slaughter him," Titus said, shooting another scavenger who appeared from within a storm drain. His voice was always so soft, relaxed, which was at odds with his appearance. Not to mention the fact he was shooting Veyn with such fucking precision while looking bored out of his mind. What was even better was the fact his gun was covered in glitter, thanks to Axel and a few hours with some glue. He had chosen various shades of grey and silver because he wasn't a monster. It went with Titus's style of black, black, and black.

"Do you see him dead?" Sythe muttered. "I'm just having a little fun with our boy here."

"You're all going to die," the man said, but it wasn't really the man who had spoken. His mouth was open, throat unmoving as the voice projected itself from deep within the shell. A puppet with a hidden ventriloquist.

"Oh, thank the Fates," Sythe said with a dramatic sigh. "I thought my existence would never end."

The man screeched, bending back until he was almost

in half. His head turned, neck at an impossible angle. "*He's coming for you all.*"

"Fuck, I think we need to call a chiropractor," Sythe said, cocking his head to better meet the man's red, empty gaze.

"Release your vessel," Titus said calmly. "This one's already broken."

The man snapped his teeth together, hard enough one cracked. "Not until you submit to us. Imagine what we could do, together."

Axel pulled himself to his feet, quickly checking his stomach. He'd stopped bleeding, and was already healed enough that he wouldn't pass out. Probably. There was no pain from the wound, in fact there was no pain at all thanks to whatever he'd smoked earlier. His beast for which he shared his soul was still present, a static energy that never rested no matter how many drugs he took. It was constant, a violent buzz across his entire body. When he wasn't on narcotics it hurt, every muscle on fire while his beast ravaged his mind. Then there were the relentless whispers, white noise and intrusive thoughts that were just as maddening.

Unlike his brothers, he had never heard his beast communicate, not in words or even desires. Nothing other than the pain and persistent discordance.

Something was broken between them, and had been since the ritual when he was forced to take the beast into his body as a child. He had no choice then, and he had no choice now. The beast would be forever with him until death.

Which was looking more and more appealing each passing day.

"Submit?" Axel chuckled. "I'm sorry, Ti likes to be the dominant one in the bedroom. What's it Cousin? Ropes and paddles?" His grin stretched when Titus shot him a pointed glare.

The possessed man straightened, and Axel cringed at each click of his spine realigned. Not many of the vessels survived the possession, and the man was already looking like hammered shit. The longer the Daemon controlled them, the more they started to deteriorate. The man's skin was relatively clean, no evidence of decay but his left arm was broken, the bone protruding sharply. There were cuts along his face, the surrounding area red and puffy as infection had set in and some of his fingers were bent at the wrong angle. If he was released, he still had to survive his injuries.

The man looked between them all, his movements uneven, jerky.

Sythe crossed his arms, his sword carefully pointed to the cobbled stones. "This is pointless. We'll just force him out."

"Fine by me." Axel shot across the space, tackling the man around the waist as they both fell to the hard ground. He ignored the punch to his side, feeling a rib break at the borrowed strength that pumped though the man's skinny arms. "Stop. Fucking. Moving," he snarled as he straddled the man, his arms pinned beneath Axel's knees.

"Effective," Titus said dryly.

"Fuck off and write the fucking glyph." Axel clenched his thighs, trying to keep the man from bucking him off, like it was some sort of rodeo. Titus was right, it wasn't the most glamorous way of restraining someone, but it worked.

Sythe laughed, a full belly chuckle that had him bending almost in half. "The guys aren't going to believe this. If you needed to get laid Axel, you could have just asked. I know a few guys who would happily wrap their lips around your –"

"Shut the fuck up," Axel growled. "Do the fucking spell before I beat your arse too."

"Okay, calm down there, Pretty Boy." Sythe's smile remained as he dropped down beside them, reaching into the man's pocket for his wallet. "His name's Rodney Collier, forty-two, and lives in the city. Oh look, he's a member of the Church of Light. " He tossed the wallet to the floor. "Makes you a big fucking bigot there, Rodney boy. I'm not even that upset that you're possessed, you probably deserved it considering you follow a faith that dictates anyone not entirely human as inferior."

Titus grumbled, "I didn't even think that church was still going, wasn't their leader killed or something?"

"You know people like that always crawl out of the fucking dirt, like little cockroaches." Sythe smirked. "Rodney, if you're in there and can hear me call you a worthless little twat, blink twice."

"Like he's going to be able to answer you right now," Titus muttered, eyes constantly scanning their surroundings. Shadow-Veyn would have scented the Daemonic blood, even if it wasn't full blooded. They were wild creatures, but they loved to serve their masters. It probably reminded them of their home in The Nether, Hell.

Sythe brushed a finger down his blade to collect the blood, and with his other hand he held the man's jaw, keeping him immobile as he carefully drew the glyph on his cheek.

"This is not the end, you will all fall to *Him*," Rodney, but not Rodney said, his movements slowing as Sythe finished the first half of the symbol. "*He* will be the new God, and he will make even the Fates fall to their knees."

With each circle he completed, the skin burned, the stench sickening as he went slack beneath Axel's grip.

"We don't give a shit about the Fates," Sythe said, a line

between his brows as he concentrated. "They left us a long time ago."

The red in Rodney's irises flickered, revealing a warm, honey brown. They knew instantly when the Daemon released Rodney's body, able to feel the darkened energy dissipating like prickles against their chis. That and Rodney's full-bodied scream.

"What happened?" he cried, head tossing from side to side as Sythe stood to his full height. His eyes levelled on Axel, and Axel couldn't get up fast enough as Rodney let out another scream. He began to scramble away, but his broken arm was useless as he tried to support his weight. He finally managed to sit up, cradling his arm across his chest.

"Calm down, you were possessed." Titus slowly knelt to Rodney's level, placing his gun in the holster under his arm. He must have looked terrifying to the human, his blonde hair obscuring his face by the wind, his large body hidden in dark fabrics and shadows. He had even painted black under his eyes, emphasising the delicate almond shape inherited from his maternal grandmother. When you added the tattoos that covered almost his entire skin, bar his face, and the piercings, he looked like Death.

"Possessed?" Rodney echoed.

Titus touched the ring that went through the centre of his bottom lip, a frustrated gesture. "Yes Rodney, keep up. Now I need you to tell me everything you can remember."

"Remember?"

"Oh for fuck's sake, I think he's broken." Sythe cleaned his bloody blade against his thigh.

"Rodney, can you tell me the name of the Daemon who possessed you?"

Rodney's eyes widened, frightened gaze flicking between all three of them. Axel slowly crouched; his smile friendly. "Hey, we're just trying to help you." His words calmed Rodney, at least enough that the edge of fear had disappeared from his lips. "Now, can you tell us what happened? What's the last thing you remember?"

Rodney took his time replying, his eyes taking in every inch of Axel's face. He knew what he saw, bone structure that even the most handsome of models would die for. It was his face, and he hated it, a reminder of what his mother was. Out of all the Breed, his father just had to fuck a succubus, a faerie literally designed to consume men though sex. He had tried over the years to make himself less appealing, but her DNA was in him as much as that of his father's.

"I'm human, you can trust me." The words were ash in his mouth, but if he was a member of the Church of the Light it was the one thing that would calm him enough to speak.

Rodney visibly relaxed.

What a fucking prick.

"They said it wouldn't be like that," he commented, tears burning down his face. "They promised they wouldn't take over entirely, just enough that I could carry out my mission unharmed."

"Who promised? What mission? I need details Rodney if you want me to help you." Anger kissed his bloodstream, and it took everything to keep himself under control.

Rodney gasped, and the scent of piss just added to the overall stench of death. "You're not... you're not."

Titus sighed, and only then did Axel feel his beast push at his mind.

Oh, fuck.

His eyes had changed to silver, eyes no human could ever possess.

"Good cop routine working well I see," Sythe chuckled.

"You heathens!" Rodney screeched. "What are you? What have you done to –" His words were cut off by billows of black smoke. His eyes rounded as thick arms wrapped around him from behind, and before anyone could react, he disappeared into the darkness with a violent yank.

It took less than two seconds, and all three of them looked at the little puddle of blood left behind, dumbfounded that a Daemon could drift Rodney away so quickly.

"Well, hot damn," Sythe said. "That was pretty impressive, actually."

"He knew he was going to be possessed," Titus said, crossing his arms across his chest. "Maybe even invited it."

"He was bloody strong, and fast," Axel added, fingering the hole in his stomach. "More so than usual."

Sythe sheathed his sword. "Possibly because he willingly gave over his body?"

"I have no idea, but it can't be good." Titus rolled his shoulders. "Honestly, who willingly gives their body over for possession?"

"Idiots who believe they're superior?" Axel looked around for the blade that had sliced him, finding it beside the bins a short distance away.

"It makes no sense," Sythe muttered as he pulled out his phone. "But we can update the guys when we get to the bar, we still have a few hours before it closes."

Axel stepped to the side, checking for any pills left. He felt his cousin's presence a second later, quickly bending to grab the knife as he slipped his hand, empty, back out of his pocket.

"What are you –"

"Nothing," Axel interrupted. "And before you ask, I haven't taken anything." A lie, but one he told often. Besides, he couldn't even remember what the fuck he had smoked. It was probably a joint, but it definitely had something extra. "So, are we going out tonight or what?"

Titus narrowed his eyes, jaw taut. "We're going to Blood, everyone's playing tonight."

Of. Fucking. Course we're going there, he thought. Not only was he avoiding the place because of his situation with Sam, which he remembered vividly, but he couldn't risk buying drugs with all his brothers present. Which meant he had to wait, and hope he remained numb against the pain.

"Great," he said with a strained smile. "Let's get going."

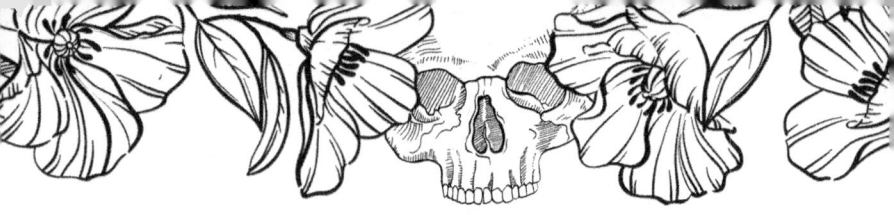

CHAPTER 3

SAM

S am matched his voice to the rock song, butchering the lyrics while Payne watched with a raised brow.

The bar had been invaded by a bachelorette party, and while they didn't have exclusive access, they were the majority of the crowd as they danced with their inflatable sex dolls and bright pink tutus. The bar itself had been pretty quiet since the bride ordered everyone in the room several shots. The party were now happy to just dance the rest of the night away on the small dance floor, which was – Sam looked up at the clock – only a few hours.

"I bet they would give you a big tip if you danced on the bar," Payne said.

Sam sniggered, hearing the dare in her tone. "Let's make a bet. If I get over one-hundred in tips you have to curtsey, and smile at every single customer you serve for the next week."

Payne stared intently, but he noticed her upper lip twitch. "If you get over one-hundred in a *single* tip, I will smile at every customer on my next shift."

"And curtsey?"

"And curtsey," she growled.

Sam winked, hopping onto the bar. "Deal."

Payne hid her smile, turning to the media station to change the song. It gave a few seconds of silence, and that was when Sam whistled over to the dance floor. "This is for the bride-to-be." The heavy beat started, but he was already moving, borrowing the grace from his leopard as he danced, rolling his body to the music.

The bachelorette party squealed, rushing over to get a better look as he danced, using the entire bar to showcase what he could do. Teasing his fingers at the edge of his t-shirt he pulled it up to show his abs, his jeans already low on his hips. He waited for the response, going by the crowds excited scream before he pulled it fully off to expose his scarred chest. The pale marks no longer bothered him, but some of the women reached as if to touch, and he twisted out the way with a teasing wink.

The song ended, but Sam continued, making sure to match his rhythm to the next one, getting lost in the music. He allowed it to take over, his body like liquid as the crowd cheered. It took him a while to remember the bet, scanning the crowd until he found the bride at the far end, screaming and holding out money. Her face was flushed, eyes wide as he dropped to his hands and knees, crawling slowly towards her with his back arched the same way he would if he were in leopard form.

"Hand me a bottle," he said to Payne, who watched with a quiet, amused smile. She immediately handed him vodka, and Sam gave the crowd a smirk before returning his attention to the bride.

She was all but panting, the princess crown on her head that read 'BRIDE' glinting as he stole it, placing the shiny piece of plastic on his own head and tilting the bottle to his lips, tasting the burn. He leaned forward, and her lips parted as he passed the shot into her mouth. The surrounding women, and even a few men roared, clapping, singing, and dancing as he slowly pulled back. Sitting on his heels, he poured another shot's worth of vodka down his chest, and the bride-to-be immediately climbed up to lick the liquid, catching the droplets that had reached low on his stomach. Just as her tongue swept up to his pecs, Sam instinctively felt himself going predator quiet. He couldn't stop himself, his gaze darting to the door just as Axel passed through, his hand slapping against Titus's back. He grinned, speaking to his cousin as his head turned, and their eyes met.

Heat. Desire and much more passed between them, hot enough Sam's stomach clenched. There had always been an attraction, but nothing like that, as if there was an intense awareness of each other.

Forcing himself to look away, he swung his attention back to the bride. "Congratulations," he said, his voice huskier, and not because of the bride, as he slipped back behind the bar. "He's a lucky man."

Payne placed a rag in front of his face, and as he wiped the remaining alcohol from his chest she held her hand to the crowd, accepting the money.

The party quickly returned to their seats, or back to the dance floor to finish the celebrations. "So?" he asked as Payne counted the notes.

She looked up, lips tight. "I have to curtsey and smile on my next shift."

Sam barked a laugh. "Have you ever asked what I did before this?"

"Oh, I knew you were a stripper." Her eyes glistened as she handed him half of the tips, the rest going inside her back pocket.

"Wait, have I just been hustled?"

She blinked up at him innocently.

"Fuck's sake," he chuckled, pulling his t-shirt back on. "That's the last time I accept a bet from you."

"Why? You won and we both made money." Her eyes glanced over his shoulder, her expression darkening. With a quick movement she pulled a coaster from beside the sink, carefully placing it on the wood. Sam dropped his gaze to the red explanation mark before turning, immediately noticing a man amongst a crowd of women dancing. He had pressed himself against a single woman, arms wrapping around her waist from behind. She looked upset, and although her friends were trying to pull her away, he seemed to follow. He gripped his hand on her upper arm, pulling her against him despite her clear protests.

"Shall I call one of the brothers?" Payne asked, ready to press the emergency button hidden beneath the bar. There were no bouncers, generally because they didn't get too many problems, but then again, the bar had a reputation of removing troublemakers with more force than necessary.

"Yeah, it may be worth..." Sam didn't get to finish his sentence, not when he noticed the sudden rage darkening the man's expression. He was over the bar, and through the crowd before he'd even realised he'd moved, claws teasing his fingertips as he grabbed the guy by the back of his shirt and pulled.

The man came too easily, which meant he'd had a drink or two. Sam was strong, stronger than the average man, but compared to other Breed he was nothing special. He couldn't tell what the guy was from his scent. Possibly human by the way sweat coated his skin, except his odour had a slight rotten edge.

"Listen when someone says no," he growled, releasing the man so he could turn. They were the same height, which put him just above six foot, but that didn't stop the man from trying to square up.

"I was just dancing," he snarled, a red ring circling both his irises. "The bitch wanted it."

Not drunk, Sam thought. *High.*

"Get the fuck out of the bar," Sam growled, sensing the man's weird energy, one that made his leopard uncomfortable. "We have zero tolerance for drugs and gobshites who don't understand consent."

Sam kept a cushion of air around them, their voices muffled beneath the loud music.

The man's face scrunched up, and Sam jumped out of the way just as he launched forward with a cry. Catching the man's shirt once more, he changed his trajectory, sending him into a poseur table in the corner. It crashed to the ground, the glasses that were perched on the surface shattering on impact.

Sam turned back to the bar and waved to Payne just as the man stood, his face as red as his eyes, humiliation fuelling his anger as he clenched a meaty fist.

Sam tensed for the impact, but before the knuckles could connect, a hand caught the punch, and Sam suppressed his growl as Axel stood there, looking pissed.

AXEL

Axel didn't believe in the Fates, had never in fact believed in the women whom his Breed revered. But right then, he prayed to the three sisters, hoping Sam wasn't working. He just wanted to continue his charade long enough until he could sneak home and wallow in his self-pity. And probably smoke again, because the pain was starting to come back, and soon he wouldn't be able to hide the tremors without another hit of something even stronger.

"You mess with my gun again, and I'll fucking kill you," Titus muttered as they passed the front desk, waving a hello to the cloakroom staff.

"What?" Axel laughed, patting his cousin on the back. "You didn't like the glitter?"

"I swear, one of these days," Titus growled. "You just fucking wait."

Axel grinned, Blood Bar a heap of activity as they walked inside. Most of the seating along the walls and in the corners were taken, as were many of the tall tables that were a recent addition. He wanted to keep his attention on the highly shined wooden floor but was unable to stop himself from sweeping his gaze across the room, drawn to the bar where he found the one person he didn't want to see.

A princess crown glittered on Sam's head, his blonde hair a straight curtain long enough it draped down his back, as a woman dressed all in white licked down his chest.

His very much naked chest.

What. The. Actual. Fuck.

A vibration of awareness, Sam's eyes hardening when they met. Even his beast had grown quiet, the audio dissonance that was a constant buzz lessening at the intense connection. Except Sam looked away, and Axel fought the urge to cross the room towards him, and force his attention back. Which was just fucking fabulous.

Axel finally tore his eyes away, jealousy an emotion he wasn't used to. What the fuck was he even jealous of? Sam had worked on and off at the bar for a few years, and they had quickly become friends. Never once had there been anything sexual between them, because Axel wouldn't allow it. Sam was the earth, people gravitating towards his friendly smile while Axel was a black hole. There had been attraction, but sex complicated things, and his life was already complicated enough.

The alley had been a mistake, an error in his judgment. The brimstone he had injected must have been laced with something else, because not once had he given into the urge to take Sam's lips. And now he couldn't get Sam's taste out of his head.

Titus touched Axel's shoulder. "You guys fallen out?"

Oh, I just corned him in a dark alley and stole a kiss, Axel thought, teeth clenched. *And what's worse is the fact I can't stop thinking about doing it again.* "No, we're fine," he said aloud, turning to smile at his cousin.

"Well, come on," Sythe added, coming up the rear. "We playing, or what?"

He didn't wait for a response, the crowd immediately moving out of their way, eyeing them warily as they both strode towards the door that stated, *'employees only.'*

It wasn't uncommon for the Guardians to part crowds, not just because of their sheer size but because they all had an aura of danger. They blamed their beasts, and even shifters knew something was different, something wrong and not to be messed with.

Yet when Axel moved towards the door he felt the air stir, had already moved out of the way as a woman tried to brush her fingers down his arm, clearly ignoring Axel's 'fuck off' vibes.

"No, thank you," he said, nudging past, once again hating his face, and hating his mother for giving it to him.

"I just want to buy you a drink," the woman insisted with a magically enhanced pout. "Or if you prefer, we can go straight to the bathroom?"

For fuck's sake.

"I don't do girls." Sex had always been served to him on a silver platter, ever since he'd came of age. Men and women had flocked like moths to a flame, and after quickly figuring out that sex was an empty, pointless exercise that resulted in nothing but disappointment, he had chosen celibacy.

Which was a major *fuck you* to his mother, considering he was already a disappointment, having been born male. Not that she had been around in a while to remind him of it.

"Excuse me?" Surprise marked her pretty face. "But I was told –"

Axel carefully moved her to the side, not wanting to touch her any longer than he had to. The lack of sex had never bothered him, not when he numbed himself with pills anyway. It had been over seven years since he last took someone up on their offer, his cock not stirring once at the invitations. No, it seemed any carnal urges he had, had been locked away in a deep box somewhere in the recesses of his mind. Except when it came to a certain fucking cat who had no business being so desirable.

Laughter filtered from beneath the employees only door, and as Axel pushed it open all eyes turned to him.

"About time, we've been waiting.'" Jax said with a glare, arms crossed with his usual pissed-off expression. "You guys couldn't have fucking changed?"

"Oh, I'm so sorry your Highness," Sythe said, taking one of the seats at the large table. "We were out fighting crime while you were, what? Baking cakes or some shit?"

"Scones, actually," Jax said, turning his icy stare towards Sythe. "And they were fucking delicious."

"Chocolate chip," Lucy added with a grin. "They had soggy bottoms. Apparently, that's a bad thing?"

"Eva's rubbing off on you," Axel chuckled, taking the remaining seat at the end.

Jax grimaced. "Bloody hell, don't say that in front of Kace."

"Speaking of K, where is he?" Titus asked. "I thought we were all playing tonight?"

It was Riley who answered, his hands a blur as he expertly shuffled the cards. "He's with Eva."

The entire table groaned, not needing details on what they were doing.

"They better not be doing it in the kitchen again," someone muttered.

"Or on the cars! I had to wash them all down only last week," another added.

Everyone laughed, Lucifer the loudest as they waited for the cards to be dealt. Riley had recently renovated the room by knocking down two storage closets to create one, large room. The walls were still used for storage, metal shelving specifically created to fit the size perfectly, but the rest of the space was left for poker, with a table in the centre designed to fit ten. They were still shoulder to shoulder, but at least the room could host all the Guardians as well as a few guests.

Axel relaxed in his chair, picking up the two cards. Fanning them between his fingers he silently cursed, his hand shaking. It was slight, probably unnoticed by his brothers. "I just need to grab a drink," he said, putting the cards face down before sliding his chair back.

"What? Now?" Sythe whined. "We've only just started."

Titus's gaze burned; cards bent as he held on to them too tightly.

"I fold." Reaching over, he tossed the cards onto the pile of chips. "I'll be a few minutes, I'll play the next one."

Not waiting for anymore objections, he quickly made his way back into the main room, the music a cover he wanted to wrap himself up in. Looking down he checked his hands, the tremor worse as lightning shocked down his arms. He was out of pills, and only had a single smoke. If he didn't get something, anything into his system soon he was going to break.

"Get the fuck out of the bar."

Axel's head snapped up at Sam's snarl, spotting him in the centre of the dance floor.

"We have zero tolerance for drugs and gobshites who don't understand consent."

Axel turned towards the man that held Sam's attention, his beast pressuring the forefront of his mind, a growling mess as it sensed something wrong. Something Daemonic. Yet there were no Daemons, or Shadow-Veyn or even possessions on the property. Well, except Lucy.

Their beasts would have sensed something, and yet the man definitely had a dark aura that set him on edge. There was a second of tension, and Axel was already parting the crowd as the man launched himself at Sam. The leopard twisted at the last second, sending the assailant careening into a tall table, shattering the glasses on top.

He was up in an instant, but before his knuckles reached Sam, Axel had caught them in a fist. Rage overpowered the pain along his skin, the crunch of bone beneath his fingers satisfying as the man howled in pain. He knew they were drawing stares, but he didn't care as he took out his pain on the worthless piece of shit.

He couldn't speak, and Sam's biting anger was a caress against his senses as he pulled the man towards the front entrance. He took pleasure in shoving him to the cobbled stones, crouching down so they were both the same height.

"You're banned," he said, surprisingly calm compared to the internal turmoil that raged in his chest. "If I find you inside again, you won't be walking out of here on your own two feet."

Sam was an intense presence at his side, but Axel dared look at him. "He's wrecked, leave him."

Axel continued, his voice closer to a growl. "Understand?"

The man grimaced, a red line around swollen pupils.

What have you taken? Axel thought.

The man's teeth were clenched, the skin on his hand already darkening with a bruise. "Fuck you!"

A pressure on Axel's shoulder, the warmth from the single touch seeping beneath his bloody and ripped t-shirt. The pain noticeably lessened, the noise inside his head decreasing to a gentle, manageable hum. He wanted to moan, to bury himself into Sam until all he felt was his heat, his skin and lips. It was his mother's succubus instincts, that's what the weird sexual chemistry was and nothing more. Nothing real. So, instead of giving in he rolled his shoulder, dislodging the connection.

"I'll deal with this piece of shit," Axel said as he stood, stepping away.

"Hey, you're hurt." Sam closed the distance, a frown marring his brows as he knelt. "What happened?"

Axel froze, breath quickening at Sam on his knees. "I'm fine," he managed to get out through clenched teeth. "It's fine."

"Aye, fine he says." A warmth against his stomach, Sam's fingers pressing gently around the wound. "You have a fucking hole where there isn't supposed to be one."

Axel swallowed his groan, trying desperately to ignore Sam brushing along his abs, even though the fabric of his t-shirt. Squeezing his eyes shut he called on his beast, but the fucker was just as infatuated with the caressing touch.

Closing his eyes was the worst decision, because now he had nothing to distract himself from the connection, and all his imagination could conjure up was of Sam. He had moved like liquid silk, such feline grace in a human body.

Fuck! He needed to get away before he did something he couldn't take back. Like dragging Sam back up so he could taste those lips again.

Tension twisted between them like an abrasion, a rope wrapping around his throat until there was no air.

"I said I'm fine," he bit out, hoping his eyes were as hard as his tone when he steadied his gaze on Sam. "I don't need your help."

Sam's own eyes glowed, his leopard apparent in the tension along his shoulders. He said nothing as he stood, jaw clenched. The space between them grew, and before long the pain was once again stinging along his skin. There should have been hours before he needed narcotics to numb his discomfort, and yet there he was about to crumble.

Weak. Pathetic. Broken.

Sam's eyes dipped, and Axel realised he was shaking. Crossing his arms he gestured to the man who still remained on the cobbled stones. He needed his medication, and he needed it now.

"I'll deal with him, you go back to dancing on the bar or whatever the fuck you were doing."

"Excuse me?" Sam hissed. "What the fuck is that supposed to mean?" His Irish accent thickened with his anger. Usually it was subtler, and Axel wondered whether he should piss Sam off more just to hear it.

Agony shot down his spine, and he locked his knees to stop from falling. "Go do what Riley pays you for." *Please,* he mentally added. *Leave.*

"You're a fucking arsehole."

Sam stormed inside, and Axel flinched, wanting to chase after him.

He agreed, except he was probably a lot worse than an

arsehole. Ignoring the cold that had settled in the pit of his stomach, he reached for his remaining joint. He lit it quickly, holding the first drag in his lungs for longer than necessary before releasing the cloud directly at the man's face. Blood was fragrant at the back of his throat, and he reached up to wipe at his nose as the first drop spilled.

"You," he began, lowering his tone as if there was anyone else around so late at night. "I need to know exactly what you've taken, and if you have any left."

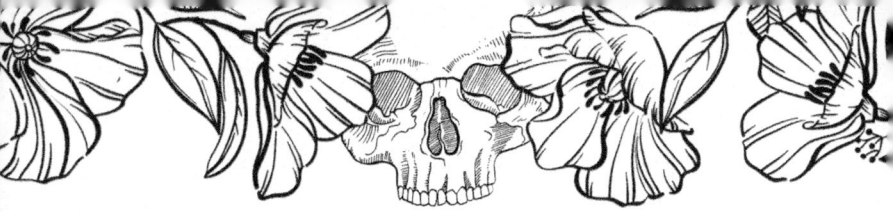

CHAPTER 4

SAM

There was such a thing as being too warm. Skin touched every side, a sandwich of flesh where Sam was the centre. Groaning, he stretched, opening his eyes to see a man to his left, and a woman to his right. He had no idea what the fuck their names were, the heavy weight in his head indicating he'd drunk more than he should've the night before. But it didn't matter, because he was a once, maybe twice casual sex kinda guy. He didn't do commitment, so learning their names seemed pretty pointless.

The woman awoke first, her lips luscious as Sam took them in a long, languorous kiss. She tasted of blueberries. Sam hated blueberries, but her little moans were worth it, as were her nails that scratched down his abs to dance an inch from his already hardening cock.

"Hmmm, morning," the man at his back murmured, his hand coming around to caress the woman's beautiful curves. His lips brushed Sam's shoulder, and Sam pushed himself back into the hard body as...

A bell rang, and it took a second for Sam to recognise the sound.

Oh, fuck.

"Ignore it," the woman moaned when Sam pulled back, jumping up from the bed to look over the mezzanine bannister to the living room below. "Everyone needs to get out," he said, his voice hoarse. "Sorry, party's over."

Clothes were everywhere, thrown haphazardly on his rug, sofa, and coffee table. Even a pair of boxers had somehow caught on the edge of his TV.

"Come on, everyone needs to go," he repeated, louder this time. "Look, it's been fun and all but seriously, I have shit to do."

The man was the first to react, his lips curved into a smirk as he prowled with confidence down the stairs, his bare butt flexing. The doorbell rang again, and frustration forced a growl from Sam's throat.

"Who's at the door?" the woman moaned, pouting her lips.

"My wife," Sam snapped. "Now will you leave?"

"Wife?" she squeaked, grabbing the sheets to cover herself as she ran down the stairs to her clothes. "You never said you were married!"

"It's complicated," he said dryly as he heard the key turn in the door, and Alice was stepping inside. "Welcome home!" he said with a grin.

Alice shot him a scowl, her fractured irises seeming to glow in the early morning sun. She didn't care that he was naked, not after living together for most of their lives. But he still reached for his jeans, which he found draped over the lampshade, yanking them on over bare flesh.

Alice waited, foot dramatically tapping on his freshly waxed floor as his guests left without even a backwards glance.

"Don't," he warned, needing caffeine before she started to chastise him.

"I didn't say anything."

"No, but you were thinking it," he said, narrowing his eyes at her.

"Maybe." Alice bit her lip. *I'm worried about you.*

Sam wanted to close his eyes, look away from the concern he could read clearly across her face.

You don't need to be, he replied the same way, a wordless conversation between two people who knew each other better than themselves. It was something they had mastered as messed up kids, being able to read the most subtle expressions like an open book. It made talking about someone in public super easy, but it also meant she saw more of him than he sometimes wanted to give.

"I'm okay," he said aloud, moving towards the kitchen.

A door creaked, and they both turned as a pretty little red-head stepped out of the bathroom. She smiled shyly, a blush blossoming on her cheeks. "Sorry, I'll just let myself out."

Sam watched the woman leave with a smirk, laughing when he turned back to Alice. "What?"

"You didn't even know she was in there."

Sam's grin grew. "I knew –"

"Lies!" Alice thrust a bag at his chest, and he instinctively caught it. "I love you, but that's disgusting."

"Aw, baby girl." Placing the takeout onto the counter he reached for her, burying his nose in her hair, and centring himself in touch. His leopard immediately purred, wanting to drown in the familiar scent of family. Alice was everything, had been his pack since they first met all those years ago at group therapy. She had been a tiny, mute five-year old, and Sam had immediately found himself needing to sit beside her despite being four years older. Amongst all the other kids, who had suffered their own traumas, she'd seemed scared and alone. Yet he hadn't been able to help himself as he'd reached for one of her plaits, his leopard fascinated with the blonde strands a few shades darker than his own.

She had turned to him with giant eyes and smiled, and from then on, she'd been his rock. She knew all his secrets, his nightmares and worries and she loved him anyway, flaws and all. And there were many flaws.

"I've missed you," she said, crushing her arms around his waist.

"You only saw me the other day," he said, kissing the top of her head.

She sighed into his embrace. "It's not the same."

Sam snorted. "I'll always be here for you, baby girl." It had hurt when she had mated, because that meant she had to leave him. But he was so fucking proud that it hurt, because she had overcome so much shit to be happy. And she deserved to be happy, even if that happiness wasn't directly from him.

"I didn't expect to walk into an orgy," she said, not releasing him from the hug. "But at least I've brought breakfast. From that show I think you'll need it."

Sam's chest shook with laughter. He remembered the night in flashes, the hot breaths and frenzied kisses. He remembered the pleasure, which was the whole point. His goal was always for his partners to come first, only allowing himself to finish once they had. But recently he felt empty afterwards. Like something was missing.

Maybe next time he'd add a fifth person.

"You want to talk about it?"

Sam blinked, releasing her with a last squish. "Talk about what?"

"Whatever just put that frown on your face." Alice pursed her lips. "Come on, Starlight."

Sam reached for the bag, finding breakfast burgers and

hash browns inside. "Don't starlight me." The affectionate name from their years of therapy. "I've already said I'm fine. I like sex, I'm not going to apologise for it."

"Bloody hell, I'm aware that you like sex, I've caught many people sneaking out of your bedroom over the years." Alice rolled her eyes theatrically. "I'm not trying to shame you, Sam. I just want to make sure you're not using sex to hide something else."

"Like what?" The mug slammed against the counter hard enough it cracked. The sound echoed, and neither of them acknowledged it. "What are you trying to say?"

"You keep doing this," Alice said, exasperated. "When did you stop talking to me?"

Sam tipped the mug, checking the bottom to see the hairline break. "We're talking right now." Tossing it into the sink he grabbed another.

"Yeah, with your back turned so I can't see your face."

Sam paused, kettle halfway to the running water. "I would never stop talking to you." He finished filling the kettle and flicked it on before he spun. "But I don't know what you want me to say? I'm living my best life. I've just finished renovating this place, I love my job because I get to see you all the time and I can fuck whoever I want. Honestly, baby girl, I'm living the dream."

Her lips pursed. "I see you, Samion Murphy. Something's bothering you and –"

"Alice, stop it," he interrupted. "You need to stop obsessing over everything I do."

"Do you truly believe your goal to sleep with every living thing is healthy?"

"I don't need you to look after me, I'm an adult who can take care of himself, I've done it my entire life."

Sam reached for the takeout bag, shoving a burger at her before she could say anything else. He loved Alice, she was the sister he'd always wanted, but since they had stopped living together she'd grown more concerned about his choices. He was the one who was supposed to protect her, his instincts calling for it ever since he was nine. Except she didn't need his protection anymore, not because she was mated to a scary bastard but because she was a fucking badass who could take care of herself.

"I'm an adult," he reiterated when she frowned. "Older than you, might I add. I make my own choices. I'm happy."

Alice's gaze could cut. "Are you though?"

Sam licked across his lips as he reached for the coffee jar. "Yes," he replied, but even he heard the lack of enthusiasm.

He was happy. Wasn't he?

"Fuck," he muttered, clearing his throat. "I'm out of coffee." He set the jar down carefully, taking a steady breath. "You want an almond latte?"

Alice nodded, a small smile on her lips that told him she wasn't finished with the conversation. "Yeah, sure. Let's walk to that place on the corner."

"No, you stay here and eat before the food gets cold and you get hangry. I'll run, won't take me ten minutes." Grabbing the packet of cigarettes he flicked the lid open, sliding one between his lips. "Caramel?"

The smile that was on her face had disappeared, and he struggled not to comfort her. "Sure."

Sam slipped outside, pressing himself against his front door for a few seconds as he lit his cigarette and took a deep inhale. He savoured the slight burn, his lungs filling with smoke before he let it all out in a single exhale through his nose.

He just needed a few minutes to himself. To figure out how to deal with someone who saw too much, saw more than even he knew. There had been dark times over the years, times he would rather have forgotten, where he buried himself in anything that would make him feel something. Feel anything. Alice had always brought him out of his self-pitying episodes, and he hadn't had one in years.

"Hey, what can I get you?"

Sam blinked up at the barista, realising he had walked to the coffee shop without even realising it, lost in his own thoughts. Mumbling his order, he waited, making sure to add a slice of cake for Alice. He didn't want to upset her, even if he couldn't agree with her observation.

He hadn't lied, he was happy enough with his life.

He definitely didn't feel sad.

Accepting the hot drinks and cake Sam turned, the sun bright through the glass door. Working in a bar had messed up his sleep cycle, and with the sun's position, he assumed it was late morning touching on afternoon, not early like he first thought.

How long had he been fucking those strangers for last night?

"Hello, Son."

Ice in his chest, his hands clenching so hard on the coffees that they spilled scalding liquid onto his hands. But he couldn't feel it, not when he looked up and saw the man sitting in the corner table. Sam found himself frozen in place, his legs locked.

"It's been a long time," his father said, gesturing to the opposite chair. "Sit."

Sam sat, following the order, numb. He didn't even notice when the barista came over with napkins, taking away the ruined cups and cake from his still clenched hands. If he had commented, Sam wouldn't have heard. Not when all he could do was stare at the man with whom he shared DNA. His father looked exactly as he did all those years ago, his recollection pristine despite it being a child's memory.

Short blonde hair, darker than Sam's and eyes of umber that glowed like that of his leopard, an amber ring around the iris. His brows were thick, his lips cruelly pinched as he stared with a hatred that burned.

The last time Sam saw his father was when he was thrown into the ocean, bleeding and broken after days of being passed around like a toy. Hurt in ways no one, especially not a child, should have been hurt. For years he'd suffered at the hands of the people who were supposed to love him, his pack. All with the encouragement from the man who sat before him.

The salt had scorched, sealing his wounds so they had scarred. Every mark of the whip, cut of the blade, and burn of the poker forever immortalised on his skin.

"Oh, how you've grown. It's been a long time Samion," his father said, appraising him slowly. "I can feel your influence, it's even more beautiful now that you're an adult."

Sam swallowed, his throat dry as his father pulled an aura, demanding Sam acknowledge his dominance. It was an abrasion against his skin, but the power flowed off him like water, just as it had as a child. He hadn't been born with the instinct to bow to those more dominant than himself, because in reality he was neither a dominant, nor a submissive. He was different, outside the usual pack hierarchy. He wasn't more dominant than the Alpha, but he wasn't beneath him either.

Equal, and for someone like his father, that was unacceptable.

His father's face creased, lip lifting into a snarl. "You left us, now everybody's dead, and it's your fault."

Sam was still silent, his heart an ache that pressed against his ribs in a powerful beat. Their pack had been unusual, consisting of many different predatory shifters rather than a single animal. It was rare, and for good reason. Many shifters, unless mated into the pack dynamic, didn't get on, their animals too different, which would usually result in deadly conflicts.

"You owe me for leaving."

"I owe you nothing," Sam said, his voice a harsh timbre when he finally spoke. "You left me to drown."

"I did no such thing," his father sneered, his accent strong and reminding him of his childhood. "You were being punished. I wouldn't have allowed you to die, not when I needed you to help balance the pack. And now, because of you I had to kill them all."

"I was a child," Sam continued, fist clenched so tight on top of the table that his nails pierced into his palm.

"Eejit, you know it was for the good of the pack."

His father cocked his head, and it was a gesture that broke through all his years of therapy, years of learning to love himself for something more than an empty shell that was made to be used. He was yet again a child, standing before his father who would beat him with a belt for the sake of it. Twenty years had barely aged the man, a few spots of grey and an extra wrinkle or two. His eyes were the same, hard and without care for his only son.

"How did you find me?" Sam asked quietly.

His father smiled, and Sam knew he wouldn't get an answer.

"Why are you here? Why now?"

"Like I said, Samion. You owe me for leaving." He shifted forward, hand reaching to grip Sam's clenched fist. The chair scraped and fell as Sam shot to his feet, his breathing erratic as he dragged in large gulps of air.

If he wasn't careful he was going to shift, and if he did, he wasn't sure if he would be able to stop himself from killing the man who'd almost ruined him on a deep level.

Rage coursed through his veins, a violent wave that stole his words, forcing him to concentrate on breathing as his father stood too. Sam was no longer a child, but a strong, proud leopard. He had built a life for himself from nothing, and he wouldn't let his father destroy it.

"There's something you need to do for me," his father said. "It's the least you can do."

"Fuck you, I owe you nothing."

"You're my son, and you will do this, or else."

Sam growled. "Refer to my previous statement."

"I need help with my new pack," he continued as if Sam hadn't spoken. "I've set a meeting this week. You'll be introduced properly, before we welcome you within our ranks. I'll send you the details." He took a step to pass, and Sam stiffened every muscle to stop from flinching. "I don't need to remind you what happens if you disappoint me, Samion. It's a nice little life you've set yourself up here, and that witch I've seen around your place. She a mate? I'll be sure to say hi next time."

"She's not my mate," Sam said, reacting instantly. "But go anywhere near her and I'll kill you, that's if she hasn't already burned you to pieces."

"Aye, we both know you could never hurt me, Son. But I'm sure she will be all too interested to know the exact details of what you allowed to happen. The disgusting things you enjoyed."

Dread tightened its grip around Sam's throat, but before he allowed it to consume him he snarled. "You're a sick fuck."

"I'll send you those details," his father said with the confidence of someone who had never been told no. "It was nice to see you, Son."

Sam stood immobile long after his father had left, only moving when he felt bile burning. Rushing outside he puked, coughing up nothing but water. Snot covered his face, tears streaming angrily as he raced back to the place he called home. He almost ran Alice over as he pushed open his front door with a violent shove, only to slam it closed seconds later.

"Sam?"

Sam choked out a sound, pressing himself against the door as he slowly fell to the floor, legs suddenly weak.

"Sam? What's happened?" Alice dropped down beside him, panic spiking her tone. "Are you okay?"

Pulling his knees to his chest, Sam wrapped his arms around them, pressing his head back forcibly into the hard wood. The pressure helped him think, helped get his scattered thoughts together. "It's my father," he managed to get out.

Alarm brightened Alice's eyes. "He's dead, Sam. That private investigator promised us that Conor Murphy was dead."

Sam scrunched his eyes closed, feeling the heat from his tears brush gently down his cheeks. His chest ached, so painful it was hard to breath. But it was no longer fear that soured his tongue. He wasn't afraid of his father, not anymore. He had had two decades, half of that with a therapist, to understand what had happened to him as a child wasn't his fault. That his father wasn't a gigantic monster who would come in the dead of night and snatch him in his sleep.

His father was just a man. A pathetic man who preyed on those smaller and weaker than himself. Sam was no longer small, or weak.

"Sam, please?" Alice's hand brushed at his hair, and Sam revelled in the gentle caress. Touch grounded him, reminded him that he was there, in the present and not locked in a dirty room, pinned to a filthy mattress.

"Well, they lied." He licked the salt from his lips, meeting Alice's gaze. "Because my da's very much alive, and he's found me."

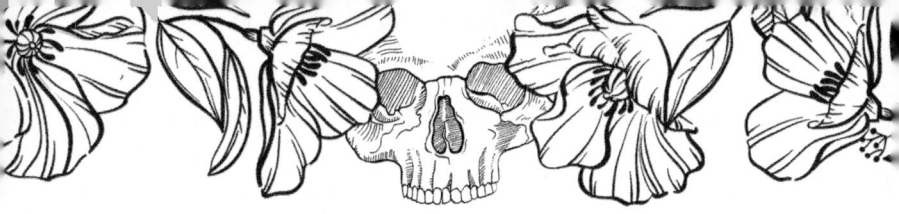

CHAPTER 5

AXEL

"That's fifty-two to forty-eight," Titus said with a grin, sweat a fine gleam across his bare torso. "What about whoever hits triple digits first is the winner?"

Axel sucked in a breath, his skin just as slick. They had been running the obstacle course hidden in the clearing behind the estate for the past two hours non-stop. Their movements were a blur as they followed the wooden structure Jax had built a few years ago to improve their reflexes. It was actually a pretty ingenious design, with certain parts of the obstacle connected by gears, and if someone pulled the crank it caused the obstacle to move. Columns would turn, blunt poles would stick out at random angles that you had to dodge when walking across the slim plank. It was crudely made, yet they all loved it.

Titus and Axel were alone in the clearing, which meant the course remained static. They had to run, jump, and slide through the race, the winner usually the person who completed it the fastest. Axel was faster than Titus on a sprint, but they didn't exactly play by normal rules.

"I think a rib's broken," Axel said, lifting his arm with a grimace to check the bruise blossoming.

"You shouldn't have tried to grab my ankle, then maybe I wouldn't have kicked you." Titus stretched his shoulder, a cut splitting his heavily tattooed skin. Out of all the Guardians he had the most ink, and not just glyphs. His entire chest was shaded as a skull, the black and grey so detailed it was hard not to study the intricate markings that Kace, their brother had created in the bone. He'd made it look as if it had been carved, echoing the glyphs that surrounded the design. A Chinese dragon curled around his left arm, starting just below his shoulder with the head finishing on the top of his hand. His other arm was covered in the glyphs they all wore, as well as his back, both legs and hands.

A silver ring glinted in his left nipple, the piercing, along with the matching ones in his face, Titus had done himself. No one else understood, mainly because of their increased healing ability. His body would reject the jewellery, pushing it out and Titus would simply pierce somewhere else.

Axel sucked a breath in through his teeth as he stretched, his ribs protesting the movement. "You wanna spar instead?"

"So, you're giving up then?"

"No!" Axel barked. "Let's go agai –" Lightning across his skin, the pain a shock that pushed a grunt from his throat.

"Hey, you okay?"

Axel fell to his knees, his calves spasming as he clamped his teeth to stop from crying out any further. "Fine, I must have overdone myself on the course," he lied. "Cramp."

"A cramp?" Titus dropped beside him, hand reaching

out to touch his shoulder before Axel flinched. "Are you seriously bullshitting me right now?"

The pain went as quickly as it came, a wave through his body that constricted every muscle. His hand shook when he let out a breath, so he clenched it into a tight fist. "Calm down, Tit. It's just a cramp, I'm not dying."

Titus's expression darkened at the nickname he despised. "Don't call me that, Pretty Boy," he growled. "That wasn't a cramp."

Shit. Guess the name didn't distract him.

"Maybe I ate some bad fish? I don't know." Blood coated the back of his throat, and seconds later the familiar heat dripped out of his nose.

Axel sat back on his heels, staring up at the sunlight that glittered through the leaves high above. He'd been going less and less between hits, his medication no longer taking away the edge. It meant he was back at square one, trying to figure out what combination of drugs and herbs would numb him the longest. At least the whispers weren't as prominent, his beast unusually still.

He wiped his nose with the side of his hand before gesturing to where they had placed their t-shirts and jackets. "Grab me a joint, would you?"

Titus glared.

"What? It helps me relax."

Titus reached for the smoke, placing it between his lips and lighting it before handing it over. "You're acting weird," he continued, concern an emotion Axel didn't need, or want. "Weirder than usual."

"Says the man who just pierced his own nipple," Axel muttered, taking a heavy drag before holding it out.

Titus refused, instead crossing his arms. "You left the poker match the other night. You went missing, no explanation. Just vanished."

"I was tired."

"And then this shit with Samion –"

"What the fuck has Sam got to do with anything?" Axel interrupted, finally climbing to his feet. His legs were steady beneath him, no echoes of the earlier pain, and his nose had stopped being a faucet.

"I've been hearing things –"

"Then stop fucking listening!"

Titus growled. "You're bullshitting me again. We both know you haven't looked at anyone for years, since you started taking whatever shit you've been taking."

"I haven't –"

"I've caught you so many times," Titus interrupted, brushing back the hair that had escaped from his bun. "You were so fucked up, I doubt you even remember. It's probably the reason why you're not interested in sex, because you numb yourself with all that fucking poison."

The tremors were getting worse, moving up his arm. "I don't –"

"And then there's you staring at the bartender like some teenage boy with a hard-on, and I thought maybe *he* would get it into your thick skull –"

"Titus, stop jabbering on and listen to me. I haven't taken anything." *In a few hours,* he mentally added. "And I've never taken anything with the intention to get high." Which was the truth.

"You're literally smoking something right now."

"Get off your high horse, you smoke this stuff too."

A muscle in Titus's jaw twitched, but he remained silent as Axel continued.

"Anyway, what's with your obsession with my sex life? I abstain because I want to, not because of anything else."

Titus chewed on his bottom lip, twirling the silver ring

that pierced through the centre. "Being celibate to get back at your mother isn't healthy."

"Probably not, but that doesn't change the fact I'm fine. I haven't taken anything, I promise."

Titus's eyes narrowed. "You're an arsehole, but I have to trust you."

Axel's stomach tightened. "Of *course* you have to trust me, we're blood. Now, come on," he said taking one last, long inhale, hoping he could hide the tremors. "The first to triple digits is the winner."

———

The brown paper bag fell to the footwell when Axel slammed on the brakes, his finger automatically lifting to flash the driver who had cut him up. He wasn't even sure why he had a fucking car in London, not when the roads barely moved from traffic. Not to mention the speed limits that were slower than walking.

But then he would have had to take the trains, or buses and Axel knew he couldn't deal with the attention on any sort of public transport. Reaching down, he grabbed at the ingredients that had fallen from the bag, catching the ball of dried oleander as it rolled. Placing everything back on the passenger seat he knocked the centre console, accidentally flicking the air conditioner as he turned down his road.

The car coughed, and a fine powder shot out of the vents. "Fuck!" Axel swerved to the side, blinking rapidly as he pulled over. Glitter, he was covered in fucking glitter. "Titus you prick!" Grabbing his phone he dialled his cousin, relaying the curse as soon as he answered.

"Told you not to touch my guns," Titus chuckled down the receiver. *"Besides, you started with the glitter."*

"I could have died."

"Unlikely." An amused tone.

"I could have killed someone else, Ti!"

"I trusted your instincts." The laughter didn't fade. *"You finished with your errands? I thought we could go another round on the course, considering neither of us are on rotation tonight."*

"I have some stuff to do at the apartment, but I'll be back to destroy you later."

"We both know you can't beat me," Titus chuckled. *"But I'm happy to slow down for you."*

"Yeah, yeah," Axel muttered, frowning at the mess inside his car. "Only because you cheat."

"It's not cheating if we both agreed to the rules before-hand," Titus said. *"Oh, I forgot to mention earlier, but Lǎolao was asking about you. You haven't visited her in a while."*

Axel hesitated at the mention of Titus's grandmother, the woman that essentially raised them both. She was a soft woman, one who only saw the sunshine and never the storms. She was the person who was tricked into signing them up to become Guardians, not knowing or under-standing what would happen. She hadn't been brought up amongst their Breed, and after her husband died, she was easily manipulated by the Archdruid.

Titus and Axel had agreed even as kids that they would never tell her what they had suffered, the severe training or the ritual of their beasts. They never blamed her, but they knew she would blame herself.

"Axel?"

"I'll ring her later," he replied, clearing his throat. "I've just been..." *Too busy trying not to be consumed with pain.* "Busy. I've got to go, I'll see you soon."

"Axel, stay out of my –"

Throwing the phone onto the seat beside the bag Axel

brushed the glitter from his face. "Pink, of course he chose pink," he muttered as he moved back into traffic. A few minutes later, he pulled into his designated space in the underground parking garage.

The apartment he shared with Titus was nice, and very expensive. They had bought it between them almost five years ago, thanks to Titus bringing in silly money with his computer skills, and Axel with his inheritance.

His father had been rich, and when he'd died Axel had inherited every single penny at just six years old, much to his mother's annoyance. He sent her money, hoping it would keep her away long enough to finally have the daughter she actually wanted and leave him alone. But even after twenty-nine years he was still an only child. That he knew of, anyway. It wasn't exactly like they had a normal mother/son relationship. She got pregnant, gave birth only to find a penis, and that was the end of her maternal love. His penis shouldn't have been a shock, considering it was common knowledge that druids could only sire males and she'd specifically hunted his father. It was how their entire Breed survived.

The lift to the thirtieth floor was quick, the black chrome doors opening to reveal a dark burgundy carpet and clean, pale walls. They'd chosen the place because of the security, the extra thick walls, and specialised team available in the entire building twenty-four seven.

Not that they really stayed there anymore, not since Riley mated and encouraged everyone to stay at his family estate. It made sense, all the Guardians together in one place. But first it was Riley, then Xee, and now Kace. They were all happy and mated, and while Axel was so fucking happy for them, all he cared for was his next hit. The house was getting busier, which meant it was getting harder to hide when the relief from the drugs faded, and the pain returned.

He didn't even have time to think about his curse, how he had to find a mate before the hundred years were up. Soulbind himself to someone or suffer an eternity as his beast down in The Nether, also known as Hell, a slave to the very fucking man who had cursed them in the first place.

Both options sucked.

Axel already had to deal with his fucked up beast, two souls in one body. He couldn't imagine adding another. There was already something broken in the binding magic, so he doubted he could even soulbind to anyone else anyway.

There was no point wasting valuable time thinking about it. He lived in the now, and didn't like thinking of the future past planning his next shot of medication.

The front door opened easily, unlocked via his hand-print. Axel thought it was pretentious, but Titus had checked the internal servers and had assured him they were safe and secure. Not that Axel had any idea what the fuck his cousin had meant.

Dropping the paper bag onto the dark oak table, he strolled into his bedroom, quickly grabbing the glue he had hidden in his bedside drawer before moving to Titus's room. He tried to keep out of his cousin's bedroom, a mutual agreement between them both. Except Titus had used *pink* glitter, and Axel was feeling a little pissed about it.

He ignored the black satin sheets, the fabrics shiny and perfectly made. The entire room was black, with a few varying shades of dark grey to accent. It looked like a generic room, just one maybe Dracula would have preferred. But Axel knew of his cousin's tastes, and opening up the armoire beside the wall-length mirror, Axel couldn't help but grin. Inside were various collars, ropes, paddles as well as other objects he had no intention of touching. He was sure they were clean, but he really didn't need to add a memory of touching Titus's sex toys to his ever-growing list of fucking nightmares.

Lifting the first paddle, Axel touched the spiked edges, the flat side made of a soft leather that looked worn. Titus enjoyed inciting pain from women during sex, which was also another reason they'd jointly chosen that particular apartment. Sound-proofed walls.

Unscrewing the cap from the glue, Axel got to work on sticking everything he was willing to touch down. It was quick drying, which meant it didn't take him more than five minutes before he had stepped away from the armoire and closed the bedroom door behind him.

"Teach you to mess with me," he muttered as he picked up the paper bag and made his way to his own room. In contrast, Axel's bedroom was light and airy. White sheets, light green walls, and a fluffy rug with bright yellow smiley faces that he'd ordered online once when he'd been out of it. He had nothing personal, because everything that meant something to him was back at the estate where his brothers were. With his family.

It wouldn't bother him if he never had to step foot in the room ever again, except he needed it. Because hidden in the en-suite was a chemistry set, essentially a child's toy he'd found in a shop. Over the years, he'd added to it, researching online how to break down narcotics to their basic elements. What once had started as a few glass beakers and a pipe, had grown to cover the entire bathroom.

He only ever returned when he needed a refill, or when he wanted to experiment. The joint had helped with the tremors, but the pain had started in his bones only a few hours later. So he was back, needing to go over his notes and try different combinations of herbs, and hope he found something that lasted. He didn't want to self-medicate, but it wasn't like he had many options.

Foxglove – ~~three flowers.~~ Two flowers max or risk heart burn
~~Ecstasy ($C_{11}H_{15}NO_2$) – ¼ tablet~~ < Could see colours.
~~Cocaine ($C_{17}H_{21}NO_4$)~~ – Doesn't mix well. No benefits.
Valerian root ~~(dried)~~ – 15 g use fresh.
Cannabis – Smoked – works for short periods of time.
Brimstone ($S_{16}C_6H_{12}O_6$) – Liquid (when heated above 100°C) Crystallises if cooled too quickly.
Stable around 95.5°C. Most reactive to herbs and longer relief.
~~Capsaicin (chili seeds)~~ < Stupid idea.

Axel crossed out foxglove entirely, hoping the oleander's pain relief benefits worked better along with the brimstone. He had first tried the usual prescription pain relief such as acetaminophens, ibuprofens, and naproxen, but they'd all been a failure. He'd quickly turned to illegal narcotics, finding more respite in the shit mixed with fuck-knows-what than medication actually designed for pain relief. Brimstone, however, seemed to be the best, the catalyst when cut with fentanyl and natural herbs.

The dark yellow liquid bubbled immediately when Axel flicked on the flame, the fan overhead keeping the room well ventilated. He had over fifty notebooks that were filled with recipes, formulas, and general scribblings. He wrote down every combination, every instruction and failure depending on the base drug he used. Five years or so of work, and he had only managed to create something that lasted forty-eight hours at most.

He was still working on the perfect combination that didn't mess him up, making him too high. It wasn't an addiction, because it wasn't the euphoria he craved. It was the reprieve. He would rather have not used any drugs raw from a dealer, not knowing exactly what was in the little white pills, powders, or liquids. But there were always emergencies, and it wasn't like he could overdose or get an infection. He knew, it would have happened by now.

Without the narcotics his skin would become tight, so sensitive even the slightest feather would cause agony. His bones would ache, lightning would shoot down his arms at the barest movement and then there were the fucking whispers, a discord of ravishing sound that only he could hear inside his head, intrusive thoughts that mangled together. It created a deep throbbing behind his eyes, making it hard to concentrate on anything but the idea of clawing at his own flesh until he could scrape his nails against his skull.

Short of blowing his own brains out, nothing could stop it, and he'd been close to trying that before he'd discovered the harder stuff. It worked, not stopping the pain entirely, but enough that he could breath. That he could live.

Now that could become addictive, the feeling of nothing. Pain free.

Something popped, a hairline splinter cracking the beaker. "Shit." Axel turned off the flame, but it was too late, the glass shattering as the molten hot liquid gushed out. "Fuck!"

Black smoke burst from the shards, the fire alarm singing seconds later.

Opening up the closest drawer Axel shuffled through the contents, only finding empty packets and vials. Crushed hogweed, nettles and other herbs lay forgotten on the bottom. Mostly dried, but the ingredients that had been fresh had started to decay. The stone mortar and pestle were filthy, and Axel couldn't even remember what he'd last crushed in it.

Desperation forced him to grab it, his tongue flicking out to lick the sludge at the bottom. The taste was vile, acidic. The tiles cracked when he threw it across the room, landing in the long unused bathtub. It clattered, knocking against some of the measuring cylinders he had stored there.

Panic gripped his lungs, and already he could feel the slight echo of pain at the back of his skull. He would need to find a dealer, and hope they had strong enough stuff to keep him going for a while. Dragging a hand down his face he sighed, his fingers spasming as he pressed them harder.

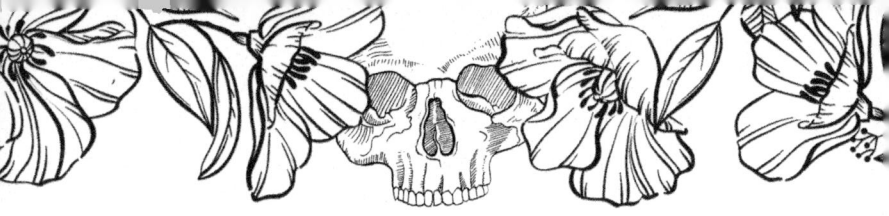

CHAPTER 6
AXEL

A xel's boots ate up the few steps to the townhouse. It hadn't been hard to find the residence, so decrepit that it was almost a neon sign that said 'drugs sold here.' He wasn't unfamiliar with the place, and he ignored the curious stares of the few men and women who sat against the walls, hypodermics sticking out their arms. Dirty mattresses, drink cans and broken needles littered the floor, what was once carpet ripped up to reveal the cushioned underlay or concrete.

"You're new here," a man grunted as Axel moved further inside the derelict house. "What do you want?" He crouched in the corner by a large rucksack, cap pulled low over his brow. He watched warily, muscles tensed as if ready to bolt.

Axel swallowed, fists clenched as he approached. "Brimstone, or anything that's strong." His skin stung, a thousand needles stabbing into his pores. He didn't care what it was, he just needed something. Anything that could help him for a few hours until he could sort himself some more medication. He had the herbs to try, he just needed the base.

"How do I know you're not from the Met?"

Axel reached into his back pocket, pulling out a fifty-pound-note. "I said I wanted brimstone."

The dealer sucked air through his teeth, taking his time to slowly open the rucksack at his feet, revealing a pile of clear plastic bags not too dissimilar to the ones he'd left in his drawer. Each was filled with various powders and pills, all the colour of dirty white, as well as a few illegal charms and vials of blood.

"Axel?"

Axel turned at his name, his heart a rabbit in his chest at being caught. Hunter stood at the base of the stairs, his face pink as if he had been crying.

"Does Kace know you're here?" he immediately asked with a growl. "This place isn't somewhere for a kid."

Hunter's upper lip curved into a snarl, the pain that was in his eyes disappearing under a flare of anger. "Does Red know *you're* here?" he snapped back, calling Kace by his fighting name.

"I told you to get out of here!" a feminine screech came from the floor above. "If you're not buying, get the fuck out, Hunt."

Hunter flinched, shoulders tightening. "Red doesn't control what I do. I can do what the fuck I want." He went to take a step towards the door, but Axel caught him by the arm. Yanking up his sleeve Axel checked for track marks, releasing a breath he wasn't aware of holding when he saw clean, unmarked skin. Usually on a shifter any evidence of using would be healed when they changed to their animal, but Axel knew Hunter had been refusing to shift.

Hunter jerked out of his grip, his jaguar teasing the edges of his Prussian blue eyes. "Don't touch me." he growled.

"Your ma told you to leave," the dealer said, standing up

from his crouch. "Don't come here and distract my customers, boy."

Axel shot the dealer a glare, his voice dropping in warning. "This isn't your concern." Returning his attention to Hunter, he grabbed the front of his hoody, dragging him down the steps and back to the street. "Go wait by the car, I'll take you home." Releasing his grip before Hunter could scratch down his forearm, he pointed to the adjacent road, his SUV parked a few minutes' walk away.

Hunter's slim jaw clenched. "You didn't answer my question."

Patience wearing thin Axel growled. "Kid, go wait by the fucking car."

"I'm not listening to an addict, I've been brought up amongst them and I know none of you can be trusted."

"I'm not an addict," the words came out before Axel even thought to respond. "I'm nothing like the —"

"Says the man buying drugs." At Axel's silence Hunter continued. "Can you even go a whole day without taking anything?"

"You know nothing, you're just a kid —"

"You're an addict," Hunter interrupted. "Even if you won't admit it to yourself."

"Go wait by the fucking car, I'll be there in a minute."

Hunter sniggered, pulling his hood up to shadow his face. He turned, disappearing around the corner as Axel stood, the wind whipping up the surrounding leaves. "Why did Kace have to take in a stray?" he muttered quietly, dragging a hand down his face, feeling the roughness of his stubble. His muscles twitched, the ache behind his eyes intensifying as he returned to the dealer.

"Brimstone?" he barked, grabbing the cash from his back pocket.

"All out of the normal stuff," the dealer said, crouching

by his backpack. "But I have the new Crimson Mist, it just came in." His hand disappeared into the bag, pulling out a handful of small, metal canisters.

"Crimson Mist?" Axel picked up one of the canisters, thumb brushing against the embossed insignia on the side. The metal was cool beneath his touch, the image of a skull with antlers surprisingly detailed. He recognised it from the same stuff the guy at the Blood Bar had taken the other night. Axel had been desperate, resorting to searching the guy when he'd refused to hand over anything he had left. He had found nothing other than the empty canister.

"It used to be that red crystal brimstone, but after there was a hiccup with the supplier it changed to gas." The dealer shrugged. "It's some good fucking stuff, and the first lot is on the house."

"Of course it is," Axel muttered, pocketing the canister.

It was a familiar tactic used to get people hooked, offering them the expensive stuff for free first. Except Axel wouldn't get addicted to the brimstone, unlike what Hunter believed.

"Let me have all of those pills too." He hadn't bought from there before, usually finding the small-time dealers in a few of the rougher clubs in the city. He tried not to go to the same place too often, not wanting to be recognised if he could help it.

"All of them?"

"Did I fucking stutter?" Pain was making him impatient, as was the blood that was slowly dripping from his nose. "Here, this should cover it." He handed over a few grand, knowing he needed to replenish his stock for making the medication. He'd never run out before, usually making sure he had backup in case of an emergency. He was distracted, so fucking busy with the increasing Shadow-Veyn.

"Happy returns, friend," the dealer said with a grin, handing over a pack of balloons too.

Axel didn't bother with a reply, quickly making his way back to his car, unsurprised Hunter was nowhere to be seen. Relief softened his shoulders, but after he jumped into the SUV, he quickly sent Kace a text to check in on his kid. Hunter may have not been biologically his, but his brother sure as fuck treated him like he was.

Reaching into his pocket he found the canister, lifting it up to look at it once more in natural light. "A gas," he mused, wondering how he opened it. "What are the balloons..." His hand spasmed, a sharp sting shooting to his fingertips.

Grunting a curse, Axel reached for the glove compartment, grabbing a knife he kept hidden inside before settling back in his chair. He wanted to laugh, the reality that it was broad daylight, and he was about to consume fuck-knows-what in open view. He never believed he would get to that point, but there he was, carefully piercing the top of the canister with the tip of his blade.

A high whistle echoed in the interior as Axel shoved it against his nose and inhaled. It lasted a second, the air frozen as it stuck at the back of his throat, causing it to spasm. Coughing, he closed his eyes, reclining his chair and waiting for something to happen. Anything, as the pain across his body began to consume him.

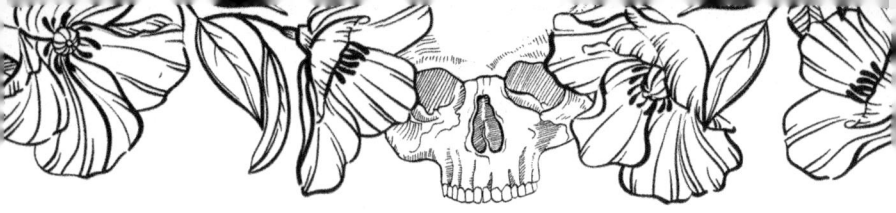

CHAPTER 7
SAM

The wind was cool, the leaves on the tree that shadowed the bench rustling gently. The park was quiet, a few shouts from the kids playing on the brightly coloured apparatus while their parents watched, but other than that the surrounding area was calm. A burst of green in a city of steel and glass.

Sam scented Hunter well before he stepped into view, his skinny body covered with a black hoody several times too big. He hid his hands in the sleeves, his jeans clean and his trainers looking brand new. Bright blue eyes greeted him, his charcoal black hair tucked behind his ears.

"Why'd you ask me to meet you in such a random place?" Hunter asked, pulling his hood lower to obscure his face. But Sam had already seen the tears.

"Neutral territory." Sam leaned back on the bench, stretching his legs in front of him. "It's an open space so you don't feel confronted, trapped."

Hunter's lips twisted. "You sound like Eva's therapist."

"Aye," Sam chuckled. "Probably the years of going to one myself."

"You went to a therapist?" Hunter finally sat on the edge of the bench, body rigid. "Why?"

"Many reasons," Sam said, letting out a gentle purr to help calm Hunter's jaguar. "But mainly to help me understand that what happened to me wasn't my fault."

"What happened to you?" Hunter sat forward, his eyes no longer wet, but still swollen.

"Talk to me about your animal, and I'll share with you some stuff about me."

Green teased Hunter's irises, his jaguar possibly reacting to the purr, or the situation. Either way it was something, progress.

"How's Eva's therapy going?" Sam asked, just trying to get the kid to talk. They'd been trying to meet for weeks, but Hunter was so tightly wrapped, he'd barely gotten a word out of him that wasn't general chit chat.

Hunter blinked, and his jaguar disappeared. "She says she doesn't need it, the therapy. But Red takes her anyway." He pulled at the bottom of his hoodie, fingers finding a single thread.

"We both know if she really didn't want to go, no one could make her."

Hunter frowned, looking down. "Maybe."

"It's the same with you meeting me. I'm not forcing you to be here, and neither is Kace... I mean Red," Sam corrected, using the name Hunter called the Guardian.

"No, but Red told me I have to. I don't want to –"

"Disappoint him?"

Hunter clenched his fists, lashes dropping to hide his eyes. "Maybe. I don't know."

Sam waited, letting Hunter relax a fraction further. "Did you see your mam?"

A single nod.

"How's she doing?"

"Why are you asking about my mum? You're supposed to be asking about me." Hunter shuffled his feet. "That's the point of these sessions, isn't it? The reason I'm being made to meet with you."

Well, this is going well, Sam thought.

"Next you'll ask me to piss in a cup," Hunter said angrily.

"I'm not going to ask that." Sam couldn't control his wince. "But because you're strangling your animal and –"

Hunter shot to his feet, his blue eyes merging into a bright emerald. "I'm clean, just like I tell Red every time he asks when I visit her."

"He's just concerned –"

"*You* can tell Red, because he clearly isn't listening to me, I am clean, just like I say I am. My mum doesn't force me to take the drugs, I say no. He isn't my father –"

"Are you finished?" Sam replied, deadpan. Moving slowly, he shuffled forward on the bench, leaning on his knees. "Red may not be your da, but he loves you anyway."

Hunter growled. "Fuck off, I don't do guys."

"What a childish fucking comment," Sam shot back in return, his leopard apparent in his tone. "It's actions, not always blood, that makes you family. Kace may not be the man who knocked your mam up, but he's done more for you than anyone else. Take it from a guy whose da hated him."

Hunter's lips thinned, his eyes widening. "Your dad hated you?" he asked, his voice quiet. "Why?"

"Even after all these years I still don't know."

"Is that the reason for the therapy?"

"Yes." Sam calmed his sudden anger, allowing another purr to rattle through his chest.

Hunter took a step back. "Stop it."

"Stop what?"

"Stop doing whatever you're doing," he growled. "It's not fair, you're making me feel weird."

"I don't mean to," Sam said, telling the truth. "Maybe that's one of the reasons my da hated me."

"Your dad sounds like a cunt."

Sam couldn't help the smile that curved his lips. "Aye, he's not a good man, and he's the reason I went to therapy for a long time, to learn that the abuse I suffered wasn't because of me, but because he was an insecure cunt."

Hunter bit his lip, fists no longer clenched so tightly. "I think my mum hates me."

Sam increased his purr. "What makes you say that?" His words were slightly muffled through the vibrations, but clear enough. "Has she told you?"

A hesitant nod. "She isn't like us."

"A shifter?"

"A cat," he said. "She doesn't like that I'm not a wolf, like her."

"Does she tell you not to shift?"

Hunter remained silent, nibbling on his bottom lip.

"It hurts, not to shift. To strangle your animal. I know because I was forced to stay a boy rather than let my leopard out."

"Is that what happened to your eyes?"

"I think so," Sam said, opening his eyes wider so Hunter could see his permanent amber irises. "I was once told it was a direct result of not allowing my leopard spirit free. Shifters are one with their animal. We're a single soul, but if you don't allow the connection between your human nature and animal nature, you can risk a divide. You may lose a part of yourself that you can't get back."

"Your eyes are badass."

Sam chuckled. "Maybe, but they're a reminder of the

abuse I suffered as a kid. I would rather have normal eyes and had a happy childhood."

Hunter thought for a moment. "I don't want to shift, are you going to make me?"

"We've been over this before, I can't make you do anything. You have to decide for yourself."

"And if I never shift again?"

"You risk permanent damage." Sam clasped his hands together, keeping himself a head lower than Hunter. He sensed the alpha potential in the kid, but he would never grow up to be a strong dominant if he continued strangling his jaguar. "Do you believe Eva would have survived her situation if you hadn't shifted and protected her?"

"She was still hurt," he said. "I didn't do anything."

"That's not what Eva says."

Hunter frowned, fingers playing with the loose thread.

"Your jaguar isn't the enemy, despite what your ma probably says. You are one and the same. Rather than run from your nature, embrace it." Sam stood, placing a hand on his shoulder. "You embraced it before, and because of that Eva survived. *You* survived."

Hunter leaned forward, and Sam got the hint and pulled him into a hug, allowing touch to centre his animal.

"I'm sorry about my earlier comment about Red," Hunter mumbled, looking away. "I didn't mean it."

"I know. You'll learn that love is love, regardless of what your partner has between their legs."

Hunter blushed, face scrunched up, and Sam laughed.

"Sometimes I forget you're only fourteen. Do you want to keep meeting?"

Hunter hesitated a heartbeat before he nodded, pressing himself against Sam's chest, replicating the purr. "Please don't tell Eva I said 'cunt.'"

Sam smirked. "I won't tell Eva that you swore, if you promise me you'll try and shift your hands."

"My hands?"

"Yep, just your hands." Sam pulled back, calling his claws. They pierced through the tips of his fingers, and just as quickly they returned to normal. "That's it."

"Fine," Hunter grumbled, shrugging his shoulders as he stepped back. The wind strengthened, flapping at his hood as he turned to face the younger children playing in the park. "The therapy, did it help?"

Sam paused, answering honestly. "It helped enough. I now have better adjectives to describe my dark thoughts and emotions."

That brought a small smile to Hunter's lips, one that lasted only a second. "Sam, can you keep a secret?" he asked after a few minutes. "I saw Axel today."

Sam ignored the flutter in his chest. "Yeah?"

Hunter swallowed hard. "He was with a dealer."

"Oh." Sam couldn't think of another appropriate response.

"It's not like it's a secret that he takes that shit, he's always high. But he seemed... different. Desperate. I'm not sure what to do."

"Have you told anyone else?"

"No, I didn't want to just rat him out to Ti. I know what it's like to be addicted to that type of stuff, you don't think straight." Dark brows drew together. "Do you think I should?"

"Why don't you let me deal with it? I'll talk to him, see if he's okay."

"But what about –"

"If he's suffering," Sam added. "I promise I will tell Titus, and we will get him the help he needs."

"Okay." Hunter pulled his sleeves down, hiding his

hands. "The Guardians have helped me, you know? I don't want any of them to hurt."

Sam smiled. "You're a good kid, Hunter."

"Ugh." Hunter pulled the hood further down, shadowing his entire face. "I'm not a kid," he grumbled.

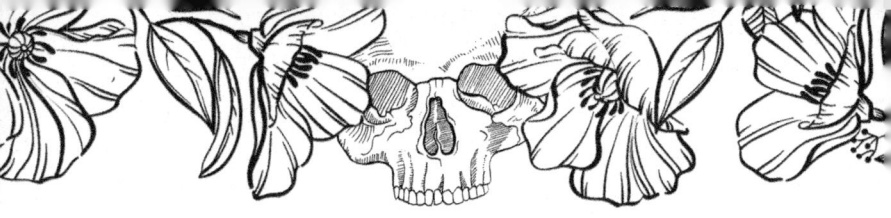

CHAPTER 8

SAM

S am barely contained his leopard as his landlord, Mr
Gibbson, handed him the new tenant details.

"This is bullshit!" he argued, scrunching the
paper into a fist. "You can't just quadruple my rent, that's
theft!"

"That's the agreement," Mr Gibbson said. "You got
discounted rent while you did up the place, and you've
done a great job. So good in fact I can charge my tenants a
hell of a lot more. Plus, I've already got a few of the packs
signing up interest, and they will happily pay the increase if
you don't."

Sam growled. "I have rights, you can't just kick me out
of my home."

"Actually, I own the property, Mr Murphy." Mr
Gibbson crossed his arms, his animal flashing behind his
irises. "And what rights? You're a rogue, you don't even have
a pack to back you up who could move in here and help
with the costs."

"I'm not a rogue!" Sam mirrored Mr Gibbons posture,
stopping himself from punching the smug smile from the

bastard's face. "I'm a registered loner with White Dawn. I'm allowed to be here."

"Get yourself a pack, or a mate even, and maybe you'll have more rights. Until then, I can charge what the fuck I like, because I doubt Councilman Xavier is gonna give a shit if you complain."

Sam bit his tongue, knowing he was right. Shifters were generally autonomous within their packs, with only extreme situations calling for the involvement of the tiger who represented their entire Breed on The Council. Sam was without a pack, which meant he was fucked unless he went to the human housing regulator. But that could take months, if not longer.

"You agreed to sell it to me. That was the deal. I've been saving for well over a year and I've got a bloody meeting with the bank next week."

"Well, life isn't fair."

"This is the last time I go with a shifter landlord!" Sam shouted as Mr Gibbson opened the front door, his chubby belly brushing the frame when he turned.

"Four weeks, Mr Murphy. Otherwise, I'll get the pack to personally give you a visit." Mr Gibbons walked down the steps, hand reaching up to touch some of the faerie lights Sam had strung from the tall hedges. "Four weeks."

Sam slammed the door closed, claws prickling his fingertips. He loved his house, having literally restored it from the old, decrepit train station it once was to a warm, welcoming home. He'd knocked down walls, redone the bathroom and even sorted the garden all by himself to save money. There were still tracks that once worked hundreds of years ago, and now were connected to nowhere. The house had history, character. He had planned to live there forever, and Mr Gibbson had just fucked him over.

"Bloody hell," he groaned, pressing his palms into his

eyes as he rested against the door. First his father, and now this?

Bad luck better not come in threes, he thought.

The door vibrated behind him, the knock loud as Sam opened it with a hiss. "What more do you bloody –"

Sam caught the profanity at the edge of his tongue, realising it wasn't Mr Gibbson who stood on the step.

"What do you want?"

Axel cocked his head, his eyes a silver that seemed to swirl like liquid. They were beautiful, and Sam wanted to explore them further until he realised that red tinged the edges. The hair at the back of his neck stood on edge, his leopard motionless.

"Axel?" Sam looked behind him, seeing no one else through the small gap between the hedges. "What happened?" His t-shirt was ripped to shreds and spotted with blood, his jeans torn at the knee and there was a faint red smear beneath his nose and along his jaw.

Sam stepped to the side, waiting for Axel to enter before closing the door behind him. Axel turned, a frown marring his face.

"Have you taken anything?"

"Taken anything?" His voice was dark, deeper than usual with a slight rumble at the end.

Sam reached to grip Axel's chin, tilting his head to better see his eyes. The red encircled his entire iris, so bright he had no idea how he hadn't spotted it immediately. Axel relaxed under his touch, and Sam instantly knew something was wrong.

Fuck. He was aware of the Guardians curse, once witnessing one of their 'beasts,' a weird wolf-lion creature that looked more at home in the Fae realm.

As a shifter he had already known there was something else, something primal and animalistic, so it hadn't been a complete shock to learn about the beast in which they happened to share a soul.

Shifters were different because they only had the single soul, both the man and animal the same person. The higher the dominance, the more attuned to their animal's instincts. More submissive shifters struggled with their natural urges, which was why it was rare to find a submissive without a pack. They required the hierarchy for control, otherwise they risked letting their animal spirit overpower their human mind, a wild animal in human skin.

Not much too dissimilar to Axel right then.

Sam knew that the Guardians' beasts were different, a distinctive entity that had their own thoughts and instincts. Two souls, one body. And Sam was pretty confident it was the beast who was currently running the show, and not Axel.

Beast seemed to know once Sam made the connection, a deep rumble echoing from his chest as a smile curved his lips.

"Are you okay?" Sam dropped his hand, only for Beast to step closer, almost chest to chest. "What did you take?" he asked, looking down at his arms. "Was it pills?"

His smile dropped, lines appearing between his brows. "I did not."

"Okay." Sam made sure his words were slow, clear. "What about Axel? Did *he* take anything?"

Beast blinked, a few seconds passing before he answered. "He hurt us."

"He hurt you?" Sam calmly stepped back, wary of the strength Beast held. "Is Axel there at all?"

"Where would he have gone?" His voice brushed across Sam, so low it was like rich velvet. It teased at his leopard, who was pressing beneath Sam's skin, wanting out.

"Can I talk to Axel?"

Beast shook his head.

"Do you take over often?" Sam had no idea whether it was normal for their beasts to take charge while as the man.

Another gentle shake of his head. "No."

"Okay, I'm going to call Titus." His phone was just out of reach, resting on the table beside the sofa. "I'm sure he'll be able to help."

He didn't make it, Beast tackling him against the wall, thick arms framing either side of his head.

"No," he growled, and Sam couldn't help but remember being in the same position with Axel all those weeks ago.

"What are you..."

Beast nuzzled against his throat.

It was a vulnerability he would never have allowed with anyone else. An intimate skin privilege, and yet his instincts were to give easier access, reacting with desire rather than panic.

"No Titus." A grumble against his pulse, and Sam groaned as his body reacted at their vicinity.

"Aye, okay, no Titus." Sam tried to move, but was met with resistance. So instead he went predatory still, wary of Beast as he pressed himself closer. Heat seeped into Sam's skin, the air thickening with the heightened tension growing between them, suffocating with every passing second.

And then he felt teeth, and Sam let out a soft exhale as blood rushed in his ears. His eyes closed as his entire body warmed, his attention on the blunt pressure on his throat just above his pulse. It wasn't a threat, the teeth not even cutting skin as he was pinned between the wall and a solid chest, Beast's heart beating so hard Sam could feel it between them.

Beast growled, and Sam moaned out a husky noise as his jeans tightened painfully, his chest heaving up and down in quickened breaths. Hands brushed against his sides, and Sam couldn't control his flinch when they began tugging at the hem of his t-shirt. He didn't resist when those fingers went beneath, moving slowly over his stomach, tracing each and every ab before reaching for his jeans.

Beast finally released his throat. "Mine."

Sam's eyes snapped open, not sure what he had heard as there was a pop of a button, the whoosh of a zipper and then Beast's hand was inside.

"Fuck," Sam swore, his cock jumping as Beast palmed him, hand hot as the other tugged the fabric further down. "What are you doing?" A whisper, as if he raised his voice the hyper-tension between them would be broken, and reality would continue, where he was soon to be homeless.

No, being pinned to a wall by a man who looked like a sex god was a much better distraction.

Beast paused, only for his attention to settle on the pearl of arousal leaking from the head of Sam's cock. He gave a single pump, and stars burst in Sam's vision as he pressed himself harder against the wall, controlling his breathing in heavy pants as lust tightened his stomach. They had barely done anything, and he had never been so turned on in his entire life, his body on fire as the rough grip of the hand slowly moved up and down.

His eyes had drifted closed once more, his hips thrusting along as he chased his release. The hand worked him perfectly, knowing exactly the right grip, adding a little twist at the head that made him dizzy before he felt an entirely different heat. Sam peered down just as Beast attempted to wrap both their cocks in his one hand, but unable to hold their combined girths.

Sam groaned, feeling his cock grow impossibly bigger as it was pressed against rigid, molten flesh. Beast's hand moved up and down them both, and the added friction of the other cock quickly brought Sam close to the edge.

74

But it wasn't Axel who was pulling the pleasure from him. Axel wasn't even aware it was happening, and that thought caused his arousal to flicker.

"Stop." Sam released his claws, pressing the sharp edges to Beast's chest when he continued his long, languorous strokes. "I said stop."

Sam's claws dragged down to part skin, and only then did Beast stop moving his hand.

"Axel." He was so close, his balls aching to the point he wasn't sure what beat louder, the pulse inside his head or the angry vein down his cock. "Bring Axel back."

Beast tilted his head, his grip tightening for a fraction, forcing a moan from Sam's throat before his eyes of silver shifted into warm hazel, showing part confusion, and part lust.

Axel's lips parted a little, and Sam wanted nothing more than to close the distance between them. To taste the tongue than had dominated his mouth all those weeks ago.

"Sam?" A gruff sound as Axel's eyes widened, a groan vibrating his chest at the sight of them both in his hand.

Sam panted, claws pulling back to leave a line of red through Axel's intricate tattoos. His orgasm coiled tightly at the base of his spine, and he knew that one more movement and he wouldn't simply explode, but go atomic.

One more stroke, but as he shifted his hips to take himself over that edge Axel pulled back with a gasp, bursting into a bright white light.

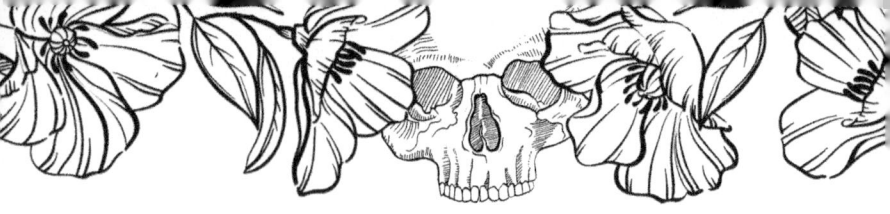

CHAPTER 9
AXEL

H e wasn't in his own bed, he knew that because it was too soft, the pillow beneath his head feathers rather than cotton. The mattress felt like a cushion of air, and the sheets beneath his bare skin satin.

Axel felt his entire body go rigid, and then immediately relax. He was in no pain, his muscles loose and bones content. There wasn't even any whispers, everything silent. He hadn't heard complete silence... A long time.

Something must be wrong.

Axel moved in a single blur, jumping up only to crouch on the floor, his senses on full alert. He definitely wasn't in his room, the walls painted a moss green, with plants stacked on a rustic wooden frame beside the bed. A silky throw blanket in a similar shade had fallen, pooling on the floor by his feet while a vintage-looking dresser was pressed against the opposite wall, covered in framed photographs and a large, oval mirror.

A grumble, followed by a leopard's head popping up to blink sleepily at him. Axel remained stiff, watching in awe as the beautiful predator stretched, the light rippling over his rosettes as claws pricked the pale sheets. The leopard yawned, showing off sharp teeth as he jumped down to brush his side against Axel's arm, tail flicking against his face.

"Sam?" he asked, keeping his voice low as the leopard sat before him, amber eyes angry. He wanted to reach forward, to stoke through the fur, but knew right then he risked losing a few fingers.

He remembered... Sam. His head had been thrown back, pressed hard against the wall. His breathing had been erratic, face flushed, and lips parted with pleasure. Pleasure from Axel's hand around his...

"Fucking hell."

Sam blinked, his fur parting to reveal bright red flesh as every cell transformed. His snout shortened, ears folding back as he began to morph into the man. Axel had never witnessed a shifter change, the magic old and highly protected due to the vulnerability it left the person in. So he remained exactly where he was as he watched every muscle ripple in painful waves, conscious of the agony as Sam's body changed. Bones snapped, realigning with audible cracks as his paws stretched back into fingers. Black claws slowly retracted, disappearing until nothing was left but blunt, square nails.

After thirty seconds or so, Sam crouched, naked and covered in a fine layer of sweat.

The transformation was both horrifying and beautiful, and even with Sam glaring from beneath the blonde strands of his hair Axel felt the air sizzle with electricity, and just a touch of animosity.

Without a word Sam stood, and Axel lifted his gaze to stop from staring at the man who was just as physically gracious in his human form as he was in his leopard. His body was all built with sinuous lines and hard, lean muscle.

Then there were the scars, fine lines that were a mess against his chest. A story, one he wasn't sure whether he had the right to ask.

Axel's stomach twisted, a strange fire burning deep in his gut that he couldn't seem to extinguish.

Without a word Sam padded towards the stairs, descending on silent feet.

Well. Fuck.

Axel counted to ten before he moved, peering over the edge to the area below. Sam's bedroom was on a mezzanine, almost the entire house open plan, with the living, kitchen, and dining all in the same space. Everything was decorated in natural woods and greens, with bursts of complimentary pinks, purples and yellows in the soft furnishings and art. It reminded him of the forest, not just in colours but in textures and serenity too. There was a faint musk scent, not unpleasant, but strange.

Sam appeared below, having pulled on some shorts as he quickly climbed back up the stairs. "Here," he said, thrusting fabric into Axel's hands. "Now get out."

Axel's fists clenched, teeth grinding at the tone. "We need to talk about this."

"Talk about what, exactly?"

Axel pointed to the rumbled sheets on the bed. "Like why I woke up in your bed?"

"We didn't have sex, if that's what you're worried about," Sam said when Axel looked away.

"Wait, we didn't?"

"No." Sam rolled his eyes. "Just look in the mirror."

Axel prickled at the demand, but followed the instruction as he moved the few steps to the dresser. He ignored the happy photographs, peering at his tired face in the reflection. It took him a second to notice his irises were encircled in a bright, angry red.

Panic constricted his lungs, his hands reaching up to yank at his hair to check if he'd suddenly grown horns as well.

"You turned up at my door, high." Sam glowered behind him, leopard still present in the tension along his shoulders. "I'm not some toy to play with, and I definitely don't enjoy edging."

"Edging?" He only remembered the pleasure on Sam's face. Everything directly before, and after was a blur.

"What did you take?" Sam asked, his voice more of a growl. "Seriously Axel, what was it?"

"I –"

"Don't you dare lie to me," Sam hissed. "You owe me that much."

Okay, more than angry, Axel thought. *Furious.*

"Some gas," Axel replied mechanically. "A canister." He had been in his car, and then nothing.

Sam stepped forward, violence crackling between them. "You don't remember, do you?" At Axel's silence Sam continued. "You turned up at my door, but it wasn't really you, it was your beast."

Axel took a second to understand his words. "My beast?"

"He wore your skin." A hollow chuckle. "And when he was done with me, he shifted."

Axel felt the colour drain from his face, a cold lump settling heavily in his chest. He had no control over his beast, only allowing him to take over in severe circumstances, and he had never taken over as the man. He wasn't even sure that was possible.

A growl at the back of his skull, the first audible communication from the creature in question without any pain.

Never do that again, he thought, not sure whether his

79

beast understood until he replied with a huff, claws gently prickling the edges of his mind.

Fuck. Me. That's new.

"Did he hurt you?"

Sam narrowed his eyes.

"Answer the question," Axel said, dread making him step forward, tone hardening. "Please."

"He didn't hurt me, he just pissed over everything. Now get dressed," Sam said with a fierce stare, "and get out. You've been hogging my bed for almost eight hours."

Axel yanked on the t-shirt Sam had handed him, the fabric tight across his chest. The jogging bottoms went on next, fitting a little better with the elastic waist. Despite them both being almost the same height Axel was wider, with denser muscle compared to Sam.

"I don't know what happened," he said, not sure what the fuck was going on. "I'm not sure why I'm here."

Sam dragged a hand down his face. "You have a drug problem, whether you admit to it or not, I don't care."

"It's not a problem. I use them for pain relief, and nothing more."

"Pain relief? Aye, sure," Sam said, his smile mocking. "You do you, Axel. I have no idea what this thing between us is, because right now I don't even think we're friends. But you can't just show up and –" A phone buzzed on the bedside table, turning Sam's head.

Axel clenched his fists, quelling the urge to touch him, comfort him. "I'm sorry."

When Sam turned back his lips were set in a stubborn line. "No, you're not. If you wanted sex, you could have just asked. You're not exactly bad on the eyes."

Axel bristled at the sarcasm. "This wasn't about sex."

"So you go around randomly grabbing people's cocks then? How can you not see that you have a problem? You don't have any memory of coming here because you were high as a fucking kite."

"I haven't got a problem, I'm not fucking addicted to anything," Axel growled. "I don't *need* the high."

"Aye, and I'm the king of England," Sam said in a clipped tone. "You need to admit you have a problem. Nobody can help you if you don't want to help your-fuck-ing-self."

"Says the guy who fucks everything that moves," Axel snapped.

Sam snarled, his response immediate. "Fuck you!"

"No thanks, I have more self-worth." Axel regretted the words as soon as they left his mouth.

Sam's face hardened, his eyes flickering with some unidentifiable emotion.

"Shit, I didn't mean that."

"Aye, you did." Sam's voice was quiet, controlled. "Get out, and don't come back."

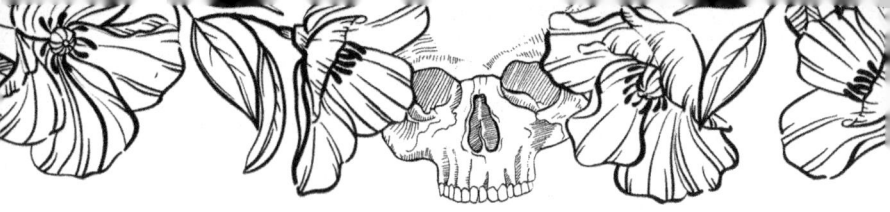

CHAPTER 10
AXEL

Axel didn't bother arguing, descending the stairs and opening the front door with more strength than needed. He was sure he left an indent of his fingers in the handle, but right then he didn't care. Nor did he care the fact his feet were bare, the stones cold as he walked the darkened streets. It must have been early morning, early enough the sun was only breaking through the horizon, and the moon still dominating the sky. Streetlights illuminated the silent paths, but he wasn't paying attention to where he was heading. He just needed to get away, the cool breeze welcome against his skin as the scent of rain threatened.

There was still no pain, his beast was content and he hoped it would last. He'd finally found something that worked, except Crimson Mist had a side effect that he couldn't compromise on. There were many things he would give up to be pain free, but his control wasn't one of them.

The first drop of rain hit Axel's cheek, and he stopped walking to close his eyes. Just wanting to feel, for the water to cleanse away his mistakes.

He had no idea why his beast sought out Sam, and

while the pain was gone, for now. It was replaced with the almost violent urge to turn back, to finish their argument until he was spent and there was nothing left. He wanted to spill all his secrets, to lay himself bare, which was a vulnerability he could never afford. Not when no one understood. They saw an addict and nothing else.

Something dark brushed against his chi, a ripple of awareness that snapped his attention to the side. The rain had turned torrential, no longer a gentle sprinkling but a sheet as it obscured his vision. But even through the heavy beads he noticed the Shadow-Veyn stalking in the dark, the hellhound opening his jaw to grin, venom dripping from its fangs.

Perfect timing, Axel thought. Crossing the street to follow the hound. He had no weapons, but that didn't stop him as he picked up the pace, the hound scratching against the brick as it backed up with a snarl.

In any other situation he would have allowed his beast to take over, to destroy the hound, but right then he wasn't feeling particularly happy with the creature lurking inside him.

"Come here, you fucker," he whispered, the hound wrapping shadows around its monstrous form. Axel smirked, the glyphs he had tattooed on to his body allowing him to see through the glamour for which they were named.

The hound let out a high-pitched howl, loud enough it bounced off the surrounding stone, brick, and concrete. There were no extra bones along its spine, nor where there any scales beneath its jet-black fur that Axel could see. Its size was relatively small, larger than a wolf but smaller than a bear. It was a classification B, maybe even a C. Nothing he couldn't handle alone.

The torturous bay ended, and for a single beat all there was, was the torrential rain battering against them both.

And then, he heard them, the returning howls. Two, three, possibly more. He couldn't be sure, not with the rain muffling the sounds. Which meant he wasn't against a single hound, he was against a pack, and he was unarmed and without a way of communicating with his brothers.

The Fates really knew how to fuck him over.

'Anyone out hunting tonight?' He stretched his mental connection, hoping one of his brothers were close enough to receive his call. He was met with silence, which wasn't entirely surprising. *'Cool, so I'm about to get eaten,'* he continued as if one of them could hear. *'But I've had a good run.'*

The hound snarled, hind legs pressing against the brick-work, body tensed as if ready to pounce. Red eyes glowing in sockets, the majority of its face pure bone with bursts of matted fur. There was no nose at the end if its snout, just two ragged holes that black vapour wafted from, moving around to dance between the exposed ribs at its side.

Axel rolled his shoulders, feeling the muscles bunch before he flicked out his hand and called his chi. He wasn't a fan of using magic, preferring to physically fight his opponents, but the warmth of pale white arcane coating his palm was comforting.

Druids in general had weak magic, born from the earth, and emphasised with the natural ley lines that ran like veins throughout the world. His chi, just like the rest of the Guardians', was heightened, as was his strength, agility and ability to survive ridiculous damage that would otherwise have killed a normal person ten-times over.

The tattoos beneath his clothes hummed to life, giving out a matching pale light. The ball of arcane pulsed, and just as the hound leapt he threw, catching the creature square in the face. It dissipated on impact, tearing through fur and muscle to widen the exposed skull. It forced the hound to shift trajectory, coming side on rather than teeth bared. It hit Axel in the chest, knocking them both back as he felt claws dig into his skin, ripping and tearing as it tried to scramble back to its feet.

Axel wouldn't let it, knowing that once he got a good hit in it would try to run away, at least until it had back up. Reaching up, Axel wrapped his arms around its neck, turning his face as the stench of carrion and rotting flesh assaulted his nose. Something cracked, and Axel tightened his grip until his muscles strained. The dark vapour swept out from the nostril holes, prickling against his skin as it tried to seek out any wounds and heal.

Which meant it was a classification C. Not as bad as D, but still worse than a B.

Fuck. My. Life.

Axel strained his arm as the hound flailed in his hold. Putrid green saliva dripped to the pavement as the hound struggled, hissing like acid until the rain washed it away. He needed to finish it quickly, because without a weapon he was seriously in trouble if the rest of the pack turned up. His brothers would be picking pieces of him from piles of shit for weeks.

Not the most glamorous way of going out.

Who would have thought that once he was stone-cold sober he would still be making such stupid mistakes? No sane person would have engaged in a fight without a weapon. Riley was going to have his head if he survived this.

A fang caught Axel's wrist, tearing through flesh with a shock of agony followed by burning. His grip loosened a fraction, and it was enough for the hound to wrench itself free. It limped, left leg dislocated as it tried to knock it back into place against the brick wall.

Axel climbed into a crouch, ignoring the throbbing ache on his wrist as the venom began eating at his wound.

Lightning brightened the sky, a shock of light splitting the dawn, followed by a rumble of thunder. The rain hadn't lightened, a sheet that drenched him to the bone. Another bolt, and with this strike the hound knocked its shoulder back into its socket, red eyes rolling freely within its obsidian hollows.

Axel tensed, the hound letting out another howl.

The call was cut short, turning into a yelp. Axel hadn't sensed another threat, his heartbeat a drum when he turned to find Sam baring his teeth, a brick clenched tightly in his hand. He threw it, and just like the first it hit the hound in the head, hard enough a visible crack appeared in its exposed skull. Axel didn't have time to ask what the fuck he was doing there, moving as fast as he could as he grabbed Sam around the waist, pulling him to the side as the hound roared, leaping up to snap his jaws just inches from Sam's throat.

The hound soared past, skidding across the wet floor before twisting back around to face them both.

"What is that?" Sam shouted through the rain, hair plastered to his skin as his cat eyes reflected back the limited light.

Axel swallowed, not understanding why the hellhound wasn't fleeing when it was wounded and outnumbered. "It's protecting something."

"What the fuck does that have to protect?"

Axel took a second to sweep his gaze at his surroundings, realising he had chased it to a dead-end alley. Buildings towered over them on three sides, the rain pouring from above.

The hound pawed at the ground, impatiently swinging its head from side to side. The crack in its skull had already started to close, the vapour that floated from its nostrils and ribs covering the damage.

Howls echoed in the distance, the sound like spiders crawling along his spine. Gritting his teeth he called as much arcane as he could to his palms, forming a perfect sphere of milky air. It sparked, and the hound reacted, jumping with little warning. Axel released the ball just as the hound reached them, twisting in mid-air to miss the magic and land on Sam. It took them both to the ground.

"No!" Axel yanked at the hound's legs with all his strength. His beast roared, and he was seconds away from changing, fur pressing beneath his skin and threatening to come out. Anger jerked his movements as he pulled the hound closer, reaching for its thick neck. Fangs tore into his arm, but he couldn't feel it as he heard a click, the hound going limp in his arms before he dropped it to the sodden stones.

Sam watched, eyes wide.

"Did it bite you?" Axel asked, rushing to Sam's side. "Did it bite you?" he repeated when Sam remained quiet. "Samion?"

"No, I'm fine." A fine layer of green splattered his cheeks, and Axel gripped his jaw to angle his face towards the rain, allowing it to wash away.

Sam jerked out of his hold.

Clenching his jaw, Axel returned his attention to the Shadow-Veyn, knowing a broken neck wouldn't kill it. Turning it on its side he found the exposed ribs, able to see its blackened heart through the gaps the vapour failed to hide. With a grunt he punched through the bones, ignoring the squelching as he tore through everything until he reached the organ. Death was immediate, the darkness that had polluted his senses dissipating as the hound's body began to break down, returning to The Nether.

"What was that thing?" Sam remained seated, the rain finally letting up.

Axel rolled his shoulders, his wrist aching, but other than that he was still pain free. "That was a Shadow-Veyn," he said. "And the fact you could see it, meant it wasn't hiding. Either because it was cocky, or more wounded than I thought."

"You were bit." Sam jumped to his feet, his white t-shirt stuck to his torso like a second skin.

"I'll heal." The wound had already began closing, his body repelling the venom. "What were you thinking? You could have been killed."

Sam bristled at his tone. "The correct words are, 'Thank you.'"

"Thank you?"

"Thank you for saving my arse!" Sam yanked at the wet strands of his hair.

"You shouldn't have even been here, one bite and it would've killed you. What the fuck were you thinking?"

"What was I thinking? What were *you* thinking?" Sam's voice could cut glass. "Are you trying to get yourself killed?"

Axel let out a frustrated sigh. "Go home, Sam."

"No, I'm not finished."

"Well, I am." Axel opened his arms wide, the rain finally stopping. "I don't know what to say, last night was a mistake. I can't tell you why my beast sought comfort from you, and trust me, it definitely won't happen again."

Sam chuckled, looking to the side. "What a surprise, you're still not taking responsibility for your actions."

"I don't have time for this. That hound was protecting something, and I need to find out what before..." Axel let his voice drift, crouching down until he was closer in height to the hound.

The end of the alley was cast in shadows from the surrounding buildings, and with the rain gone he was able to make out clearly the bin in the corner. The lid had been broken, hanging on a single hinge. He pushed it to the side, revealing a large hole in the brick.

"You've made your point," Axel said. "Now go home. There are other hounds hunting tonight."

"I've already told you, I'm not finished."

No longer wanting to continue that particular conversation Axel spread his awareness out, finding nothing inside the darkened hole.

"Can you smell anything?" he asked, knowing shifters had a superior sense of smell.

"No..." A slight hesitation at the question. "Nothing but rain and dust."

Axel pressed further inside, eyes adjusting to the pitch black. With a static pop the glamour that had protected the hole dispersed, and Sam let out a curse from behind.

"Bloody hell, what the fuck is that?"

Axel breathed through his mouth, the stench overwhelming as he scanned the room.

Drip. Drip. Drip.

He couldn't tell what it used to be, the walls painted in entrails and shit to the point it looked fake, a horror movie set. Everything looked too shiny, plastic. What would have been the door further into the building had been locked tight, the edges sealed with a hardened green sludge.

Drip. Drip. Drip.

Axel counted three heads, two torsos and more limbs than he cared to total piled in each corner, the centre what looked to be a bed made out of skin. The floor was tacky, red coating the entire thing as the pitter patter of blood dripped from the fresh kill on one of the piles.

"It's a nest." Axel pulled out as quickly as he could, happy to breathe in the cleaner air of the outside, despite the smell now escaping. "Was protected by glamour, which is why the scent barrier has been broken."

"You said there may be others?"

"Doubt they'll come back here now the glamour has been destroyed." Axel stood to his full height. "Do you have your phone? Because I'm going to need to call in the cleaners."

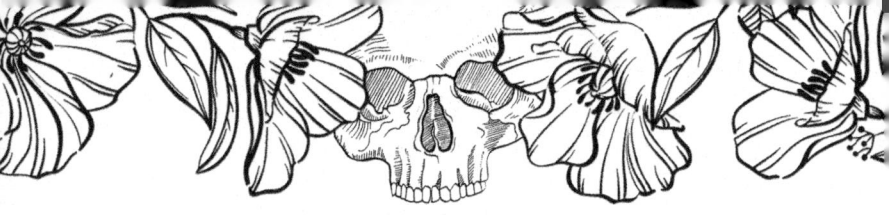

CHAPTER 11
SAM

S am wasn't sure why he still stood there, the stench of death wrapping around him like tentacles slowly forcing the air from his lungs. It was nauseating, but he wasn't finished with Axel. There was too much left unsaid, their last conversation leaving a sour taste in his mouth. Despite what Sam had said, they were friends. At least, he thought so anyway.

There was never anything more, and Axel had made it clear that there wouldn't be. Which was absolutely-fucking-fine because Sam drew a line with the Guardians anyway. Especially ones who liked to fuck with his head.

"This is the largest nest we have ever seen," Viktor, one of the cleaners said with an audible tut. He wrote something down on his clipboard, nodding to his wife who stood by his side.

"Yes," Viktoria replied, frowning up at Axel. "This is going to cost extra."

Sam leaned against the brick wall to the side, out of the way as he watched the two witches talk to Axel. They looked like dolls, both barely reaching five-foot and dressed in a pressed black suit and matching pencil-skirt dress. Not one hair was out of place, Viktoria's makeup was applied perfectly while Viktor's patent shoes didn't have a single smudge. They weren't like any cleaners he'd ever seen, not to mention their perfect upper-class English accents.

He'd been ignored for the past ten minutes as Axel explained the details, and he wasn't upset by it. Both of the cleaners reeked of ozone, their magic oozing out of their pores so much it made Sam's nose twitch, not to mention that both carried themselves with such superiority that Sam was a little intimidated. Both their irises were pure obsidian, matching their dark, perfectly styled hair, and if Sam hadn't smelt the ozone he would've put money down that they were vampires. They even moved like the bloodsuckers, each movement precise and thought out.

Viktor cleared his threat, nose wrinkling as he opened the briefcase that sat by his feet. With a click the gold clasps opened, and he rummaged inside the red velvet that was as bright as a bloodstain. Without a word he pulled out a crystal, white and about the size of his thumb.

"Da?" he asked, turning to his wife who nodded, just a single dip of her head. Reaching for his briefcase once more, he closed the claps, setting it in exactly the same place as it was before. Staring at the crystal in his palm he whispered, the words not carrying on the wind before he carefully placed it at the mouth of the nest.

The stomach-recoiling stench stopped, and Sam had never been so thankful for clean air.

"You," Viktoria barked, turning to face him. "Who are you? Civilian?"

Sam flicked his gaze at Axel, who refused to meet his eyes before returning his attention to the witch.

"Does he need to be taken care of?" she asked Axel, but remained facing Sam. "That will be extra, too."

Sam's spine stiffened before Axel said, "No. He's with me."

Viktoria sniffed, upper lip curled. Her next words were muffled, and it took a second to realise she was speaking in Russian. Sam blinked dumbly, wondering if she was speaking to him until Viktor replied in the same language.

"We accept the job," Viktoria said, returning to English, her accent once again perfect. "We will send the invoice to Mr Storm, as usual."

"Of course," Axel said, bowing his head slightly. "We appreciate your discretion, Viktoria. Viktor."

Viktoria dismissed him with a flick of her hand. "Be gone, druid. We need to work, and swiftly," she grumbled. "You called us too late. That will cost extra."

Viktor nodded, brushing his palms down his already perfectly pressed lapels.

Axel pursed his lips, gaze to the ground as he stepped towards Sam, gesturing for them both to leave. Sam followed in step, only turning to look back down the alley when they reached the road. Except he could see nothing, neither witch, hole nor remains of the hound. Nothing but perfect, unmarked brick.

"Those guys are fucking terrifying," Sam said when Axel paused beside him, a shock of heat against his skin that his leopard wanted to wrap himself up in. It was a confusing reaction, one he had never really experienced. Not with the people he slept with, and not even with the single boyfriend that was a failed experiment.

"You should be." Axel cleared his throat. "There's a reason they're on retainer and paid big money." His attention dropped to Sam's t-shirt, expression not changing.

It read *'Monday hates you too.'* It was fucking hilarious.

Sam waited for Axel to comment, but when he didn't, Sam closed his eyes, letting out a heavy sigh. The sun had started to push against the moon, but it was still cold as chills shook his bones, clothes soaked through. "I –"

"You should head home," Axel said, interrupting him.

Sam's stomach twisted, fists clenching. "Why do you do this?"

Axel finally looked up, a frown pinching his brows. "Do what?"

"Act like you're alone, that you don't have people around who would drop everything to support you."

Axel blinked, mouth opening to reply but Sam stopped him.

"I don't know how to help you, Axel. Because you need help, even more so because of your complete denial that it's normal to what? Self-medicate with drugs?"

Axel stiffened. "You don't understand –"

"Then help me understand." Sam moved until they were face to face, Axel's lips opening a fraction. "Help me understand. Tell me why you get high, why you poison yourself with all that shit."

Axel's body remained as rigid as granite. "I don't need to be fixed."

"Who said I wanted to fix you? I care about you, you fucking idiot." He wanted to scratch his claws across Axel's chest, just so he would react with something other than such indifferent bullshit.

Axel's hazel eyes were hard, empty when they steadied on his. "Look, you have your own stuff to deal with, and I have mine. Let's leave it at that."

A growl vibrated his chest. "Fine."

Axel's features remained frozen, not a single emotion as he stepped away. "Fine."

Sam ignored the ache developing behind his ribs. He was no longer able to feel the cold, his body numb as he slowly walked back to his place. His frustration had gone well past worry, and now sat sternly at anger.

Axel wasn't his problem, and yet why couldn't he shake him from his thoughts?

"Bloody idiot," he mumbled beneath his breath, strides quickening as he turned down his street. Sam understood addiction, the comforting familiarity of doing the same thing over and over. A compulsion. What he didn't understand was not wanting help in breaking the impulse, the need to hurt himself.

There must have been something more, because he had a support system. He had his cousin as well as the other Guardians, and yet he was in a free fall.

The gate to his home squeaked, and Sam halted. His front door was ajar, and he was confident he had slammed it closed before he had chased after Axel. Slowly approaching he listened, ears straining for movement inside.

Walking on silent feet he opened the door the rest of the way, stomach dropping when he noticed the words smeared in black across his wall. Heart thundering he swept the place, finally able to breath when he confirmed he was alone.

"Fuck," Sam muttered, reaching over to touch the paint that was still wet.

436 Lower Parade.
11.a.m
Don't be late.

"Was this really necessary?" Alice asked as she pushed the wet rag across the wall, wiping away the words. "What could he even want after all these years? Your father, I mean."

"He wants me to join his pack, I think," Sam said, back pressed to the opposite wall as he watched, Poe purring in his lap. "Apparently I'm this hot commodity, baby girl," he said, hiding the growing panic.

"Humble too, apparently," Alice said, catching his nerves.

"You're right, I should work on that," Sam said, smiling sadly as his best friend shook her head. "I've told you not to bother. I'm going to be looking for another place soon anyway, so I was going to leave it as a parting gift for Mr Gibbson."

"Your landlord's an arsehole," Alice said, puffing out a breath. "I said this when we first moved in, but I can't just leave this here where you can see it every day."

"Aye, he is an arsehole, but there isn't anything I can do about it. Not without a pack, and even then it wouldn't be worth it." Poe stretched in his lap, drawing his attention. "No, it's not worth it, is it my little poet?" he said in a high-pitched voice. The little bundle of black fur had gotten fatter, his mismatched eyes blinking up at Sam expectantly.

"Don't talk to him like he's a baby," Alice said, rolling her eyes. "If we have joint custody, you can at least talk to him normally."

"I gave you full custody because shifters don't keep pets," he said, his voice still high-pitched. They thought it was cruel, being they were part animal themselves.

"Oh, so we should release him?"

"No!" Sam pulled Poe closer to his chest, replicating a purr. "He's an idiot, he would never survive on the streets."

Alice shook her head, wiping the rag against the wall before she jumped back with a squeak. Sam was up, Poe on the floor before the thought even registered.

"What happened?" He gently touched Alice, rubbing his hands across her shoulders and down her arms while she stared at the wall. "Alice?"

"There's something in the paint," she said, eyes widening. "Magic."

"Magic?" he repeated. "What kind of magic? Can't you just throw salt at it or something?"

Alice frowned, a crease between her brows. "That's not how it works."

Sam shrugged. "What? That's how you usually deal with stuff, I've watched you for years just throwing salt at things that have gone wrong, hoping it'll fix it."

Alice shot him a look before she returned to the wall, her hand hesitant as she held it out. "I don't think this is paint."

"Then what the fuck is it?" He moved closer, his nose unable to pick up anything.

"I'm not sure, and I don't recognise the magic either." Hand closing, she pulled it back to her chest, frown deepening. "You can't stay here."

"Like fuck I can't. My father isn't going to do anything."

Alice ignored him as she headed towards the stairs, going up to his bedroom.

"Baby girl, stop. I'm not leaving."

"You're coming home with me." Alice pulled open his wardrobe, finding a rucksack at the bottom.

"Alice, I'm not leaving."

"That house is a fortress." She began pulling t-shirts out and stuffing them in the bag. "You kept saying you wanted a sleepover."

"Alice –"

"We could watch those horror movies you love, like we used to," she continued without a pause. "And go shopping for some more of your silly t-shirts."

"Alice –"

"Or we can –"

"I'm not leaving my home." Sam pulled the bag from the bed, ignoring Axel's scent on the rumpled sheets.

A single blink before Alice said, "Then I'll stay here with you."

Sam tightened his grip on the bag. "What will Riley say about that? I don't fancy taking on an angry druid because his mate has decided to sleep over at a friend's house."

Alice dismissed the comment with a single look. "Don't be an idiot, you know Riley loves you almost as much as I do."

"Aye, he said so last time I threatened to remove his bowels with my claws if he ever hurt you."

Alice pursed her lips.

"Don't look at me like that. He may be bigger and stronger, but I plan to fight dirty." Sam winked, but Alice remained upset. "Baby girl, it's fine."

"Your father broke into your home, the same father that abused you for years, who..." Alice turned her head to the side, fingers sparking in anger. "You've been protecting and helping me since we were kids. Let me do that for you. Please, Sam."

"Come here." Sam held out his arms, wrapping them around her until he could settle his chin on the top of her head. His leopard immediately calmed, his purr low as Poe curled his body around their legs. "Without you, I would be nothing right now, a lost boy without a home or family. You saved me, gave me a reason not to be so angry with the world."

"You can't stay here, it's not safe." Alice pulled back. "There's a reason he wants you, Sam."

"It doesn't matter though, does it? Because he can't have me." Sam shook his head, making sure his voice was soft, but strong. *"You're* my pack. I don't need him, or anyone else for that matter."

"We need to tell Riley, maybe the guys can keep a watch out or –"

"What's he going to do? Nothing, so I'm not going to bother Riley or any of the other guys with something that's just an inconvenience."

"But maybe –"

"And you won't say anything either," he said, pointedly looking at her. "I'm not going to run from him, Alice. Not now, not ever. He can't make me join his pack."

"I don't want you to get hurt."

"Ah, baby girl." Sam crushed Alice back to his chest. "He's nothing, a sperm donor who I refuse to acknowledge. He can't hurt me anymore."

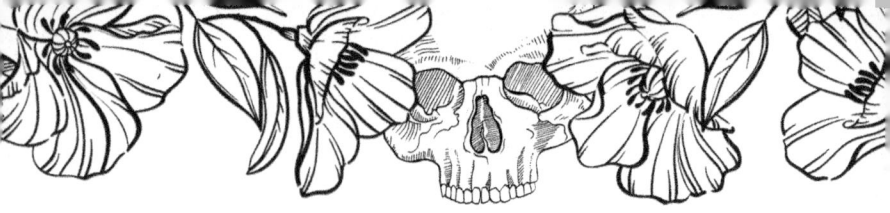

CHAPTER 12
AXEL

Axel ascended the steps, deciding to head straight to his room. He wasn't in the mood to speak to anyone, especially as the whispers were starting to return, which meant soon the pain would too. The constant noise was frustrating, distracting as he ignored the intrusive thoughts, but the pain was worse. A pill or two would help, keep the ache at bay until he figured out what to do about Crimson Mist. He couldn't take it like that again, but he could play with it a little. See if a smaller dose worked just as well when spliced with different herbs.

Then there was the beast situation, something he needed to discuss with Riley. His beast should never have been able to take over as the man, and even now, hours later, he still couldn't process those memories. It was as if he had been in a deep sleep, or more like a nightmare.

But then he had woken up to Sam...

"What the fuck do you think you're doing?" Axel shouted, finding Hunter searching under his bed.

Hunter jumped to his feet, putting his hands in his pockets. "Nothing."

"Nothing?" Hunter went to slip out beside him, but Axel caught his arm.

"Hey, get off me!"

Axel pulled his hands out, checking the front pocket of his dark hoodie before forcing his palms open. "What have you..." Inside his left hand was a single pill.

A kick to his shin, so unexpected he released his grip and Hunter staggered into the hallway, scrambling to remain on his feet.

"You need to get help," he said, knuckles white as he gripped the hem of his hoodie. "You can't keep telling yourself you're –"

"Hunter?" a voice boomed down the hallway. "Go to your room."

Hunter turned around with a snarl, the sound caught in his throat when he noticed Kace's expression. Without a word he stormed away, his feet smacking against the wood.

Axel froze in the threshold of his room, spine straightening at the rage in Kace's tone.

"Stay the fuck away from him," he said. "In fact, don't bother helping out at The Vault anymore."

"Excuse me?" Axel stepped closer, his hand clenching on the little white pill. "What the fuck have I done?" He helped Kace train at The Vault every few weeks, enjoying teaching the kids there how to defend themselves. Each of the Guardians took turns, and Axel found it weirdly calming.

"I can't have you influencing Hunter, not while he's still recovering," Kace said, voice ending in a growl. "So stay the fuck away. He's just a kid."

"Influencing him?"

Titus appeared, bourbon eyes flicking between the two of them. "Axel, Riley wants a meeting," he said, his voice soft, relaxed compared to the rising tension.

Axel gritted his teeth, the ache at the back of his skull growing. "Sure," he said to his cousin before returning his attention to Kace. "He's the one who broke into my fucking room."

Kace's eyes shifted, the liquid silver glistening as Axel felt his own beast push to the surface.

'Watch yourself,' Kace said telepathically, the mental connection locked between them.

Normally Axel would have laughed, talked Kace down from his rage but right then he wasn't feeling calm, or friendly. *'Maybe you should be watching your kid better.'*

"Axel," Titus interrupted, knowing they were seconds away from exchanging blows. "Let's go."

Kace watched Axel descend, lips pressed into a thin line.

"What was that about?" Titus whispered, following tightly on Axel's heels as he headed towards Riley's office. "What are you wearing?"

Axel frowned, remembering he was wearing one of Sam's shirts. Pulling the fabric away from his stomach he glanced at the design. It showed two arrows, one pointed up at his face and another straight down. Between them it read *'Two Seater.'*

Fucking hell.

"Nothing," Axel muttered, releasing his shirt. "It's just Kace being Kace." Pill still in hand he brushed his lips as if to scratch, covering the motion of swallowing the pill dry. He wouldn't have usually taken one so early on, but he guessed he needed the added boost, to help the noise inside his head from whispering too loudly.

He wasn't even sure what it was, and he didn't care. It took a minute or two to start feeling the effects. Everything seemed brighter, more defined as he moved through the house. The outside was gloomy, overcast with the rain running down the windows. It darkened the rooms, despite the morning sun and whatever drug he had just ingested into his system making everything seem better. Axel was more aware of every movement, even a slight twitch of his finger could be felt throughout his arm. He could almost physically feel Titus's stare, a brand against his skin as if he was suddenly hyperaware.

"It's just a sweet," he said, ignoring Titus's tension.

He shouldn't have taken the pill, not raw and without dilution from the herbs. It was a mistake, but if his options were the whispers that would soon turn to howls inside his mind, and the pain which crippled his body, or the feeling of euphoria. He knew he had little choice, but it was still a stupid, impulsive decision to have taken it without thought.

It seemed like he'd been making a few stupid decisions lately.

"I'm worried about you," Titus said, reaching over to stop Axel from opening the door. "Seriously, Axel."

"Why? I'm fine." At least he wasn't slurring, which was a bonus.

Titus grunted. "Yeah, you sure look like it." His grip tightened on Axel's shoulder for the briefest second before he released, instead opening the door with the flat of his palm.

Riley sat silently behind his desk, the computer screen creating shadows against his already hard features. The window framed him perfectly, and even with the miserable day outside it made him look powerful, a business mogul. Which wasn't exactly inaccurate.

He didn't look up as Axel waited, Titus a strong presence at his back.

"I've just got the invoice," Xander said from behind, slipping past them to close the door behind himself.

He placed the piece of paper in front of Riley, and then stood to his side.

"Nice shirt," he said, upper lip twitching.

Other than Riley, The Guardians didn't have a hierarchy. Each one was equal, but Xee always took himself as Riley's second, and no one else fought him for the position. Each individual Guardian had their strengths and weaknesses, and together it made them formidable. Brothers, joined through fate and not blood.

A few minutes more before Riley looked up, a frown pinching his brows. "How big was the nest?"

Titus stilled behind him.

"Looked like it housed three, maybe four hounds," Axel replied mechanically. "From what I witnessed there were at least eight bodies."

"That's what, the second nest we've found this month?" Xander grunted, crossing his arms.

"The Shadow-Veyn don't seem to be going back to The Nether," Riley said, rubbing at the stubble along his jaw, his eyes sharp as they steadied on Axel. "But that was a good catch."

"You weren't on rotation," Xander said. "So what, you just stumbled upon it?"

Axel cleared his throat. "I chased a hound."

Riley glanced at Titus before returning to Axel. "Is it dead?"

He nodded, the subtle movement causing his head to spin.

Fuck. What was in that pill?

"I managed to kill it before the rest of its pack came back to the nest," he continued. "Then I called the cleaners before it could be discovered by anyone else."

Riley stood, the heavy leather chair rolling back to knock against the glass. "What's the first rule, Axel?"

Titus shifted from one foot to another behind him, but Axel refused to turn as Riley repeated the question.

"Never engage alone," Axel mumbled.

Daemons were powerful, as were the Veyns who crawled out of Hell along with them. They may have been trained specifically to fight, their bodies tortured and forced to control magic that wasn't natural, but that didn't mean they were invincible.

"I can sense Daemonic energy," Riley said, his voice quietened as he stepped around the desk.

"No shit," Axel sniggered. "I just found a nest, what else do you expect?"

"Careful," Xander warned.

Riley moved until they were toe to toe, silver teasing at his irises. "No, I can sense Daemonic energy in *you*."

Axel dropped his gaze, unable to watch the disappointment he was sure would flash in Riley's expression. He knew the red had gone from his irises, but clearly some remnants of the drug still lingered. "There's something else I needed to discuss. Alone, Sire."

Riley paused, head cocked before he nodded. They didn't usually call him by his title, Riley preferring they didn't, but Axel knew it was the one way to get him alone. He was their leader, the strongest and first of them to go through the ritual to gain his beast.

"I took something last night, a gas called Crimson Mist. It allowed my beast to take control while still remaining the man."

A heavy pause. "Fucking hell." Riley's growl forced Axel's head back up. "How bad?"

"It wasn't that –"

"Axel," Riley snapped. "I'm not talking about your beast. As you're still in once piece, I'm going to assume that he released you quickly enough. I'm talking about you, and

105

the fact you took some fucking gas not knowing the conse-quences. So, how bad?"

"It was nothing, something to take the edge off –"

"Take the edge off?" Riley's voice had gone dangerously quiet. "What the fuck is wrong with you? I'm aware you take some shit, you're an adult who can make his own deci-sions. But it hasn't interfered with your hunting until now."

"What do you mean?" Axel stepped back. "It hasn't interfered with anything, and especially not me hunting."

"Rule number fucking one. Do you truly believe you would have made the decision to engage in that hound alone if you weren't fucking high?"

"What is this, shout at fucking Axel day? I wasn't high!"

"Then why the fuck would you even take it? You've just admitted you've taken brimstone, and it resulted in you losing control to your beast. Talk to me, Axel. Because I know for a fact you're not talking to Ti anymore. If there's a problem, we're here to help."

Axel's excuse was ready, but nothing came out. His face had become numb, the rain that had started to come down thicker once more glistened against the window like diamonds.

"You're not even listening."

Axel blinked, dragging his attention back to the conver-sation. "I'm sorry, it won't happen again."

"It better not, because I can't risk you out on the field like this. Next time you find a Shadow-Veyn alone, you don't engage without back up. Is that clear?"

Axel dipped his head. "Crystal."

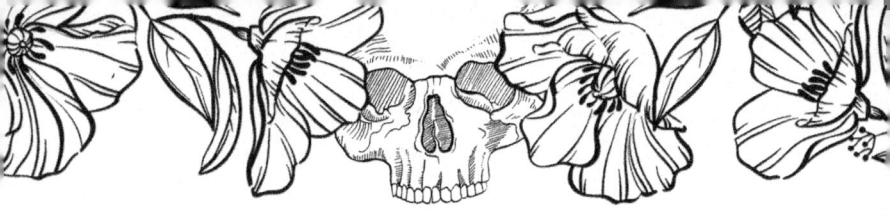

CHAPTER 13
AXEL

Something slammed, the loud crack pulling him from a deep sleep.

"Get the fuck up, arsehole," a voice snarled, and Axel felt himself be yanked up from his bed and up onto his feet. The ashtray he had balanced on his stomach clattered to the carpet, spilling ash and the remains of the joints he had just smoked.

Axel pushed at Titus's arms, loosening the grip on his t-shirt enough for him to step away. "What the fuck?" He blinked, rubbing the sleepiness from his eyes. "What's wrong with you?"

Titus stood at the side, vibrating with anger as his bourbon irises swirled the silver of his beast. "So I went to our apartment today," he said, voice a deep growl edged with ice. "To check everything was okay, considering I got a notification that the fire alarm went off."

Axel squinted his eyes, mind groggy. "Look, you shouldn't have used pink glitter, that was a dick move. It's just glue, I'm sure we can get something to dissolve it and your toys will be fine."

"What are you on about?" Titus growled. "I'm talking about your room, you know, where you've kept your fucking drugs."

"Keep your voice down!" Axel quickly slammed his bedroom door closed despite Titus's tone being quiet.

"Not to mention the bathroom," he continued. "The one where you've been hiding a fucking chem lab."

"It's no one's business but mine what I do in my own fucking room." Axel's beast was reacting to the violent current in the air, pulling him completely out of his daze.

"It's my business if you're hurting yourself. " Disappointment frosted his words. "You're family. How could I have not seen how bad it's become?"

"Ti, what have you done?" It was a whisper, panic strangling his voice. "What have you done?" The words rose to a scream.

"I've smashed it," he answered. "All of it."

"Fuck you, you selfish prick!" Axel began to pace, his movements rigid with rising anxiety. "You have no idea why I do this. The pain I'm in, the constant fucking noise in my head. Nothing helps except... Fuck." He glanced at the ashes on the floor, at what remained of the joints and wondered if he'd set them on fire, how much fumes could he inhale.

"I'm done protecting you, Axel." Titus stepped closer, forcing his attention back. "You were back up tonight, or did you forget? Again."

Axel stopped moving, remaining deadly still as Titus's words registered. He glanced at his phone, lying dead on the pillow.

He swallowed past the lump in his throat, mouth suddenly dry. "Was anyone hurt?" He wasn't on rotation, but he was on call to help if needed. Was *supposed* to be on call, and instead he had smoked until he had passed out.

Fucking. Great.

"Jax," Titus muttered. "But Sythe came when you didn't answer your phone. He'll be okay, it wasn't as bad as last time."

Axel couldn't help but glance down at Titus's chest, remembered the life-threatening wound his cousin had suffered. Axel was supposed to have been on call that night too, but instead he had been getting high at the bar. The same night he kissed Sam.

"I've been lying and protecting you for years, telling the others there was nothing wrong, hoping you'll sort yourself out and it was just a phase. I've risked everything for you, and you were sitting cooking your own shit this entire time." Titus looked away, a flush across his cheeks. "I can't do this anymore."

"The pain –"

"I'm done, Axel. Done with picking you up so high that you can barely walk and done with making excuses for your mistakes. I've tried to help you and you've done nothing but –"

"Help me?" Axel's voice rose once more. "Fuck you, you've never helped me do shit you arrogant prick. How can you help something that's beyond repair? My connection to my beast is fucking fragmented, Ti." Axel clenched his fist, so tight his knuckles cracked. "It's been ruined since the ritual. We're not bound properly. My beast isn't connected to me like everyone else, he's constantly trying to escape and it creates this intense ache and fucking whispers inside my head. The drugs, they help."

"You can try –"

"I've tried everything," he said. "I've gone to healers, holistic witches and I even tried asking a faerie down at the Troll Market. Nothing worked, the pain's still there to the point I can't take it anymore. The narcotics take the edge off, so I keep going back."

"I can't watch you destroy yourself," Titus said, his beast present in his tone. "You're going to kill yourself, and I'm not going to sit here and watch."

Something dark and twisted burned in the pit of Axel's stomach. "Stop acting like you're better than me, like you haven't got your own issues."

Titus's body tightened to granite.

"Maybe deal with your own problems rather than trying to control mine. I'm not your parents, you don't have to beg for my love and fucking attention."

"Fuck you." Titus's face smoothed to lethal calm. "You're at these crossroads, and only you can choose the right way."

Axel punched the wall. His chest hurt, his breathing coming in rapid pants as he struggled to catch it.

Titus laughed, the sound dark and hollow. "I found your car by the way, tracked it to The Bricks. I'm not even going to bother asking you why it was left all the way out there because I don't think you would tell me anyway. Three tires were stolen, and the back window was smashed so anything inside is probably missing too."

Without another word he turned, closing the door quietly behind him. Axel waited a single heartbeat before he took his anger out on his room. Picking up his laptop he threw it across the space, watching it crumple against the wall before he repeated the action with a book. Kicking out, he knocked over the bedside table, the sound of it crashing to the floor fuelling his rage as he attacked the desk next. His knuckles bled as he punched the wall once more, leaving a dent. The pain gave him a second of clarity, his pulse racing as he scrambled to what remained of the bed, pulling up the mattress to check his emergency stash. He found a single clear bag with a few pills and a hypodermic, the needle capped.

"Fuck. Fuck. Fuck." Axel's hands shook as he pulled the pills out, holding them in his palm to count.

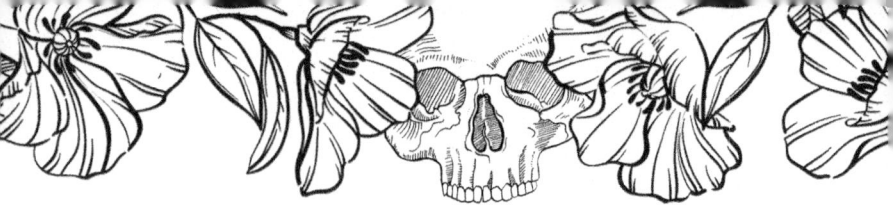

CHAPTER 14

SAM

"Whose idea was this again?" Alice mumbled as Lucifer pushed through the already busy crowd, the lead singer belting out a heavy rock song along with her band.

"Mine," Sam said with a grin. "I thought we needed a night out." *And somewhere to hide from my problems like the grown-arse adult I fucking am,* he mentally added.

Alice shot him a concerned look as if she could read his mind, which was a possibility knowing how well she knew him. Being at a concert was better than sitting at home, waiting for something to happen. Because he wouldn't be helping his father. Ever.

"Of *course* we need a night out," Lucifer added with an equally wide grin. "It's been months since we last went out."

"Didn't you recently play poker with the other guys?" Eva said, frowning up at Lucy.

Lucifer found a table at the back, snarling at the men who were currently sitting at it. They scrambled out the way, and Lucifer pumped his fist in victory. "That doesn't count because I lost." A thick dog chain wrapped around his throat, the bone-shaped tag a bright pink that read *'fluffy.'* A matching bum bag was strapped diagonally across his chest, and Sam wasn't stupid enough to ask what he kept inside, because knowing Lucy it was something ridiculous. Or dangerous. Or both.

He swept his arm towards the table, careful to not lose any of the liquid from the cocktails he held. "Ladies," Sam purred, waiting for both Alice and Eva to take their seats before he sat at the end. The music was trembling the floor beneath his feet, his body already starting to sway to the beat. He found Eva moving the same way, and he knew he picked the right place to take her.

His leopard could sense her apprehension of the crowd, which wasn't unexpected for a vampire of not even a year. His hearing was heightened, so he couldn't imagine what it would be like if all of his senses were enhanced. Overwhelming. But he knew she not only loved to dance, she needed it like her next breath. It was in the way she moved, in the way she expressed herself.

And she hadn't been able to do what she loved, her spirit diminishing with each passing week. Her confidence had been hit, and Sam couldn't help the need to fix things that were such an integrated part of her spirit. It was his nature, a compulsion to help, and Eva needed the freedom. To dance amongst a crowd and not feel trapped. She probably wasn't even aware, not really. Not until she got on that dance floor and let herself go without fear.

She was new to the Guardians dynamic, recently mating with the hot-head Kace. He wasn't exactly sure about the circumstances in which they'd mated, and it wasn't his business to pry. She wasn't a shifter, so he couldn't influence her with his calming nature, but taking her to a concert, where live bands played a wide variety of music was the next best thing.

So there they were, excitement brightening everyone's eyes as they all cheered, sipping their chosen drinks while the band rocked behind them.

"Where's Kyra?" Sam shouted to his left, where Alice was brushing her fingertip around the rim of her sex on the beach.

It was Lucifer who answered, his mojito already finished as he slammed it against the sticky table. "Had to finish a spell or something, said she may meet us here later." The stem of the glass cracked, and he stared at it for a few seconds before letting out a full belly-laugh. "Who wants another?" He didn't wait for a reply, standing up to march back across the large room to the bar. He paused to smile at a woman, who quickly looked away in fear.

"He's going to be pissed if he doesn't slow down," Eva said with a chuckle, sipping her own drink. "Ah, to be able to get drunk. Those were the days." She rolled her eyes, a smile tugging up her full lips.

Sam echoed the smile, knowing vampires couldn't become intoxicated no matter how much alcohol they consumed unless it was mixed with fresh blood. Unfortunately, not many places provided it, except Blood Bar, and he wasn't stupid enough to offer his wrist knowing her mate would probably create a necklace with his ribs if he even tried. Which would actually go quite well with the vampire fangs that currently hung elegantly from Eva's ears.

"How are you feeling?" he asked her, noting the tension along her bare shoulders.

Eva's smile widened as she took another sip, relaxing a fraction. "Like I'm almost ready to dance."

"Then drink up!" Lucifer shouted above Sam's head, a

tray of tequila shots landing heavily on the table. "Then you dance while I find someone to play with." He wiggled his eyebrows, and when no one commented he added, "you know? I want someone to fuc –"

"Lucy!" Alice squeaked. "We get it," she laughed.

"I didn't think this would be your scene," Eva said, grabbing the shot from the centre of the table while Sam reached for his own.

Lucifer downed his drink, frowning at the glass. "I always go clubbing with Sam," he said, his teeth sharper than usual. Which, Sam knew from experience meant he wasn't consciously controlling his glamour. Probably because that was his fourth shot and they had been there less than thirty minutes. "I'm his... what's the word?" He turned to look at Sam expectantly, red eyes glowing.

"Wing man."

"Wing man," Lucifer repeated in his smoky tone. "Because you know, I have wings."

"That's not..." Sam shook his head. "Anyway, I plan to get both you ladies happily tipsy and safely back home. So drink up, and let's dance." He downed his shot, loving the burn of the tequila as it went down.

"Are you not having another?" Eva asked him as Lucifer gave out the rest.

Sam smiled, already feeling the slight buzz. "And who will warn away any disgusting men who believe they stand a chance with you beautiful ladies if I'm too drunk?"

"Me?" Lucifer said, his face uncharacteristically serious. "I'll just kill them."

"Lucifer, we've talked about this," Alice sighed. "You can't just casually kill people."

"No one will know it was me." Lucy's eyes darkened. "No means no."

Eva reached over to squeeze his hand.

"Okay, we need to lighten the mood." Sam finished the rest of his cocktail, knocking his knuckles against the table. "Finish your drinks, and then let's get moving."

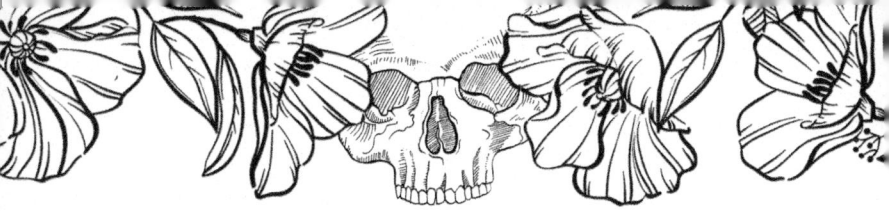

CHAPTER 15
AXEL

The treadmill whined, and still Axel increased the speed. The rhythmic pumping of his legs was soothing, his breaths becoming more rapid as his muscles burned at the constant movement. Exercise released dopamine, serotonin, and adrenaline. A beautiful mixture that helped keep the pain at bay, but only lasted a short time. Impractical compared to drugs.

Axel increased his speed, ignoring the smoke that tickled his nose.

"You're going to break the machine if you carry on," Kace said from behind.

Axel glanced up, glaring at his brother in the floor to ceiling mirrors that encircled the entire basement gym. He had sensed Kace enter, and he was more than happy to ignore him.

Kace's lips thinned as he crossed his arms across his chest. "I've just heard you've been taken off rotation."

"Word travels fast." It hadn't taken long before Riley had appeared at his bedroom door, and by then he had ripped apart the bed, the mattress torn to shreds as he searched every little crevice in his panic. He didn't think he would hit lower than rock bottom, but there he was.

Axel increased his speed, and the machine rattled dangerously beneath him.

With a grumble Kace kicked at the plug, yanking the cord from the wall.

Axel almost tripped, catching himself on the treadmill's frame. "What the fuck? You could have killed me!"

"I'm worried that Hunter may start using again." Kace said, ignoring Axel's glare. "I don't know how to stop him."

"What's that got to do with me?" Axel's ribs ached, his heart thumping aggressively as he tried to settle his breathing. "I have my own problems, if you couldn't tell."

"Don't bullshit me, Pretty Boy," Kace growled. "We both know why."

Axel finally stepped off the belt. "Why do I get a shitty nickname and you get something cool like Red?"

"Because you look like a model and I make people bleed for a living," Kace said, matter of factly. "Now, what did Hunter find in your room earlier?"

Axel reached for his towel, wiping across his face and chest to give him a few more seconds to reply. A lie was ready, but he was so tired of the lying, and the deceit. Of pretending everything was fucking fine when in reality he was at the edge, and the dark abyss was looking more and more welcoming.

"A pill." Kace's expression darkened, but before he could comment Axel continued. "I don't believe he wanted it for himself, he's a good kid. He was just... he thinks I have an addiction." Axel sunk to the ground, his legs thankful for the relief.

"Well, do you?"

"I..." He had taken that little white pill without hesitation, his instinct to swallow without thought. It wasn't about the pain, or even the whispers inside his head. He'd felt its weight in his palm, and all he wanted to was to take it, to feel the familiarity of it travelling down his throat.

"Axel?"

"I... don't know." It was the first time he didn't outright dispute it, and it was almost cathartic.

"How often did you take something when you first started?"

Axel didn't hesitate. "Once a week or so, you know, to help with the pain."

Kace's gaze was direct. "And now?"

Axel gripped the towel between his hands. "Every day or two." With a groan it ripped in two. Frustrated, he balled them in his fists, staring down at the frayed edge.

"Are you on something now?"

Yes. But Axel couldn't bring himself to admit it. "K, how did you overcome your issues with your beast?"

Kace's brow raised. "Why? Do you think there's an issue with *your* beast?"

"It's like there's a connection between me and the beast that's broken."

"If it's broken, then it can be repaired."

Axel let out a humourless laugh. "How did you do it? Your beast was a fucking maniac and yet you're... not as irrational as before."

Kace chuckled, sinking to the floor opposite. "My beast is still a homicidal maniac, but since I've mated Eva, I've better control. It's constant work, and I still crave violence. I'm pretty sure the rage will always be there, it's just not as constant when I'm around her. Eva grounds me." He smacked his chest with an open palm, just above his heart. "Right here. It's hard to explain."

"I'm happy for you, brother."

Kace's smile was small. "Out of us all, I would never

have believed there was a soulmate for me. I was prepared to be alone, always fighting against our curse until the very end."

Axel shook his head. "I don't think I could ever mate."

"Why? Because you like guys?" Kace frowned. "Same sex relationships amongst Breed aren't uncommon."

"No, no it's not that." Axel glanced at the ring Kace wore on his finger, the gold stolen from Eva's ex-boyfriend. It was an interesting choice.

"Hey, are you guys coming?" Xander poked his head through the door, Kyra smiling beside him.

Axel was thankful for the chance to settle his thoughts. "Coming where?"

"There's a battle of the bands or something. Supposed to be a fun night out and I've never been to a concert before," Kyra answered. "And neither of you are out hunting tonight."

"It sounds busy," Kace said as he stood. "I don't do crowds."

"No, but you're coming," Xander said. "Because you can't stay away from Eva."

Kace clicked his neck. "Fine, but only because I plan to seduce my mate back to our bed."

Xander looked amused, his pale eyes brightening. "What if she doesn't want to leave?"

"Then I'll put her over my shoulder and take her home anyway."

Kyra's laugh echoed around the gym. "She'll bite you."

"Oh, I hope so." Kace smirked.

"I take it back," Axel muttered. "You're still a maniac."

Kyra shook her head, still laughing when she turned to Axel. "So, are you coming or not?"

"He's coming," Kace answered for him. *'Sitting in self-*

pit isn't going to help,' he added, the mental connection sharp as Axel pushed him from his mind.

Xander's knowing gaze was heavy. "Then let's get going."

The room was uncomfortably electric, the atmosphere thick tendrils that wrapped around him like a suffocating blanket.

Agreeing to the concert was a bad idea. He was already unstable, his thoughts splintered after his realisation that his self-medication may not have been as simple as he wanted to believe. Even now, with the last of the pill in his system gone, all he could think about was his next fix, the panic starting to build before the pain could return in full force.

So was that addiction?

Or was it more fear?

'You can't return until you're clean.' Riley's voice brushed across his memory. *'I can't risk you being on the hunt when you're not in control. You could hurt yourself, or someone else.'*

Axel fought the shame. He wanted to be alone, somewhere where there wasn't a crowd who could all see the disappointment that was an aura surrounding him. His sole purpose, the reason why he was fucking created, was to fight against Daemons and the creatures that escaped along with them. Now he was nothing. Useless.

The band on stage effortlessly moved to their next song, the pyrotechnics flashing across the crowd as the balls of arcane flames were carefully controlled by the lead singer. She stood in the centre, the microphone pressed to her lips as she sung, wand stretched to point to the fiery orbs that danced along with her voice. It took impressive control, especially with the anti-magic sphere that was suspended from the ceiling. It was aimed away from the stage, but Axel could still feel the strength of the deterrent vibrate against his chi. With magic came chaos, so it wasn't uncommon to see the expensive preventive measure in such a large venue.

Xander and Kyra stopped to look at the show, Xander's arms moving to wrap around his mate's waist as he whispered something intimately into her ear.

"You all make me feel sick," Axel shouted to Kace, who in return smirked despite the tension along his muscles. "You can't just go from wild barbarians to domesticated house-husbands. It's unnatural." He gestured to Xander, who shot him an amused look over his shoulder.

"Who said we're domesticated?" Kace replied.

Kyra turned, frowning until Xander explained the conversation. "Didn't you serve Eva breakfast in bed the other morning?"

"*I* was the breakfast," he growled, head snapping to the side. Kace's expression remained severe, his gaze sweeping the busy crowd, distracted.

Without a word he walked away, and Axel tracked him through the dancers. They all parted like water, a natural instinct to move out of the way of something bigger, stronger. Kace was a man of barely suppressed violence, and he wore it clearly in the way he held himself. His brother would never have put himself in a situation with a busy crowd unless it was for his mate, and he found Eva in the centre, arms held high in the air as her body danced to the music. Her smile was private, her lips silently moving before Kace reached down and threw her over his shoulder just as he had said, her laughter clear even from the distance.

Axel quickly averted his eyes, jealously an unwanted emotion on top of everything else in his fucked up mind. He hadn't lied, he was happy his brother had found his soulmate. It made three of the seven Guardians mated. Three out of seven who had broken their curses.

One-hundred years from their ritual to bind to another person permanently, or risk becoming their beasts forever, serving a fallen angel in the depths of Hell.

What a load of fucking bullshit.

"Fuck this," he muttered, keeping his eyes down as he stepped away from the crowd and into the darker corners of the club. It was where depravity lived, and that was exactly what he wanted as he searched in the gloomy booths against the walls. He could sense arousal, his body attuned to the hormones thanks to his succubus genes. When he was younger, he would have joined, sought out sex just as he was searching for drugs. But the thought of fucking strangers now caused panic to grip his lungs like a vice.

Abstinence gave him control, something he didn't really have anywhere else in his life. He hadn't chosen to be thrown into combat training at nine.

He hadn't chosen to be bound to his beast.

He hadn't chosen to take narcotics to help quell the pain.

He found exactly who he was looking for in the fourth booth, the man's hard gaze sweeping consistently across the dancers. When they steadied on his he paused, and at Axel's gesture he nodded, inviting him over.

"Yes?" he asked as soon as Axel slipped into the bench opposite.

"Brimstone," Axel said quietly, looking back over his shoulder towards the dance floor. "Whatever you've got."

He was already a fuck-up, getting kicked out of his job and losing his best friend in the span of a few hours. So he would be as well going down in flames.

The man pursed his lips, slowly assessing Axel in his dark t-shirt, jeans, and heavy black boots. At least he wasn't still wearing Sam's funny tee, because that would have gone down like a lead balloon.

With a sound of impatience Axel opened his wallet, flashing the cash stored there before slamming it closed.

"Alright, guv. Give me a minute." The man stood, stepping down from the booth. "Stay here."

Axel waited as he swept the area once more, his knee bouncing beneath the table. He couldn't see either of his brothers, not by the bar or at the edge of the dance floor. He could sense them in the room, and if he concentrated, he would be able to find them, not that he wanted to be found himself.

Axel waited, nervously flicking his gaze back across the...

Sam stood by the stage, head thrown back, eyes closed as he rocked perfectly in time to the music. He moved like liquid, and even in human form he had the effortless elegance only a cat could pull off. His long blond hair had been tied away from his face, his t-shirt tight enough to act like a second skin. He drew those around him, the neighbouring dancers just as captivated by his beauty and grace.

Axel wondered what Sam would do if he joined him, if he pressed himself against his back and danced along to whatever beat the band created. He could almost visualise it as he found himself unable to look away. Axel froze when Sam turned his head, their gaze somehow meeting through the busy crowd and across the distance.

Sound dimmed, the rock music losing all definition until it was nothing but a single, forgettable noise. Axel's lips parted slightly as their eyes locked, desire prickling.

"Here you go guv," the dealer said as he stepped back into the booth. "That will be two hundred."

Sam's amber eyes glowed, quickly shifting to the right

before returning. He gave a subtle shake of his head, but the connection was already broken.

"That will be two-hundred," the dealer repeated, tapping the table with his finger.

Axel tossed down some cash, not bothering to count as he swiped the bag and stood. His strides were quick, palms beginning to sweat as he pushed himself through the throngs of people, searching for somewhere quiet and alone. He found the bathrooms down a secluded corridor at the back of the club, separated from the main area. Thankful they were enclosed individual units, Axel entered an empty stall, turning to flick the lock.

A quiet curse before Sam pushed inside, closing the door behind him.

"What are you doing?" Axel asked, breath coming in nervous gasps. "Get out."

"I can't." Sam pressed himself against the bathroom door.

"Fine, you do you." Axel opened the bag, hand shaking as he pulled out the hypodermic needle and specialised vial of dirty brown powder. Without looking up he ripped the bottom of his t-shirt, quickly tying the scrap of fabric around his bicep. The vial was next, arcane burning in his palm as he heated the powder until it bubbled into a foul-smelling liquid, and quickly inserted the syringe. He turned away from Sam, his attention burning across his back.

A low growl, and Axel jerked his head up to look at Sam in the reflection in the mirror. The glass was fractured, a spider web of cracks all leading from a fist-sized hole, but even with the warped view he caught Sam's steady gaze.

Axel pressed the needle into his skin, but Sam came at him far quicker than he had anticipated. The tip scraped a bloody line down his arm, missing the vein as he turned with a snarl. He had dropped the vial, it shattering on the black tiles as Sam grabbed at the hypodermic.

"Fuck the –"

The words were swallowed by Sam's lips, his tongue sweeping in as he pulled the needle from Axel's grasp.

A second hesitation, a pause before Axel kissed him back. He silenced all of the anxious, guilty thoughts from his mind, locking them away as Sam pressed even closer, the feel of his thick, heavy arousal pressing against his jeans, forcing a moan from Axel's throat. Lust burned through his blood, the nerves and panic that had settled in his gut turning to something darker, more twisted where there were no consequences.

Fuck it.

Wrapping a hand in Sam's hair he pulled forward, his tongue fighting for dominance he wasn't even sure he wanted to win. Sam was ruthless in his invasion, his touch possessive, and Axel finally surrendered entirely without an ounce of resistance. He had denied himself any sort of sexual release for so long, and right then he was thankful he had waited because nothing compared to Sam's soft lips, his grip strong as he held Axel's nape, his thumb pressing just hard enough that Axel was aware of the power of the hold. And that turned him on even more, that his partner was a strong male who wasn't weak or frail. Wasn't some little mouse who would shrink at Axel's burdens.

No, Sam was so confident in his strength that it made any submission so much hotter. It made Axel want to bury himself in his heat, lose himself in his tight body until there was nothing else to crave but him.

His own, personal drug.

Sam finally pulled back, breathing in heavy pants. His pupils had swollen, nearly concealing the beautiful molten amber of his irises. Electricity crackled in the air as he yanked at Axel's t-shirt, fingers exploring the deep lines of each ab with an impatience Axel echoed. Cotton tore, the fabric falling from his shoulders in scraps before he did the same to his own shirt.

This time Axel took the lead, crashing their mouths together in a kiss just as explosive as the first, desperation and need taking over as he pushed Sam back against the cool tiles. Lust was steadily building beneath his skin, hands exploring Sam's chest before dropping down to tug at his belt.

The buckle opened, the faux leather slipping from each belt loop before Axel felt claws prickle against his forearms, pushing him back.

"Yum," Sam whispered, his voice a throaty purr as he dropped to his knees, keeping the eye contact as he reached forward to free Axel's cock.

"Fuck!" he growled, ready to combust as a pearl of arousal glistened on his tip and Sam caught it with a flick of his tongue. Legs weak Axel planted his palms on the wall, steadying himself as Sam gave his cock another long, languorous lick.

Axel was hard as a fucking rock, his skin so painfully tight as Sam dipped his head once more, licking down the length. But it was a sweet pain, one Axel welcomed as his hips jutted forward and Sam pulled back, only to circle his tongue around the crown before repeating the movement over and over.

"Fuck. Fuck. Fuck," Axel muttered, his voice a harsh curse as Sam concentrated on the head. He blew out a breath, teeth clenched as his hips flexed, and Sam took his entire length down his throat.

Nose pressed to his groin, Sam hummed, the vibration almost too much as Axel pulled back to hold his cock at the base, trying to stop himself from coming right then and there.

Sam panted, lips moist and swollen as he reached down to pump his own, thick cock. The sight was mesmerising, and Axel gripped harder, hoping the visual of Sam on his knees with his heavy cock glistening in a tight fist will be forever imbedded into his mind.

"Up," he rumbled, desperation making him impatient. He wanted to savour the moment, take his time, but if he didn't bury himself in Sam soon, he was going to combust. Any sort of intimacy had been too long, and it had never felt like this, as if his next breath relied on it.

Sam stood in one, fluid movement. Somehow losing his jeans to stand there naked, his body mouth-watering as Axel pulled him back to his lips, able to taste himself on Sam's tongue. Sam groaned into the kiss, flexing his hips to rub his cock against Axel's, both trapped between them. The friction almost sent him over the edge, each subtle shift sending little tremors along his spine.

"Mine," he all but growled, spinning Sam until he was the one who faced the wall, his palms flat on the tiles as Axel kissed along his throat.

Reaching around he slipped his fingers into Sam's mouth, allowing him to quickly suck before releasing the digits with a pop. Axel found his entrance, teasing in circles before slipping a single finger inside, his cock already slick from Sam's saliva and from his own arousal. But he forced himself to take his time.

"Fuck," he groaned, feeling how tight he was before he added a second finger.

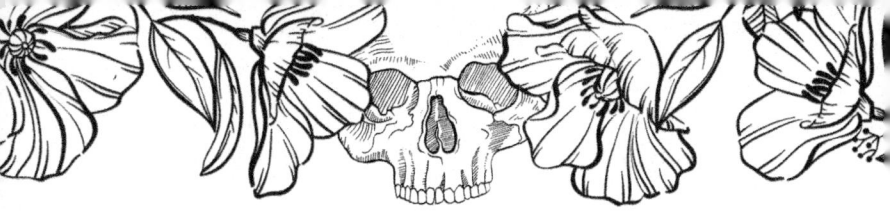

CHAPTER 16

SAM

S am thought he had never been so turned on in his entire life when Axel had first pressed him against his living room wall, but nothing compared to the feeling of Axel's hard body at his back, his lips rough against his throat and fingers stretching, preparing.

Body tightening with anticipation, he arched his back, trying to take Axel deeper as those talented fingers brushed against his prostate with such confidence that electricity shot down his cock, the tip already leaking.

He moaned at their loss, lasting only a second before Axel replaced it with something bigger, and fuck did Sam want it. He sucked in a sharp breath, the thick head pushing past the first ring of muscle too slowly for the growing sexual tension between them. The burn was delicious, just on the edge of pain as Sam bent himself lower, his breath strained as he took Axel's length in a single, gentle push.

He had never felt so full.

"Fuck, you feel so good." Axel pulled back an inch, thrusting forward with a controlled movement that brushed perfectly against Sam's sensitive spot, and had him seeing stars. But Sam didn't want restrained, he wanted rough. Axel needed to lose himself, to forget the reason why he came into the dingy bathroom in the first place.

Sam wanted him to remember nothing but his body, and his lips.

Remember nothing but him.

Letting out a sound of frustration he rolled his hips, clenching his inner muscles. "Harder."

Axel groaned, continuing his shallow thrusts. "I'm trying..." Another thrust, their groans echoing against the surrounding tiles. "Not to..."Axel moved faster, his breath coming in puffs. "Hurt you."

Sam couldn't speak, could barely think as he concentrated on Axel's cock filling him up, moans falling from his lips as he struggled to regain control. Each thrust made his cock throb, ache for a release only Axel could bring. "Please," he rasped, struggling to push the word out.

Axel finally surged forward until he was buried to the hilt, hand fisting in Sam's hair and forcing his body to bend until his back hit solid chest. Axel controlled the angle as his hips thrust with such strength that any arousal Sam had, had intensified until it crackled violently in his veins.

They were the perfect height, almost identical as Axel pinned him in place, and Sam revelled in the power as he felt himself be dragged closer and closer to the climax he craved.

Axel set a punishing rhythm, each thrust stealing the remaining oxygen from his lungs. The heat of his chest was like a full body caress, one that made Sam's leopard purr with pleasure. His cock reached places he had never thought existed, pleasure so intense colour burst beneath his eyelids as he palmed his aching cock. He moaned at how hot and heavy he had become, the skin pulled almost painfully taut as he rubbed his thumb along his slick tip.

"Fuck," Sam grunted, biting his lip to keep from crying out.

Axel finally realised his grip on his hair, only to wrap it around Sam's cock. "Mine," he growled low into his ear, stroking him at the same pace as his thrusts.

The dull ache along his skull only added to the desire as Sam turned his head, catching Axel's fractured reflection in the broken mirror beside them.

Their eyes met, Axel's irises that of his beast while Sam's glowed that of his leopard. Axel's mouth was open, lips parted and face creased with such desire that Sam almost came at the sight alone.

Sam moaned, no longer caring if anyone heard. His skin was ablaze, the pleasure pulled from Axel's strokes intense. His orgasm exploded, a roar ripping from his throat as hot liquid squirted against his abs in powerful jets. Axel's own hips stuttered, his cry a vibration that caused Sam's knees to almost buckle as he felt Axel spill himself deep inside.

"Fuck," Axel groaned, pressing his forehead to Sam's shoulder. "That was... fuck."

Ditto, Sam thought, unable to say actual words as he tried to calm his racing pulse. When he had first chased Axel down, he wasn't sure what he was doing, all he knew was that he couldn't let Axel drown by himself. He hadn't planned to kiss him, and he definitely hadn't planned to let Axel fuck him.

Not only fuck, but the best fucking sex he had ever experienced, and Sam had had a lot of it. Sex with Axel was different, it wasn't a simple joining of bodies for a mutual orgasm. It was something more, something he couldn't explain.

And that was terrifying.

He was surprised at the disappointment when Axel pulled out, at the sudden emptiness. He couldn't move, not even when Axel cleaned him up as he just breathed, his body still overly sensitive.

"I didn't mean for that to happen," he said, voice humiliatingly hoarse. Probably because he screamed. He never screamed.

Axel froze behind him, and Sam finally turned, thankful for the cool tiles against his fevered skin. Axel wouldn't look at him, and right then Sam was fine with that as he studied every inch of Axel's skin. His chest was clearly carved from stone, the glyphs tattooed there glowing a pale white light that slowly dimmed until they settled back into their fine, black, and red lines. His arms were roped with muscle, although not as big as his other brothers, but hard and defined enough that Sam wanted to explore them slowly with his tongue.

His thighs were solid, tensed and then there was his cock, relaxed and spent between his thick legs. Axel seemed just as comfortable with his nudity as Sam was, and Sam felt himself stirring once more despite having the most mind-blowing orgasm in his life.

"That was..." he erupted into laughter, and Axel finally looked up with a frown. "That was fucking amazing."

"Did I hurt you?"

Sam wiped his stomach, the effervescence bubbling through his blood fading at the quiet question. "Aye, that's why I've made a complete mess of myself." Axel's face remained hard, so Sam rolled his eyes with a smirk. "You didn't do anything to me I didn't enjoy."

"That was..." Axel seemed lost for words, and Sam understood. "I didn't mean for that to happen either."

"Well, I'll give you an A for effort." Even though it couldn't really happen again, because Sam wanted to fuck him, to bite and mark while he pumped Axel full of his seed. It was an instinct he was fighting, because Sam didn't get attached. Couldn't get attached. Not to the sex god who was supposed to be off limits.

His leopard clawed to be released, to rub against Axel and scent mark him to warn others away.

Fuck.

Sam reached for his jeans, at the same time Axel did, both tugging them on quickly. "Well, this was –"

"Thank you for –"

Sam burst into laughter once more, the tension palpable as he reached for his ruined shirt. "This was nice." – *Nice? It was more than fucking nice!* – "But I need to get back to the girls. You know, chicks before dicks."

Axel blinked, brows knitting together as he pulled on his own shirt, now with randomly placed tears. "Yeah, okay. I should get away from temptation anyway." He rubbed at his neck, and Sam wished it was his claws leaving scratches instead.

Please stop!

The drive almost overpowered his control to the point he could feel his claws prickle at his fingertips, ready to be released. "Temptation?" he echoed, voice dropping low.

Axel's lips parted as their eyes locked, electricity a violent storm between them. "See you around, Samion."

Sam waited a heartbeat as Axel unlocked the bathroom door, ignoring the woman who stood outside and scowled as he took a moment to himself.

"That definitely can't happen again," he muttered to the air, bending over the sink to splash cold water against his face. He had hoped it would dowse the hunger that twisted his stomach, desire wanting him to hunt Axel down and do that all again.

Sam had always been aware of their unnatural magnetism. It reminded him of the connections of a pack, a spiritual bond between two shifters.

But Axel wasn't a shifter.

With a frown Sam closed his eyes, visualising the threads of life. Usually only strong dominants had the ability see the pack dynamic, and despite Sam being a registered loner, he did have a golden thread woven around his chest. He was alone as a shifter, but he wasn't alone according to the magic that bonded shifters together as a group. He knew if Alice was in the same room, the golden thread would tangle around her too, connecting them on a spiritual level by magic neither of them understood. Sam guessed long ago it was a trauma response, the bond attaching itself to the first person he had ever loved, and despite them not being technically pack, the magic didn't care. His spirit leopard didn't care either.

As Sam opened his eyes he blinked at his fractured reflection, finding no other threads, which didn't explain his constant awareness of Axel.

"I'm just being ridiculous," he muttered, dragging a palm over his face. What he had to do was go back and dance, find someone else to take home just like he usually did. Except the idea left a bitter taste in his mouth.

A loud knock. "Hurry up in there, I need to go!"

Stepping back from the sink Sam searched for the needle, finding it behind the toilet, covered in grime as he carefully wrapped it in tissue. The vial had broken into relatively blunt shards when he had tackled Axel, so he pushed them with his boot into the corner for the clean-up crew later.

"Sorry," he said as he pulled the door open, the woman who had waited for the bathroom relaxing a fraction at his apologetic smile. "All yours." Carefully holding the hypodermic behind his back, he made his way towards an exit, stepping out into the cool, night air.

He couldn't dispose of it inside where anyone could

find it, so stepping down the side alley he found a large bin, breaking the needle from the base before tossing the remains in with the rest of the rubbish.

Sam closed the lid, his ears perking up as he heard a footstep directly behind. The hair on the back of his neck stood at attention as he turned, and something solid flashed in his vision.

Instincts kicked in and he dropped, the makeshift bat swinging over his head with a whoosh as he tackled the aggressor, his shoulder pushing into a hard stomach before he rolled over the top, landing on his feet.

Three more men appeared in his peripheral while the fourth straightened to his full height. Two of the four were reasonably large, with the wide shoulders and thick arms of people who frequented the gym. The other two were small and scrawny, body emaciated. But it wasn't their size that made Sam hesitate. It was their faces, which were so meticulously painted it took a second for Sam to realise their heads weren't actually stripped of skin. Unlike on Samhain, where it was common to see someone painted as a skeleton, the bone wasn't as white as paper, nor was the black poorly applied and grey. Instead, they were painted a dirty cream, the shadows smudged in just the right places to emphasise hard edges and empty holes. The black around their eyes was so dark it created a void, drawing focusing to their irises, which were all various shades of red.

Fuck.

Sam growled, his fingertips stinging as his claws pierced through flesh, controlling the parts of his body he wanted to shift. He was more powerful as the leopard compared to the man, but the time it took for him to change shape left him vulnerable.

Sam's eyes dipped to their weapons, each brandishing a blunt object designed to hurt. Their hands remained unpainted, as were their arms, where thick, black veins pulsed beneath ashen skin.

He knew he would never have been able to win against four men at once, but he would sure as hell try and make them hurt.

"You're late," a familiar voice said from behind, and Sam froze. "It seems I do need to remind you what happens if you disappoint me, Son. You've brought this on yourself, maybe next time you'll remember this before you disobey your Alpha."

Before Sam could react, all four skulls stepped forward as one, their movements far faster than he had expected. He sensed a familiar scent of animal, but it was wrong, rotten, as he took a hit to his stomach, doubling him over before another blow his across the back of his shoulders.

The next swing missed as he twisted, brick dust crumbling around him as the lead pipe hit the wall where his head was just moments before. Struggling to regain his breath, Sam planted his feet harder into the cobbled stones as his fist caught one of the skulls, knuckles connecting hard enough he felt it reverberate down his arm.

Barely a grunt, the skull's lips peeling back to reveal sharpened teeth that he snapped in threat. His tongue was black and twisted, the end raw as if it had been hacked off with a blunt knife.

A knock to Sam's head, hard enough it threw him against the wall, the pain sharp before another blow brought him to his knees.

"That's enough you eejits," his father said. "We need him alive, for the good of the pack."

Sam hunched his back, arms shaking as he spat blood on the floor. A shadow moved closer, and he growled as his father came into view.

"I'm just trying to help you," his father said, crouching

down. "You're meant to be with me, and your pack. You'll understand when I get you home, where you're supposed to be." Snapping his head to the side he clicked at the closest skull. "Bring him."

Sam tensed, ready to fight once more despite his body protesting. He glared through the strands of his hair, teeth bared.

"Sam, what are you..." Lucifer's eyes flicked from Sam, to his father, to the skulls all within a single second as he stepped into the alley. With a roar he exploded, horns piercing through his hair to curl down towards his jaw while his wings burst from his back, far larger than the space provided. He bounced on the closest man, and without any hesitation tore his head clean from his shoulders.

Sam rocked back onto the heels of his feet, controlling his breathing as the other skulls ran, dropping their weapons as Lucy called after them.

"You scared little cunts!" he screeched, dropping the head at the same time his foot came up in a kick. The head shot down the darkened alley, and only then did Lucy twist to face him.

Sam tried to smile, his father long gone. "You're the best fucking wing man."

Lucifer rolled his shoulders, his wings disappearing into his back. "You never stated fighting in this role of wing man. I love it." He dropped down to Sam's height. "You look like shit."

Sam chuckled. "I feel it." With a groan he climbed to his feet, using the wall as leverage. "What are you going to do about that?" He gestured to the headless body.

Lucy clicked his tongue, opening the bright pink bum bag strapped across his chest. Inside he pulled out a ball, which he threw carelessly towards the corpse. It exploded with a burst of white, and Sam coughed as the cloud settled to reveal nothing but glitter, and a slightly scorched hole in the centre of the dead man's chest.

A bomb. Lucy had had a bomb in his bag. One with glitter.

"Looks like I'll have deal with it," he grumbled. His eyes flashed further down the alley. "Probably shouldn't have kicked the head, though." Lucifer shrugged, retuning his attention to Sam.

"Get me home, Luce," Sam said on a pained exhale. "And you better not tell anyone about this."

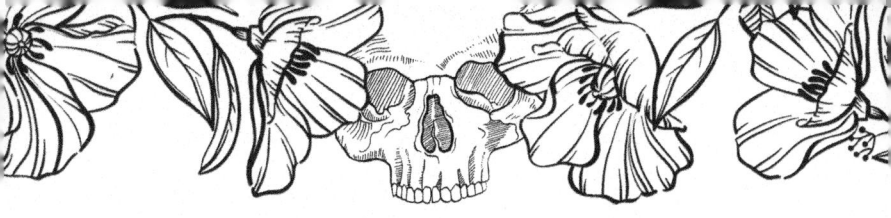

CHAPTER 17
AXEL

A xel looked at the empty needle sticking out of his arm, the rush of the brimstone already over. Thirty seconds, that was how long the euphoria lasted. Thirty seconds, and it hadn't done anything but make him feel weak.

He had woken up with no pain, his body relaxed, and even the whispers had quietened to almost nothing. He felt... revitalised. But still, he found himself in a dirty bathroom in a strip club at the edge of The Bricks at eight in the morning.

"Fuck!" he cursed, yanking out the needle and throwing it across the small room. It shattered against the black painted wall, the same dire shade as the toilet and sink. It hadn't even taken him twelve hours before he sought it out, the pills that rested in his pocket not enough.

When did he get to that point?

Impulsive. Reckless. An Addict.

"Hey baby, you done?" The women who had sold him the brimstone leaned casually against the wall, lines of white powder smeared on the basin, her skirt so short her lace thong peeked from beneath the fabric. "Or did you need something else?"

Self-loathing burned, even more so when he looked into the grimy mirror to find his pupils blown wide. "No," he grumbled, flinching when she reached over to touch his shoulder.

"Are you sure?" she purred. "We don't usually get people who look like you in here."

The shit he had just injected was weak, cheap. He needed his own stuff, brimstone carefully mixed with valerian root, fentanyl, and any other herbs he had to hand. He didn't even need relief, and he already knew the shit he had just taken wouldn't have helped any of his pain. He had taken it because it was all he could think about, that and Sam. But it wasn't like he could hunt Sam down and take out his needs on him.

Take his anger out at breaking his celibacy on him.

"I won't even charge you."

Even high he would have had no problem denying her request. The door to the bathroom opened with a creak, the corridor dark as he turned the corner to the main floor. Even so early in the morning there were people dancing, twisting their bodies around poles while an audience watched. The men and women may have been beautiful once, but they weren't anymore. Sores, inflamed veins and blackened palms; Track marks visible even beneath the poor lighting, the dancers trapped by their own dependences.

Axel was aware that if he didn't have glyphs tattooed, he would probably look the same. His skin would be scarred and broken, a visible reminder of his weakness. Maybe that was what he needed, rather than his body healing the needle marks instantly.

Ignoring the glares from the bouncer, Axel stepped out

into the early morning sunshine, squinting his eyes as he began his walk towards Chinatown. That was where he was supposed to be, where he intended to go, before he found himself standing in front of 'Paradise Strip.' It was as if he was pulled there by a force, his beast scolding him as he made his way inside. The fact his beast communicated should have broken through his compulsion, but instead it made his need to self-sabotage worse.

An angry huff, pressure at the back of his mind.

Shut up, he growled in reply.

The walk was bitter, and it wasn't long before the quietness of the morning was disrupted by busy commuters. Agitation made him impatient as he followed the red lanterns hung high across the buildings. Familiar scents and colours should have been calming, and yet, as he found himself in front of his childhood home, all he felt was shame.

Lǎolao wasn't directly his blood, connected only by being Titus's maternal grandmother, but that had meant nothing when Axel had found his father dead, and Titus his only remaining family. Having already taken guardianship over Titus from a young age, she opened her arms for Axel too, and he would always adore her for not letting him go into the system. She owed him nothing, the nephew of the son-in-law she despised, and still she welcomed him as if he were her own.

He could already envision her disappointment for the drugs that coursed through his veins, or the ones that burned a hole in his pocket. Could imagine the conversation, how she would blame herself for his poor choices.

Axel paused, staring at the worn, red paint of the door as he debated whether to press the bell or not.

Lǎolao's flat was above a bakery, and a place he ate at

frequently as a boy. Both Axel and Titus had offered to buy her somewhere else, a place where at eighty-nine she didn't have to climb so many stairs every day, but she'd refused with a stern warning each time. She'd always explained she'd met her husband only a street away in the main market of Chinatown, and they'd lived in that flat for over fifty-years before he'd succumbed to his old age.

"Are you going to see that old-bat or not?" a familiar voice said from behind. "I assumed she was dead by now. Humans have such disappointing lifespans."

Axel closed his eyes, breathing through his nose before he turned to face the beautiful woman who stood across the street. She was almost as tall as he was, with curvy hips and slim legs most models would kill for. Her dark brown hair hung loose around her shoulders, thick lips ticked up in a smirk.

Of course she was here, he thought. *Like a fucking bloodhound.*

"Well?" she said when he remained silent. "Is that any way to greet your mother?"

"What are you doing here, Thallia?" he grunted, stepping down and away from the door. If Lǎolao saw his mother here she would beat her with a pan.

Thallia pursed her lips, and a man passing seemed to trip over air at just the sight of her.

Axel couldn't stop the roll of his eyes.

"I've come to check on my son," she said, her tone a touch harsher. "That's what a mother does."

Axel's laugh was humourless. "It's been five years, and the last time you turned up without notice all you cared about was money."

Purple eyes hardened, but he remained where he was as she crossed the street and stroked her hand down his cheek. "You've grown into such a handsome man, so much

142

like your father." Bitterness edged the end of her sentence.

"It's been five –"

"You know how it's like in Asherah," she said with a flippant wave of her hand. "Time runs differently. For you it was five years, for me it was a matter of months. You have no idea how hard it's been to come back since the doorway's been closed."

"What do you want? Is it money?" Axel turned on his heel, walking swiftly towards the food market, where he hoped to lose her in the crowds. "I'll send you your usual cheque."

Thallia's face reddened, anger flashing. "I'm not here for money, I'm here for you," she said, keeping up with his long strides with ease. "You're my only young, so I must know you're not starving yourself."

"Does it look like I'm starving?" Axel scratched down his arm, his skin stretched tight. He felt so aware of the drugs in his pocket, his hands itching to grab them. Trying to improve his high was much better than having to deal with his narcissistic egg donor.

Nails caught his wrist, pulling him to a stop with a surprising show of strength. "Axel, I'm your mother."

Axel ignored the enamoured stares by the crowd for the women who had birthed him as he gently pulled out of her hold. "Why are you really here, Thallia?" he asked, his voice hushed. "Because you've never been a mother to me. The instant you pushed me out you left."

"I left you with a father that was capable," she said, frustration seeping into her voice. "When I found out he had... I came back, but you were already happy with that old bat."

"Watch yourself," Axel snarled, "Lăolao was nothing but kind, something I never received from you."

"Sometimes the best thing for your child isn't you."

Axel swallowed his next comment, not sure whether she was being genuine or not, as she looked away. He could feel the stares, some for him, but mainly for his mother. She was truly beautiful, even more so when she wasn't glamouring her natural glow. Which made sense considering she was a succubus, a faerie who fed off sex. Her beauty was nothing but a trick.

"Just because I never planned to have a son, doesn't mean I don't care for you," she continued, flicking her hair over her shoulder. "But now you've come of age, I need to enlighten you about your Fae genes."

"You're a few years too late, and in case you've forgotten, I'm one-hundred percent druid." He couldn't hide the resentment. "Not my fault you fucked a Breed who could only sire males."

"No, but you still share my genes, which means you'll likely have some succubus tendencies." She grabbed him when he went to turn away. "I've been sending you toys to play with, but you've refused them all. You must feed, spread your seed or risk starving yourself."

"Oh, for fuck's sake." Axel gently pushed her away from the market, not wanting the conversation to be overheard. "So that's what you wanted? To breed me?"

"Stop acting like a child," she snapped. "This is your nature. Not only sex, but intimacy and affection. I've sent you every gender, and not once have you taken any of them up on their offers."

"I can't do this right now." Axel pinched the bridge of his nose, trying to stop the headache from forming behind his eyes. He was already coming down, which just made everything worse. His choices. His mother. "I just... go back home to Asherah of Far. You've done your motherly duty for this decade."

He didn't hear her reply, wanting to get as far away from her as possible before he finally lost it.

Axel carefully placed the broken side table beside the rolled-up rug. He'd spent the last few hours cleaning his room, picking up the remains of the furniture he'd broken in his rage. His bed was fixable, but two side tables, his desk, a chest of drawers and a mirror had been removed and positioned with the rubbish outside. His room was now empty, but it was what he needed.

A fresh start.

A place to get clean.

Axel leaned against the broken furniture, listening to the wind whistle through the surrounding trees. Grass danced in the distance, and Axel grounded himself in nature. It was calming, especially since the effects of the cheap brimstone had finally dissipated from his system. He could already feel the need rising, his skin itchy, stomach clenched with the compulsion to seek out more.

But he wouldn't fall.

His beast hummed in agreement, and Axel smiled at the easier communication between them.

Riley was a man of his word and removed him from rotation for hunting, which was the wakeup call he needed. His mistake that morning proved he had a problem, that it was more than self-medication. He would need to find another way to relieve the pain. One that didn't compromise himself, or his brothers.

"You look weird," Lucifer commented as he returned from his run, his bare chest slick with sweat. "You're smiling, but I've just been told you've been kicked out of The Guardians."

"I haven't been kicked out," Axel growled. "I've been *temporarily* removed."

He couldn't help himself from tracing the tattoos, which were so similar to the Guardians', across Lucifer's skin. He had almost as many as Titus, the swirls and lines old, reflecting a history of druid and Daemonic magic. Normal druids couldn't handle more than a few glyphs tattooed around their wrists to help stabilise their chi, but Daemons went beyond most druidic boundaries. Which was likely one of the reasons his brethren ascended into dark magic.

"Sure," Lucifer said with a chuckle. "Welcome to the losers club."

"I'm not a loser," Axel said, hardening his voice into steel. "This is just a hiccup."

"Whatever helps you sleep at night," Lucy said with a mocking smile, cocking his head. "Hey, do you have a thing with Samion?"

The change of subject made Axel frown, a migraine beginning to ache. "Sam?"

"So you won't mind if I have a go with the cat then?"

Axel almost burst from his skin, his fist snapping out to knock Lucy's jaw with a sharp crack. The ferocity of his attack surprised him, especially considering Lucy didn't retaliate.

Anger lit the Daemon's eyes, his hand coming up to rub the already bruising mark. "I'm convinced you're all fucking idiots."

"Stay away from Sam," Axel said, his voice deadly calm despite the burst of violence.

"Do you think that was a normal reaction? I'm not inter-ested in the leopard, you prick. But clearly you are." Lucy dropped his hand, his face uncharacteristically devoid of humour.

"I'm... It's not what..." Axel's voice drifted off.

146

"Sam was one of my first friends up here in the light, and last night he was attacked at the concert."

"Attacked?" Blood turned to ice in his veins.

A smirk slashed Lucy's face. "Sam asked me not to tell anyone, but I'm an arsehole so." A shrug, a knowing glint in his eye. "You better go check on him."

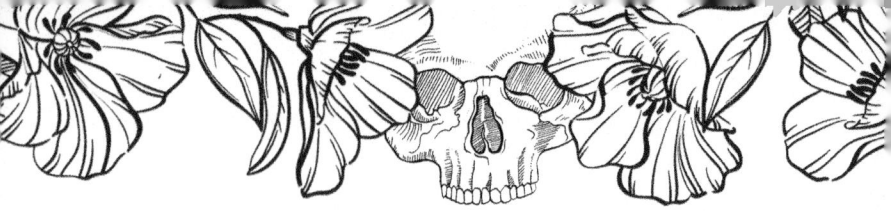

CHAPTER 18

SAM

Bang. Bang. Bang.

Why the fuck was someone knocking on his door like a bad-tempered child so early in the morning?

Sam groaned as he rolled out of bed, blinking at the light that seeped through the curtains. *Okay, so it wasn't morning,* he thought with a frown. Waiting for his legs to stop shaking, he passed the mirror, quickly turning to check he had all his appendages in the right place. The bruises had already lightened to yellow, the ache from them just a memory as his body readjusted to standing on two legs rather than four.

Bang. Bang. Bang.

"I'm coming," he grumbled, sucking in a pained breath as he descended the stairs. He'd lost count how many times he'd shifted, healing any wounds that would have otherwise required medical attention. He'd taken a few dangerous hits to his head, but bar the headache he, was confident there wasn't any permanent damage. Probably.

Bang. Bang. Bang.

"I said I'm..." Axel stood on the doorstep, the sinking sun creating an angelic halo around him. "Coming."

"I can see that." Axel raised a brow, eyes taking their time to slowly trace down his body. His eyes darkened at each bruise and cut, but he seemed to hesitate when he got lower.

It was then that Sam remembered he was naked. "Looks like Lucifer has a big mouth," he muttered, leaning against the edge of the door to better steady himself. "Remind me to buy him coal for next Winter Solstice." He didn't bother to hide himself, not because Axel had already seen it, but because he was a shifter, and nakedness just wasn't something that bothered them. Bodies were beautiful, every size, shade, wrinkle, mark, and scar. And Sam's was covered in scars.

"I'll help you pick out the biggest one," Axel said before his attention flicked behind him, his entire body stiffening.

Ah, shit. Sam let out an exhale, turning back inside. The paint was still smeared across his wall, the words barely readable.

"What happened?" Ice cooled Axel's voice.

"My father," he replied with a humourless laugh. "He wanted me to join his pack. I said no, so they decided to hit me with several blunt objects."

"Why didn't you tell me?"

"Aye, I'm sorry, when did you expect me to do that? When I caught you trying to hurt yourself, or when you were busy fucking me?" Sam flinched at his own bitterness. "Why are you even here?" He turned, faced with a beautiful man with an expression carved from stone.

"Because, I'm not going to keep pretending like you don't matter to me." Axel stepped closer, a wall of masculine heat. "Because I can't get you out of my head, and the sheer fear I felt when I found out someone had hurt..." He cleared his throat. "I've lost everything. I can't lose you too."

Sam licked at his lips, and Axel's attention dropped to the movement. "This is just sex." He waited for Axel to close the distance, tension strung taut between them.

"Is it?"

The beginning of panic gripped Sam's chest, stirring confusing as desire raced through him too. "That's all I can give you." He'd tried a relationship, quickly realising he couldn't commit to a single person. Sex had become a crutch, a way to cope with his past.

"I'm not asking for anything." Axel shifted the bag in his arms, one that Sam hadn't even noticed. "Your bathroom through there?"

Sam blinked, startled by the sudden shift in conversation. "My bathroom?"

Axel turned towards the kitchen, opening doors until he found what he was looking for. Within seconds Sam heard water running, steam quickly escaping.

"What are you doing?" he asked when he found Axel kneeling by the freestanding bath, pouring what looked like milk into the water. The subtle scent of lavender drifted from the bubbles, and Sam felt the strain on his shoulders already relaxing.

"What does it look like? I'm trying to look after you."

"I thought you had come over to..." He couldn't seem to finish his sentence.

"You thought I came over to What? Have sex? Hours after you've been attacked?" Axel looked horrified. "Bloody hell Sam, I'm fucked up, but I'm not that fucked up. I was celibate until last night, I'm not –"

"Celibate?" Sam's smile faltered. "I... fuck. I didn't know. I wouldn't have –"

"I don't regret it," Axel interrupted, his voice a deep

timbre. "I realised I was using the celibacy as a weapon, and it wasn't healthy." Turning off the tap he checked the water, his fingers creating ripples as he gently broke the surface. "I've realised a lot of things that I do that aren't healthy." Axel sat back on his heels, waiting with patience as Sam hesitated in the doorway. "It's not easy, you know, admitting you have a problem."

Sam flicked his attention to the glistening water before returning to Axel.

"I've added some special oils, they'll help the aches without risking scars." Axel's eyes dipped to Sam's chest. "It's an old Chinese recipe," he continued when Sam remained uncharacteristically silent.

"You're not Chinese."

Axel's upper lip twitched.

An unrecognisable emotion wrapped around Sam's chest, tightening with every step closer to the bath. The temperature was hot when he finally sank into the water, and he immediately let out a moan. "Thank you."

Axel shrugged, leaning against the edge. "It's just a bath."

Sam shifted his legs, too tall to fully submerge himself. He sat up, the milky water pooling at his waist. "So... why were you celibate?"

Axel's lashes dropped low over his eyes. "At first it was a fuck you to my mum, but after a while I used it as a way to control a single aspect of my life." He scratched his nails down his jeans. "It's hard to explain."

"No, I understand completely." Sam clasped his hands beneath the water, his hair drifting forward over his shoulders to create a protective curtain. "You said I fucked everything that moves, but that's not entirely true."

Axel cursed. "I didn't mean it; I was angry and wasn't thinking."

Sam shook his head. "It doesn't matter, but I don't sleep with just anyone, actually I'm very particular who I fuck."

"You don't need to explain to me."

"Please, let me finish." A knot formed in the pit of his stomach. "I need to finish, to explain, because I understand the need for control. Control over my body was taken from me when I was young. I fuck a lot of people, but I *choose* who I fuck. It has to be on my terms."

The silence was cutting, and Sam dared look up as his fingers twisted uneasily.

"My old therapist once told me that sexual promiscuity after abuse, especially as a child, is a way for the victim to gain power in a situation they had no control of when they were young." A gentle shrug. "So aye, I understand where you're coming from."

Axel reached over to brush Sam's hair from his shoulder, combing his fingers through the strands. "We're a unique pair."

The water had cooled, and Sam pulled his knees up towards his chest. His skin was as soft as silk, his bruises no longer aching as much.

"We're too fucked up; it would never work." *He* was too fucked up. Sam knew he needed constant validation in order to feel, and Axel wouldn't be enough. He'd made peace with never settling down, content in never committing. But right then, there was a sadness, an emotion buried so deeply, he hadn't even realised it was there.

"Sam, look at me."

Sam clenched his jaw, but he followed the gentle command only to find Axel had moved closer. And just like that Sam wanted him, lust bursting through all the uncomfortable emotions that were forcing themselves to the surface after being suppressed for so long.

"Kiss me," he whispered, his voice raw, vulnerable. "Please."

Axel moved closer, his lips a temptation. "I'm not going to ask you for more, because I know that right now you can't give it." He closed the distance, his moan breaking through Sam's lips as his tongue swept in. There was no rush, no urgency as they just tasted one another, Sam's left hand wrapping inside Axel's t-shirt before the right scratched along his jaw, the long stubble deliciously rough. Only their lips touched, but sensation stretched tight across his skin, making him lightheaded as he savoured every shared breath, every caress and moan.

This wasn't about sex, it was about intimacy and support, which was something Sam had never really experienced before. Creating a connection emotionally, rather than physically wasn't something he'd ever wanted, yet he found himself rising from the bath, water dripping down his chest to pull Axel closer, using his touch to fight against the memories that threatened to unravel him.

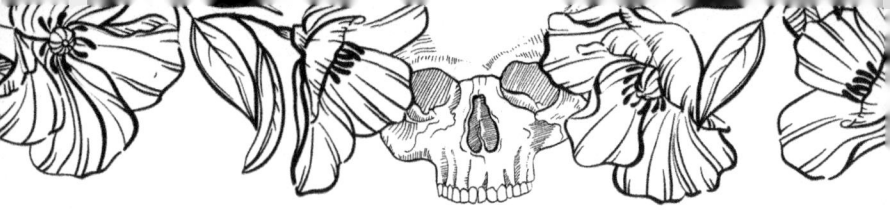

CHAPTER 19
AXEL

Sam had been passed out for hours, his breathing steady and even. Axel had made him shift twice more after his bath, the results knocking him out to the point he'd almost had to carry him to bed.

He wasn't supposed to stay the night, watching him sleep like some creep, but he couldn't seem to bring himself to leave. It was strange to lie beside someone else, their warmth more comforting than the blanket that pooled low on his hips.

But he was too hot, his skin stretched painfully. Tugging at his t-shirt didn't help, nor the sweat that dripped down his forehead as his fingers itched, searching for the pills he kept in his pocket.

Carefully removing the blanket, Axel slipped out of the bed, and Sam let out a low complaint in his sleep.

Mine, his beast grumbled, the word clear and precise.

Axel pursed his lips, a heavy ache rattling behind his ribs, and despite rubbing the heel of his palm over it he couldn't seem to erase the strange sensation. It had been too long since he had poisoned himself, his body craving its next fix. That must have been it.

Forcing his attention away from Sam, he slowly descended the stairs, making sure each step was silent as he padded across the wooden floor to the bathroom. Pressing himself against the closed door, he just breathed, the faint scent of lavender lingering from before.

Dragging a hand through his hair, he carefully reached for the clear bag from his back pocket, arm shaking as he counted the three pills. One had been slightly crushed, more of a powder but the other two were fine, smiling faces carved onto the small circular surfaces.

Axel opened the bag, the pills odourless as he tipped everything into his palm.

His pulse throbbed, his was mouth dry as he scrambled to the toilet, tipping the drugs into the water and flushing. Stomach cramping, Axel pressed his forehead to the cool surface, fighting against the nausea and sudden dizziness.

Pathetic, he thought. *Weak.*

Taking a single, controlled breath, he pulled out his phone, texting the one person Sam trusted.

Climbing to his feet, Axel turned to the sink, splashing cold water against his face. Shoulders hunched he caught his reflection, not recognising the man in the mirror. His eyes were hollow, the skin beneath dark as if bruised.

A beep, his phone brightening to reveal a response. It gave him a new focus, one that didn't involve self-loathing as he finally opened the bathroom to go stand in the living room.

The sky was a pale pink on the horizon, the large windows allowing for a beautiful view as Axel waited, biting his nails, concentrating on each of Sam's breaths as he slept above. It wasn't long until he saw Alice's shadow, and before she could knock he opened the door quietly.

"He's asleep," he whispered before she could say anything. "He needs to rest."

Alice wore dark jeans and a tight black t-shirt, her Spook Squad badge pinned to her belt. "What happened?" she asked, matching his volume. Her eyes searched his, her power an uncomfortable prickle against his chi. He had known Alice for a while, fought beside her and he was always surprised with the amount of suppressed power she carried. "Axel?"

He hesitated, wondering how much he should tell her. He decided on everything he knew, hoping Sam would fill her in more when he awoke.

Her power increased along with her anger, her fingernails leaving distinctive dents in her arm by the time he had finished. But behind that anger he saw a flash of guilt, and his beast sought blood.

"You knew he'd been threatened?" Axel asked, beast deepening his tone. "What the fuck, Alice? Why didn't you say anything?"

SAM

Voices drifted, rousing Sam from his sleep.

"You knew he'd been threatened?" Axel growled, low and threatening. "What the fuck, Alice? Why didn't you say anything?"

"Don't you dare –"

Sam jumped out of bed, taking the steps two at a time. "Enough," he said, his voice like gravel, his body stiff from sleep. "Hey, baby girl." He tried to smile at Alice, but her glare could cut glass.

"Don't baby girl me, Samion Murphy!" She poked him gently in the chest, her cheeks flushed. "You were attacked and –"

Sam pulled her into a hug, the rest of her sentence muffled against his chest. He met Axel's guarded stare, Alice short enough he could rest his chin comfortably on the top of her head. "You have to protect me, because I'm sure Alice's going kill me," he joked.

Axel's face remained blank, schooled into an emotionless mask, and Sam ignored the heavy weight that settled on his chest, not sure how to handle the sudden hot and cold.

"Has she planted any endangered plants recently?" Sam continued with a tight smile. "That's where you'll find me buried by tomorrow."

Alice pulled back with a grumble. "You're giving me grey hairs."

"Aw, don't worry baby girl, I'm sure granny chic will suit you."

Axel cleared his throat, forcing the attention back to him. "I'm going to go; I just didn't think you should be alone right now." His eyes drifted to the wall, concentrating on the paint.

Sam wanted him to stay, the words at the edge of his tongue. But instead panic tightened his vocal cords, his lungs filling with cement. Maybe this was his out, a chance to create the space he usually needed. Axel coming over had changed their dynamic, and Sam wasn't sure what he wanted.

If he pursued Axel, he was sure it would end up in heartbreak. He had never felt more than a slight warmth for any of his other sexual partners, but with Axel it was different, a scorching hot chemistry that made him want to risk being burned to embers.

A heartbeat passed, and then another, time stretching until the tension overwhelmed the air between them. When Sam remained silent Axel nodded, turning to Alice to give her a gentle bow before passing through the front door.

Releasing Alice, Sam stepped back, fighting the urge to go after him.

"What was that about?" Alice asked, her voice soft.

Sam worried his lip, staring out the window as if Axel would suddenly turn back. "Fuck," he whispered beneath his breath. "Nothing. It was nothing."

"That sure as hell wasn't nothing," Alice said, brows pulled together.

Sam crossed his arms, compressing them against his chest as if it would keep him together. "I told him I don't do commitment; I can only give him sex."

"Don't do that." Alice's frown deepened as she reached over to pull at his arms. "You're more than just sex."

"Alice, I'm not good at –"

"You're more than just sex," she repeated, but Sam barely heard it.

"I need to pack," he muttered. "I'm thinking about staying in a hotel for a few days, you know, until I can figure out this thing with da."

"You're coming home with me. We'll figure it out together."

"Sure." Defeat edged his tone. "Just give me a second." He didn't wait for an answer as he made his way back to his room, stopping for a moment to take in the space he'd made his sanctuary. Independence was important to him, which was why, even as a child sneaking into Alice's room he'd made sure to leave what little money he stole on her bedside table. It was a roof over his head, and so he felt the need to pay his way.

He couldn't be a burden.

As an adult, he took it to the extreme. He paid for everything, making sure he was never in debt and always keeping a little nest egg as backup, ensuring he would never be homeless again. His own home had been a lifelong goal, and now everything was being taken away.

Anger burned through his veins, and with a snarl he swung his arms across the dresser, knocking every frame, ornament, and mirror to the floor with a crash. Tears prickled his eyes, but he refused to let them fall. Turning to his bed, the scent of Axel still strong, he shredded the sheets, knocking the headboard so hard the wood cracked down the centre.

He sensed Alice on the stairs, but he was too far gone. He wasn't sure how much time had passed before he finally felt Alice's arms around his waist, her cheek pressed against his back. It finally broke him, and as he crashed to his knees she went with him, holding him as he finally allowed himself to break apart.

"I'm going to kill him," he said, liquid salt on his upper lip. "He's made me a child again, weak and fucking defenceless."

"You're neither weak, nor defenceless," Alice whispered against him. "You never were. You punish yourself for what happened, but you know deep down you could never blame a child for the actions of an adult."

Sam closed his eyes, centring himself with touch, concentrating on her weight against his skin. He was exactly like a child, one who sought comfort from someone familiar. Someone safe.

"You care so deeply, Sam, but you disguise your pain, and I don't know how to help you. You deserve happiness. You deserve love."

"I love you," he said, voice raw. "I let you love me."

"You know that's different," she whispered, tightening her hold. "You've always been cautious of being in love, and I understand why. But you're holding yourself back. A wise man once told me you're allowed to be happy."

Sam recognised his own words, once spoken to her long ago.

"Be happy, Sam." Alice pulled back, and as he remained frozen where he was she moved around to face him.

"It's not that simple." Sam's tone was rough, the words trapped in his throat. "What... What if I let someone in, and they still leave?"

"Love is –"

"Love isn't enough!" he interrupted, body trembling. "Love isn't enough. What happened, what I went through... They loved me, Alice, and despite that they used me like –"

"That wasn't love." Alice pressed her forehead against his, cupping his jaw as tears burned down his face.

"To them it was love." Nausea threatened at the memory. "To them it was –"

"That wasn't love. I know that. *You* know that." Alice sat back on her heels, her own face wet as she reached down to grip his hands. "I know you, Samion, better than anyone else. I know your secrets, your nightmares and darkest thoughts, and still you deserve the world."

Sam closed his eyes. "I love you, baby girl."

Alice lifted their joined hands, pulling them to her chest. "I know, I love you too. But now I think it's time you spread your love to someone else. I believe some souls were always meant to be, whether its best friends like you and me, lovers, or soulmates. Stop telling yourself you're not worthy of love when your heart is so kind. You have a soul-mate out there who will love and accept you as the person you are, who'll never let you be anything but your imper-fect, beautiful self."

"Wait," Sam sniffled. "You think I'm imperfect?"

Alice chuckled, loosening her hold. "You are my

sunlight in a world of darkness, but your fear of commitment is stopping you from being truly happy."

"Bloody hell Alice, go easy on me, would you?"

"You're afraid of being hurt, because you believe committing to someone makes you vulnerable, when in reality it makes you stronger. I hope one day you'll understand, because honestly Sam, you're worth loving."

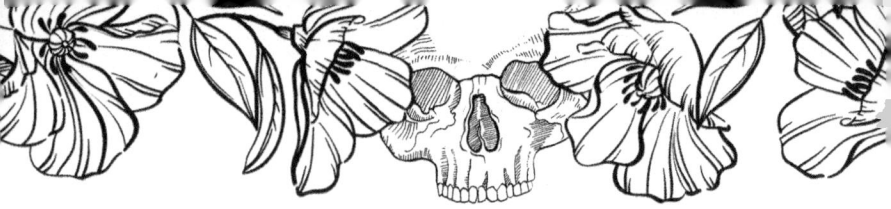

CHAPTER 20

AXEL

J ax stared at him from across the table, his dark navy
eyes icy as he sat there in judgemental silence.

"Are you going to say anything?" Axel growled,
picking at his nails beneath the table. "Or are you just
going to stare like a fucking freak?"

A single brow raised, his face remained hard as he
purposely crossed his arms, his chin held at its usual arrogant tilt.

"Axel," Riley barked. "That's enough."

Anger mixed with his growing agitation, but he bit his
tongue as he turned to face away, jaw clenched. He had no
outlet, nothing to distract himself from the need surging
through his veins. Nausea threatened, his palms sweaty as
he dragged them down his jeans.

"They're called the Undead," Lucifer said with a twist
of his lips. "That's who attacked Sam, which means you
boys have a serious problem on your hands."

Axel jerked his head to the side, meeting Lucy's red
gaze.

"There've been whispers of a new organisation cutting
through the Undercity, faces of death who've been slowly

gaining territory," Sythe said, his boots on the table as he leaned back in his chair.

"Viper territory?" Kace said, seeming to spit the name.

Sythe shook his head. "According to my team, the majority of the Vipers' territory has remained untouched due to the damage. But what wasn't destroyed was split amicably between the remaining Lords."

"Amicably?" Axel laughed. "Of course it wasn't fucking amicable. They're lords of the Undercity, they would slaughter their own children if it benefited them."

"From what I've found of the financial records I could hack," Titus said, pointedly ignoring Axel. "I would say at least two of the factions have gained some ground in the past few months."

"Should we be concerned about the Undead?" Jax asked, finally breaking his silence. "The other Lords have been leaving us alone –"

A growl, Kace banging his fist on the table.

"For the most part," Jax continued.

Lucifer leaned back against the wall, looking between the Guardians. "I have a feeling you're going to be seeing more of them soon enough."

"Why?" Axel asked, ignoring his brothers' scrutiny as it crawled across his skin, sharp as hornets. Except Titus, who purposely kept his gaze on the table.

Lucifer clicked his tongue, a smile spreading across his face. "What are you going to offer me for this information?"

Grumbles and shouts erupted, only quieting when Riley held up his hand. "What do you want?"

Lucifer didn't hesitate. "I want to join you boys on some hunts."

"You're not a Guardian," Axel said.

A harsh laugh. "Neither are you."

Axel froze for the barest second before rage ignited, his

beast snarling to the forefront of his mind. His chair toppled as he shot to his feet. "You mother fucking –"

"Enough!" Riley barked, and Axel felt a hand settle on his shoulder, pushing down.

Axel sucked in a breath, shaking the hold before moving to lean against the wall. Anxiety buzzed across his skin, and his hand shook as he dragged his fingers repeatedly through his hair. Xander moved to stand beside him, a heavy presence.

Fuck. Fuck. Fuck.

"I don't want to be a crappy Guardian," Lucifer continued, stepping forward to plant his palms face down on the table, leaning forward. "I'm bored."

"You want to kill Daemons with us?" Sythe asked. "Because we don't invite them to tea parties to discuss the weather."

Lucifer's eyes narrowed, his fingers clenching on the wood. "Tell me again when you last caught a Daemon? And not a hound or human twat stupid enough to get possessed?"

"If you were to join us on our hunts, you would be one of us," Riley said. "Which means you follow our rules."

Lucifer set his lips into a stubborn line, shoulders rigid. "I'm not a fucking idiot, I understand what you're saying, and I agree. I will put down my kind like dogs, because that's what they deserve. Right?" Resentment poisoned his words.

Riley's smile was sad. "Why do you believe we'll be seeing more of the Undead?"

"Because the skull heads that attacked Sam were Lessers."

"There are no Lessers, we killed them all," Jax said.

"Well, clearly not," Lucifer said, rolling his eyes. "Daemons are no longer stuck down in The Nether, which means they have all the time in the world to do *dastardly* things like creating Lessers. Even ones as basic as those I sensed back in that alley."

"Councilman Edwards has put out a precaution to protect druids under the Order," Riley said as he leaned back in his chair. "Which makes me believe he probably knew of this before us."

"What about the druids who don't follow the Order?" Axel asked with a frown, ignoring the stares. "What happens to them?"

"What do you think?" Riley shook his head, and Lucifer chuckled.

"And you call my kind soulless bastards. Your own councilman couldn't give two shits about your Breed unless they're the ones he has control of."

"Your kind are soulless bastards," Jax said.

"Technically the same kind if we're going to be pedantic about it," Sythe added with a shrug. "What?" he said when everyone turned to him. "It's true."

"If Edwards has regimented those under the Order to take precautions," Xander said to keep the conversation on track, "it probably means he believes druids are being taken again."

"Or druids are choosing to ascend," Lucifer said, his expression darkening. "But ascending doesn't take days, it takes months or sometimes longer. And that's if they're strong enough to accept the transition in the first place. Which is why it's likely we're going to see more Lessers, weaker versions used as disposable soldiers."

"We haven't fought a Lesser in years," Riley said.

"Because like you said, you probably killed them all." Frustration made Lucifer's voice sharp. "These pricks are something I haven't really sensed before, but they have the marker of a Lesser. They can't truly ascend into power, only druids have the physiology that could survive the ritual. But to create a Lesser takes a few days at most, and usually the only rules are the Breed has to be magic based."

"Why do you say usually?" Xander asked.

"Because while I sensed they were Lessers, I couldn't taste their chis."

"You think they're human?"

"Sounds like they're forcing corrupt magic onto those that can't support the power," Jax whispered. "What were we saying about soulless bastards?"

Lucifer turned towards him with a snarl. "Fuck you. You're all obsessed with my Breed only being about death and depravity." Lucifer's hands vibrated when he pulled them back, forcing him to clench them into tight fists. "You have no idea what every single one of us went through to make the decision to ascend, if we even had a choice at all." The energy in the room shifted, and Lucifer disappeared with a burst.

Tension strung taut between them, but it was Titus who was the first to break it. "I'll go calm him down."

Axel watched, fighting the urge to reach out until his cousin closed the door behind him.

Riley shot a pointed look at Jax.

"Fine," he growled with a scowl, quickly following Titus out the door.

Riley waited, turning to the remaining Guardians. "If what Lucifer is saying is correct, then we now know what the Daemons who've settled in the city have been doing this past year."

"It makes sense if you think about it," Sythe said. "The Undercity controls everything. Creating a faction to rival the Lords is a smart move."

"Hmmm. Until we find out more about the Undead, I've offered Sam protection here."

"We need to figure out the connection with his father," Xander added. "Do we really believe Sam being attacked was a coincidence? He's too close to us."

"I'll prioritise information," Sythe said. "Find out what I can regarding the Undead, and anything I can find on the Daemon, or Daemons running it."

Riley nodded, looking tired. "We're already stretched thin with the increased activity, so I'm going to speak to Councilman Edwards."

Sythe snorted. "Yeah, like that prick will help us. He hides at the abbey amongst his books and grimoires."

"It's worth a try, even if he refuses to provide us with support, I may be able to find out what he knows, if anything," Riley said. "But until then we'll stay in pairs. No hunting alone." The last sentence was aimed at Axel.

"I wasn't out hunting alone," Axel said, his voice edged with irritation. "I was –"

"That's enough," Riley interrupted, his eyes glacial. "No more excuses."

"No, I get to defend myself." Axel moved forward, only to be stopped by Xander. "Get off me, brother," he warned, the air charged.

"I'm sensing a little hostility here, Pretty Boy," Sythe said, slowly standing. "You want to calm your fucking attitude down?"

Axel concealed the increasing anger, jaw rigid as blood pounded in his ears. For once there was no dissonance, no whispers to conceal his beast's angry snarl, violent in the pressure against the front of his mind. If he didn't calm down, he was going to shift, and then he was really fucked.

"You need to step out?" Xander said, his cold gaze assessing.

"Go get some air," Riley said in a clipped tone, realising how close Axel was to the edge. "Now."

Axel pushed against Xander's chest, his brother growling at the contact as he quickly made his way out of the room and down the corridor. Sythe knocked against his mental shield, but Axel ignored it as he stepped outside, the night swathing him in welcoming shadows.

Chest heavy, he crouched, dropping his head to suck in deep gulps of air.

I can't do this, he thought, scratching his nails down the inside of his arms, hard enough it left deep, red lines. *I can't do this. I can't do this. I. Can't. Do...*

"You sneaking out?" a familiar voice cut in.

Axel's head snapped up, finding Sam leaning against the side of the house, a cigarette between his fingers. It took a second to find his voice, the magic that changed him from one shape to another prickling beneath his skin. "I didn't realise you were out here," he said, his beast's attention pinned to the dark silhouette.

Sam's irises were reflective against the moon, the amber glowing. His hair was a straight curtain, draped over his shoulder with his back slightly arched. He lifted the cigarette to his lips, taking a long drag before releasing the smoke in an ethereal cloud. "I can't sleep."

Axel closed his eyes, Sam's voice calming his anger to a simmer.

"So, are you sneaking out?" Sam asked once more.

Axel stood to his full height, the movement jerky. He wasn't going to fall, even if the craving was violent, taking over his thoughts. His beast growled in agreement, releasing some of the tension that strained his shoulders. "I'm not on my way to get high, if that's what you're thinking."

Sam's attention dipped to the red lines on his arms. "So you're what... enjoying the night air?"

"Why are you hiding outside?" Axel asked instead, trying to hide the already fading marks.

Sam shrugged. "This isn't my house."

"No, but it's safe."

"Is it?" Sam cocked his head, and Axel's heart raced for reasons other than anger. "Is anywhere really safe?"

"You're protected –"

"Sure." Sam's chuckle broke him off. "I feel like I've lost everything." Carefully stubbing out his cigarette he straightened. "Everything I've built, it's crumbling around me."

Axel licked his dry lips, and Sam's attention dropped to the subtle movement. "All I can think about is shooting up," he admitted, uncomfortable with the vulnerability. "And do you know what? I'm not even in pain."

"When's the last time you used?" Sam asked, voice soft.

"Not long enough for me to be craving something so soon." Axel tipped back his head, staring at the night. "Even now, I feel my control slipping. I almost lost it inside, all because I'm stupid enough to believe brimstone would help." He may have started the drugs to help with the growing pain, but he had long ignored the signs of addiction.

"Let me distract you," Sam whispered.

"Distract me?" Axel pulled his attention from the sky, finding Sam only a few feet away, the air thickening between them. "How would you distract me, exactly?"

"Any way you want." Sam reached over, his hand brushing against Axel's shoulder. "Let me make you feel good."

"Sam..." Axel ended with a silent curse as Sam's hand drifted lower. The distraction was working, his entire being pinned on the fingers that teased at the edge of his jeans.

"Let me do this." Sam stepped closer, his heat wrapping around Axel in a welcoming caress. "It's the only thing I have left."

"Bullshit, you have more to offer people than sex."

Sam's body tensed, muscles rigid. "Then help *me* forget."

Axel took a second to reply as Sam managed to slip his fingers beneath the denim. "Forget?"

"Help me forget that I've lost everything."

"You've not lost everything." Axel moved to grip Sam's wrist, stopping him from exploring any further. "How can I show you how amazing you are? You're not some body to warm beds, you're this amazing male that lights up every room he enters."

"Stop it," Sam growled, a vibration low in his throat. "This is just sex."

"Of course it is, because that's all you want," Axel said, surprised by the slight resentment.

Sam nodded, just a shallow dip of his head. It brought his lips closer, but neither of them closed the distance. "You're making this complicated. I don't want complicated; I want to fuck and be fucked so hard that I forget my father's come back from the dead. That I've lost my home, and that from tomorrow I'm going to have to rebuild with the knowledge that I'll probably never be free from him."

"Would you find someone else if I said no?"

Sam's eyes met his, the night glow brightening as the leopard prowled behind his irises. "Not tonight."

Mine, his beast roared, but as Axel stood toe-to-toe protectiveness welled within his veins. *Fuck,* he thought, not sure what he needed. His priority was to get clean, to become a Guardian once more, and fight beside his brothers.

Sam was right, he was complicating it. Sex could be just sex. No attachments. He had done it enough in the past, before the celibacy, so why was it so hard now?

"I can't get you out of my head," Sam said, voice returning to a whisper as Axel rocked forward until their lips were a single breath away. "How good you felt inside me. But you need to stop being so...hmmm."

"So what?" Axel said, his beast wanting to poke at the weakness until Sam admitted there was more between them than he wanted to admit. That he wasn't like everyone else.

Fucking hell.

"So... you."

Axel smiled, and Sam parted his lips with a soft exhale. The need to take him ignited deep within his chest, burning through the anger and frustration until there was nothing left but ferocious lust. "Kiss me," he said, repeating the words Sam had whispered to him only the night before.

He needed Sam to want him like his next breath. Want him more than every other body that he had ever taken back to his bed. Because this definitely wasn't just sex, it was so much more. More than even Axel understood.

"Kiss me," Axel repeated, watching Sam's eyes darken with desire. "And I'll help you forget."

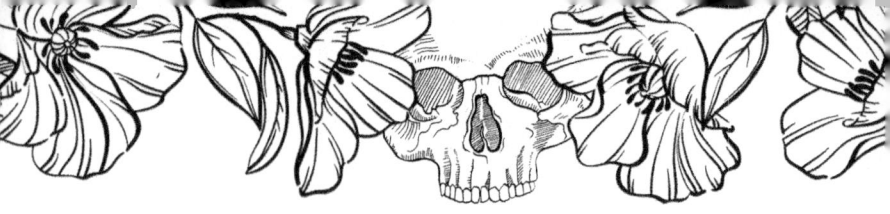

CHAPTER 21

SAM

Sam wasn't even sure how they made it back to Axel's bedroom without being spotted. The door closed seconds before he was slammed against it, Axel's slightly larger body covering his like a delicious blanket.

Their movements were frantic, as if they were both starved for each other's touch. He felt a frustrated sound leave his lips, desperation forcing him to rip at his t-shirt so Axel could easier claim a kiss to his bare flesh. He was too hot, overwhelmed, as his cock throbbed painfully against the fabric of his jogging bottoms. Axel truly knew how to play him, and already, with the barest touch he had Sam rock hard and leaking.

This is just sex, he reminded himself as Axel nipped at his skin before brushing his lips over the small hurt. *Just sex.*

Sam moaned, loving the extra length to Axel's hair as he tugged his head back, away from his throat so he could lick along those sexy lips. Axel's mouth opened, and Sam took advantage as they came together in a passionate clash of tongues and teeth. He could have kissed him for hours, savouring every hitch of breath and panting moan. But Axel pulled back, his hair slipping through Sam's fingers as he dropped to his knees.

There was no teasing, no hesitation, as Axel freed Sam's aching erection and licked down the entire length, looking up as he swirled his tongue around the head. Sam pushed back hard against the door, widening his legs further as Axel finally took him between his lips. He watched through half-lidded eyes, body strained as Axel's short beard scratched at the inside of his thighs.

"Fuck," he hissed, arching his hips so Axel could take him deeper, only for him to suck hard enough he saw stars. Sam bit his lip, trying to quieten the increasing moans as Axel worked him hard, each lick and suck driving him higher and higher until he was on the very edge of his release.

Reaching down to grip his shaft, he pulled back, seconds away from exploding. Axel dropped to suck his balls, and then lower, with the flat of his tongue, licking over and over his entrance as he prepared him with an impressive amount of patience.

Patience Sam didn't have.

Pulling him to his feet, Sam shoved him until the back of his knees hit the bed. Panting, Sam stroked himself slowly as Axel watched, eyes trained to his hand.

Red flushed across his cheekbones, hair a mess as Axel pulled off his shirt, slow enough it matched the pace of Sam's strokes. A teasing smirk curved his lips, his hand slowly tracing down his own abs until he reached his jeans, popping the button. And even just that sound was enough for Sam to let out a strangled moan, his fist tightening as he began to pump slightly faster, his thumb rubbing the slick tip.

Slipping the jeans off, Axel sat there completely naked, lounging back on his hands as Sam's mouth watered. The tip of his cock glistened, standing hard and thick enough Sam knew it would stretch him to the edge of pain. He couldn't fucking wait.

Axel tilted his head, and Sam all but crawled across the carpet, sinking between Axel's legs to lick down his length. Axel groaned as he slipped his mouth over the head, taking his time before he pushed down until the tip entered his throat, cutting off oxygen. He wanted to take it slow, to drive Axel as crazy as he had driven him. He curled his tongue around his shaft, licking the underside along with every suck. It wasn't long before Axel's thighs tensed beneath Sam's hands, his hips buckling up to fuck his face hard enough to choke.

Looking up, Sam hummed, causing Axel to curse and grip his hair in a grasp, before forcing him up and off his cock. His lips were bruising when they clashed against his, his tongue dominating as Sam straddled his lap, placing his knees either side of Axel's hips. His cock was caught between them, so heavy and aching he knew he wouldn't last much longer.

Axel reached below, and Sam lifted himself just as he felt Axel position himself right at his entrance, his thick head slick and ready. Sam dragged his fingers through Axel's hair, forcing him to meet his eyes. "Fuck me," he whispered, dropping himself down at the same time Axel thrust up.

His cock pushed through the tight muscle with little resistance, the shock of burning pain nothing compared to the pleasure that rocked his core. Axel reached places that made all his other lovers nothing but blurred memories. He knew exactly the right angle, guiding the thrusts with his hands clamped to Sam's waist, fingers dug into skin.

"Fuck," Axel cursed, teeth clenched. "You feel so good."

Sam groaned, lifting himself up and down in a brutal

rhythm that pulled him back toward the edge faster than he expected. "Next time," he said, barely able to speak through the pleasure that touched his entire body. "Next time, I'm going to fuck you."

Axel groaned. "As long as you know there's going to be a next time." There was no delicate caresses or kisses, nothing but raw lust as they rocked together, their bodies moving as one.

Axel's breathing increased, the growls and moans becoming louder as he thrust up to meet every movement, and Sam knew he was close.

"That's it," Sam moaned. "Right there." His own orgasm coiled tightly at the base of his spine, his dick soaking them both as Axel reached down with a strong grip. His fingers pumped once, twice, and combined with the intense fullness and the hard clasp, Sam exploded, throwing his head back with a shout loud enough it echoed against the walls around them.

Axel's free hand curled around Sam's throat, giving him no time before pulling him down so their lips met, swallowing the remaining cry as his cock throbbed. Axel's hips continued pumping up, his movement frantic as Sam felt him thicken, his cock pulsing deep inside until he found his own orgasm.

The hand on his cock loosened, but the one on his throat remained as Axel breathed heavily, both their bodies slick with sweat and cum. Leaning forward Sam rested his forehead against Axel's, enjoying the steady thrum of his heart. He wasn't sure how long they had sat there, embraced in each another, just breathing, when Axel finally shifted them both to the bed, Axel on his back with Sam draped over his chest. His cock slipped out, but neither moved, content to just lay there together on the sheets. Sam hadn't realised he was purring, a soothing vibration as he revelled in the afterglow of his orgasm. He watched as Axel's entire body relaxed, eyes closing.

"You make everything quiet," he whispered, voice soft. Tranquil.

Sam stroked down Axel's chest, fingers exploring every curve and hard line. The skin he touched brightened, a pale white glow emitting from the tattoos that were such an intricate design Sam felt himself mesmerised by the patterns.

"You've told me that before," Sam said, not sure what he meant. "When you first kissed me."

"Fuck, yeah I did." Axel grunted. "I still can't believe I shot up at Riley's bar, right where my brothers could see me. I guess I'd fallen earlier than I thought."

Sam purred harder, pressing his chest against Axel's arm so he could feel the gentle vibration. It was supposed to sooth other cats, a natural instinct he couldn't help.

"I was high, that must have been what gave me the push to finally kiss you. It's the one thing I don't regret." Axel turned his head, eyes opening. "You make me feel... at peace. There are no intrusive thoughts when you're around, my beast's content."

"Are you just saying this because you just had a mind-blowing orgasm?" Sam chuckled, enjoying Axel's skin reacting at his caress.

Axel frowned with a sudden seriousness that cut off Sam's purr. "You're an Omega, aren't you?"

Sam stopped stroking, fingers paused on his right pectoral before rolling onto his back, facing the ceiling. "Aye, I think so. But I wouldn't say I was a particularly effective one," he said with a laugh devoid of humour.

"You think so?"

"I've never actually been told what I was, only that I was damaged because I didn't have the natural instincts to bow to those more dominant." Memories of his father beating him because he didn't advert his eyes fast enough forced their way to the forefront of his mind. "Omegas are supposed to be the centre of a pack," he continued. "The heart, but my father thought I was more of a burden."

Axel sat up, resting on his elbow. "When did you figure out you were probably an Omega?"

A small smile, Sam remembering the young, blonde girl carrying several books far bigger than herself. "It was Alice who stole me some books when I was about ten. I couldn't read then, so she read them out loud and helped me understand. I used to sneak into her room at night, sleeping as a leopard on the foot of her bed."

Sam traced Axel's relaxed expression as he listened intently.

"It was because of her that I didn't starve to death on the streets. That I was warm and safe with a roof over my head."

"You were only a kid."

"Living rough was better than going back to my father and pack. I owe Alice everything, without her I wouldn't be here."

"She says the same about you, you know," Axel said, smiling.

Sam blinked, reaching up to brush his fingers along Axel's jaw. "I had people try and help, but for obvious reasons I had a huge distrust of adults. So it was Alice who stole the books, and that's where I learned that Omegas aren't part of the normal pack structure, that we have Alpha tendencies without the need for bloodthirst."

"A protector without the aggression."

Sam shrugged, the sheets scratchy against his back. "I supposedly have a calming aura. I think it's one of the reasons my father hated me, because he thought I was trying to influence him."

Axel pressed into his touch, the edges of his irises glimmering. "I'm sorry about your house, that you've lost everything you've built."

Sam dragged his fingers down, caressing Axel's velvety soft lips. "It's just a house. Just things. It hurts now, but I've suffered worse and will come back stronger. You should always look for the sunshine, otherwise the darkness will swallow you whole."

"That's... a great way to deal with it."

Sam laughed. "Years of therapy, baby."

Axel's smile matched his, widening as he leaned down. The kiss was soft, gentle compared to before, and Sam melted into the touch, his leopard content to wrap itself up in the affection.

He may have lost his home and security, but unlike as a child, he wasn't alone.

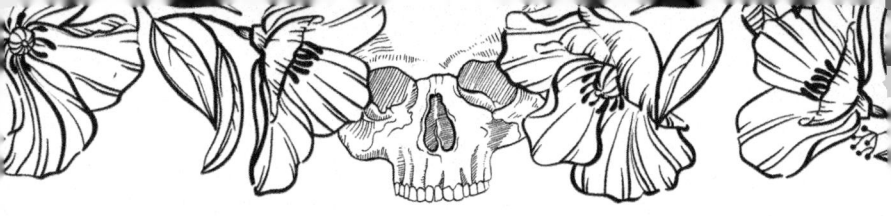

CHAPTER 22

AXEL

A xel paced, arms crossed, as he waited for Titus to open his door. "Bloody ridiculous, surely he can't still be asleep?"

He'd already waited a few minutes with no response, his patience wearing thin as he ignored the need itching the inside of his arms. Lifting a heavy fist, he thumped hard against the wood.

"Come on, Ti. Open up the fucking door!" A moment passed, and Axel let out a frustrated sound as he went to knock again. "Stop being such as petty little –"

"What do you want?"

Axel spun, finding Titus in the corridor with a bored expression. "Oh, I thought you were inside," he said, awkwardly lowering his hand. "Where were you?"

Titus mirrored Axel's crossed arms, closing himself off while Axel immediately dropped his arms to the side.

Fuck, he thought. *This is going well.*

"Look, I came to apologise. What I said... about your parents... everything. I didn't mean it."

"Yes, you did." Titus moved around Axel, opening his bedroom door and stepping inside.

Just like Axel and their other brothers, they'd all personalised their rooms, making them their own little sanctuaries. Titus's was similar to his place at their apartment, with dark colours and rich woods. His bed was fourposter, the sheets black satin with only a single pillow. Titus never brought any of his dates there, which wasn't a surprise considering all his toys were back at their shared apartment.

"What do you want Axel? I'm busy." He gestured to his ridiculously large computer, the three monitors dark except for a single white cross pulsating in the centre. Titus worked online security for all of Riley's corporations, as well as hiring himself out as an expert in his field. Not that Axel really understood what he actually did on that computer of his, the screen usually showing random letters and symbols that made zero sense. But if you wanted something hacked, money moved without a trace or a virus designed to take out a competitor, Titus was your man. Probably.

"You were right, I have a problem. I'm sorry it took me so long to realise it, that you had to protect me," he said, cautiously watching his cousin's expression remain neutral. "I'm trying Ti, I really am. It's... it's hard to admit this weakness."

"You're not weak," Titus said, reaching up to brush the blonde strands from his face. The roots were dark, his natural colour coming through. "Stupid, but not weak."

Axel chuckled, the tension he carried relaxing a fraction. "I really am sorry. I don't deserve you as my brother, or cousin."

Titus dropped his gaze to the floor, his hands tightening on his arms. "Do you actually want help?"

"Yes." There was no hesitation, not now he understood it was an addiction. "I don't know why I didn't listen, you're always right."

"Of course I am," Titus said with a genuine smile, his

own body no longer strained. "But I'm sorry too. I should have seen you needed help." As Axel went to protest, he held up his hand, moving to grab a black and gold tin from his bedside cabinet. "This is tea, it's supposed to help with withdrawal symptoms."

"Tea?" Axel repeated when Titus handed it over. "Helpful considering I'm doing this cold turkey. That's the phrase, right?"

He turned it in his palms, unable to read the Mandarin label despite studying it as a kid.

"Is this from Lǎolao?" He felt the colour drain from his face. "Ti, tell me you didn't tell her? She's human, you could have given her a heart attack!"

"Of course not." Titus scrunched up his face. "Do you think I'm an idiot? She would demand you back home, and probably make me come too for letting you get in the situation in the first place."

A beep, the middle monitor flashing white before returning to the small pulsating cross in the centre.

Titus ignored it. "How did it get so bad? We used to talk about everything, and then you just shut me out."

"I didn't realise I stopped." Axel clutched the tin to his stomach, the metal sharp at the corners. "The pain was getting worse and nothing I was doing was helping. My biggest fear was letting everyone down, unable to perform my duties with you guys." A hollow chuckle. "Which of course, is exactly what happened. I found that some drugs could help with the pain, and even better when mixed with certain herbs. So I started experimenting, resorting to stronger stuff until I came to brimstone. It helped. I could perform without being overwhelmed as long as I was... high."

"Why did you never tell me about the pain?"

"Because I didn't think you would believe me." Axel

shrugged, unable to look at Titus. "We're Guardians. We were trained to withstand pain, to fight until our last breath. I could never admit I constantly ached, that my skin felt so sensitive even a feather hurt."

"I would have –"

"It doesn't matter, does it?" Axel interrupted. "I didn't tell you, and now we're here with me grovelling for your forgiveness because I was a stubborn arsehole."

"I don't see much grovelling," Titus muttered. "Shouldn't you be on your knees?"

Axel snorted. "Like your women? No way in fucking hell."

Irritation sharpened his bourbon brown gaze. "Says the celibate."

"Are you really going to that?" Axel said with a burst of frustration. "It was a choice."

"Wait, *was?*" Cynicism coloured Titus's words.

"Fuck sake, I didn't come here to discuss my sex life."

Titus raised his brows. "So there *is* a sex life?"

"Ti!" Axel growled, pinching the bridge of his nose. "Look, I'm going to cut it off, all of it. I promise."

Titus nodded and all the joking disappeared, replaced with a resolute expression. "I know you will, but what are you going to do about the pain in the meantime?"

Axel went to reply, a frown curving his brow. "Shit." He hadn't thought that far ahead.

"Are you in any pain right now?"

"I'm... not," he said slowly. "I'm not in pain, I haven't been in a few days." *Which was weird,* he mentally added.

"And you haven't taken any drugs?"

A shake of the head.

"So, what's changed?"

"I've..." Sudden realisation hit Axel like a sledgehammer. "Oh fuck. Oh fuck. Ohhhh fuuuuuck."

"Very articulate," Titus muttered. "As always."

"I know why I haven't been in pain, but I don't want to admit it."

Titus frowned. "Why wouldn't you want to admit it?"

"Because it means my mum was right," Axel groaned.

"Wait." Laughter lurked beneath Titus's voice. "Does that mean...?"

"I've been starving myself." He had always blamed his beast for the pain, but maybe it wasn't his beast. The pain started around his twenty-first birthday, which was when druids were classed as adults and when the full transition with his beast was complete. It was also the time he had chosen to become celibate.

"Didn't I tell you that celibacy was bloody stupid?"

Axel realised exactly what had changed.

"Oh, fucking hell."

He'd started having sex.

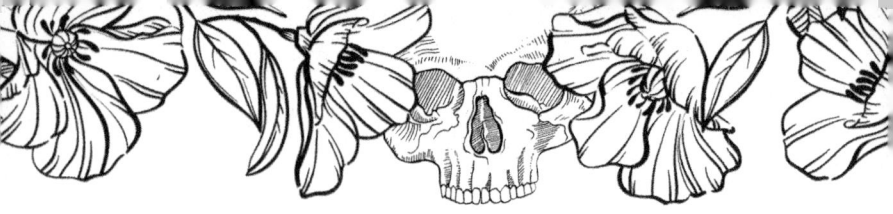

CHAPTER 23

SAM

S am quickly changed into his work t-shirt, the familiar black cotton with red embroidery comforting. Normal, as if it was just another Thursday night. The bar was reasonably busy, and he hoped his shift would be full of drunken anecdotes that kept him distracted.

He wasn't allowed to feel sorry for himself anymore, he'd already brooded around the house that wasn't his all day, bothering Alice, Lucy, and anyone else he could find.

Except Axel.

Because that was who he really wanted, to have intimate skin privileges as well as casual. To walk in a room and he be there, with his stupidly handsome face smiling at him, and only him. Axel spoke to his leopard spirit more than any other male, or female ever had, and he found himself craving his attention. Axel made him feel things, made him want things that he never thought he desired because he had been happy alone.

Alone you couldn't mess up, be told you weren't good enough or blamed for things out of your control. Alone was simple, easy.

'*You deserve love.*' Alice's voice drifted through his mind, but he pushed it away.

Love was easy too, but it came and went like the wind. He'd heard enough stories from the customers he served drinks, that love was simply a burst of chemicals in the brain that could be just as fleeting. So how could he commit to one person? When their love could just disappear by the dawn, leaving him alone and vulnerable.

Sam wasn't sure he could do that to himself.

"Oh, hey man I didn't think you were on tonight," Lewis, one of the temp bartenders said as he entered the small staff room. "I was called in to cover."

Sam closed the locker where he kept his stuff, locking it tight. "Yeah, I think it was a miscommunication with Riley. Don't worry though, we would appreciate the help now that Bianca's gone on maternity."

"Okay, cool." Lewis unbuttoned his shirt before pulling on his own black t-shirt, Blood Bar embroidered on the left pec. "Thanks man, I know you're the one who sorted my overtime out last time too."

"No problem," Sam said as Lewis waved, passing through the door to the main floor. Sam had been taking on more of a managerial role the past few months, working the bar as well as sorting some of the back-end paperwork. It seemed to be a natural transition the longer he was there, allowing Riley to take a step back from just one of his multiple businesses. Although Blood Bar was more of a passion project compared to his numerous multi-million-pound companies and charities. It amused Sam to see Riley in his full suit, knowing him as the warrior he was.

There was no band mid-week, but the music still brought a small crowd to the floor. The bar was busy, all the stools taken as Payne nodded to him in greeting.

"You're here, good. Lewis can't make a drink for shit."

Lewis rolled his eyes, used to Payne's cheery attitude as he continued to serve on his section. "I missed you too, Payne."

Payne pursed her lips. "Your face is happy, but your eyes are conflicted."

"Oh you know, the usual conundrum of figuring out what you want in life," Sam said with a tight smile.

"Deep... anyway help me clear this crowd before I blow my brains out and leave you to deal with the mess." She tossed her braids over her shoulder, the gold beads glistening.

"Always a pleasure," Sam muttered, widening his smile as he turned to the next person in his section. "Hey there beautiful, what can I get you?"

The young woman with dark red hair blushed, but proceeded to order a Pornstar Martini. Sam smiled, making the cocktail quickly before he moved on to the next customer, losing himself in the work. A few hours passed in a blur, time speeding by as Sam carefully flipping an electric blue bottle over his head for the watching audience.

"Hey," a man said as he stepped up to the bar. "Can I buy you a drink?"

Sam flipped the bottle once more, catching it before pouring the five shots that Payne had lined up along the wood. Flicking the end they bumped towards the woman who'd ordered them, her friends squealing with delight.

"Sorry, I'm working," he said, wiping down the side. "What can I get you?"

"Surely you can have one drink?" he pushed, sitting on one of the stools. "Come on, it'll be fun." The man smiled, showing off perfectly straight teeth. "What about your number? You can give that out, right?"

Sam cocked his head, studying the man's handsome face as he leaned forward. Before he wouldn't have hesitated, but now all he could do was compare. He had green eyes, not hazel and his jaw, while defined, was clean shaven rather than rough.

"What can I get you?" Sam repeated, hoping his tone remained light and friendly. It was the first time he felt nothing but indifference, no physical reaction or attraction. Not that he was attracted to everyone, but he usually felt something, even if it was just a slight effervescence in the fact someone desired him. Wanted *him*.

"The name's Scott," he said, continuing to smile, not disheartened by the rebuff. "I would love a beer, please. Whatever's on tap."

"One beer coming up," Sam said, his own smile strained. What was wrong with him? Scott was cute, and would warm his bed for at least the night. Yet his thoughts went straight back to hazel eyes and dark brown hair that held a slight curl.

Fuck. This can't be happening.

"Hey, blondie, you awake?"

Sam blinked, turning to Payne with a frown. "Huh?"

"You've been staring into space for the past five minutes," she said, a crease appearing between her brows. "It's only eight, it's still early yet."

"Fuck, yeah. Sorry."

"You okay?" she asked, shooting him a wary glance. "You're not being normal."

Sam shook himself from stupor, moving to clean the bar. "Define normal."

"Well," Payne began as she turned to face him, popping out her hip. "The sunlight that usually emits from your pores and makes me want to puke has changed."

Sam repeated her words several times through his head, still not understanding. "What?"

"Ignore I said that." Payne shook her head. "I sometimes forget who I'm talking to."

"No, wait. Changed how?"

"Well, it's still there. But you're not projecting as much, as if your sunlight is concentrated inside, more like a shield to disguise your pain from others."

"I... I don't know what to say to that," Sam said, never having heard Payne string so many words together at once. "I have sunlight coming from my pores?"

"It isn't a bad thing, just nauseous." Payne shrugged. "The change isn't necessarily bad, it's expected as you heal."

"Payne, I don't know –"

"Hey," a feminine voice interrupted. "I'm sorry, but can I get a vodka tonic, please?"

Both Payne and Sam turned to the small woman as one, the pretty redhead who had blushed at him earlier.

"I've heard Angela makes the best one," she continued, her voice nervous as her eyes darted to the side. Sam picked out a single male at the back of the room who watched them like a predator. His face barely changed when his eyes met Sam's, his expression schooled into an almost violent stillness.

"Of course," Sam said, gesturing to Payne who immediately understood. "Angela will be right with you."

Lifting herself onto the bar, Payne reached for the bell in the centre, ringing it until the entire room turned. "The first five people who reach me get a drink on the house."

The diversion worked, and as the customers rushed forward Sam gently escorted the redhead through the employee door and out the emergency exit. "Are you okay?" he asked as soon as they stepped into the alley out back. "Did you need me to call anyone?" She had used the code-word 'Angela,' meaning she felt unsafe, vulnerable, or threatened and needed help out of the situation immediately. It was a word used across the country for both men and women, and Blood Bar was one of the many establishments trained to be safe.

"No, I've already called a friend to come pick me up," she whispered, clutching her phone to her chest. "Can you... can you wait with me? Please?"

"Of course," Sam said as he walked her towards the street, finding a car already waiting for her. "Get home safely," he said, shutting her inside.

"Thank you."

Waiting until the car disappeared around the corner Sam turned, only to find the same man from the bar standing a few feet away, his face just as empty as before.

"I think it's time for you to leave," Sam growled. "You can fuck..."

The man slowly raised his arm until his hand covered his face. His fingers were spread, his eyes peeking through the gaps as an intense cold settled in Sam's chest. Just as slowly, he dropped his hand, and Sam watched as his face transformed, his tanned skin brightening until he was pale as bone, the shadows beneath his eyes deepening until they looked like dark pits void of any light.

Claws prickled at Sam's fingertips, and just before he took a step towards the man who wore the glamour of a skull, an intense heat burned against his side, an orange glow brightening the night. Screams echoed, but Sam was already running back to the bar as smoke assaulted his nose.

"Payne?!" he shouted through the crackling of flames. "Lewis?" The handle of the door was hot as he pushed it open, only to find the last of the customers running for the entrance. It took a second to realise some had passed out on the floor, amongst fallen tables and smashed drinks. Flames ate away at the furthest wall, seeming to keep themselves relatively contained as Sam continued to call out names.

Bottles had shattered on the bar, liquid dripping as Sam found Lewis collapsed behind, blood a heavy pool beneath him. Dropping to the floor, Sam crawled closer, Lewis's knuckles split and red, but his eyes were empty, his throat slit open from ear to ear.

"Fuck!" Sam fell backwards, breathing heavily as he stared at his friend.

The glass office on the floor above creaked, cracking from the heat as flames crawled up the walls, eating away at the ceiling.

A moan, and Sam immediately found Payne in the corner, clutching her stomach. A dark mist coated her palms, moving up her arms as she tried to climb to her feet.

"Payne!" Sam shouted, the smoke starting to tighten his lungs as the glass high above finally shattered, raining down, the flames moving to devour everything exposed. Heat licked at his skin, but Sam ignored it as he jumped over the fallen tables and chairs to get closer. He caught her as she sagged, her eyes rolling and head slack. The mist that had encircled her arms flickered before disappearing, leaving nothing but dark skin painted gold.

A violent whine, the beams above quivering as the flames danced. Blinding.

"Fuck!" he shouted, picking her up beneath the knees to keep her close to his chest.

The hackles on his neck prickled, his senses on full alert as he clutched her tighter. Sam turned to find three men, their faces painted like death as they watched him with an intensity just as hot as the flames. Sam eyed the exit, teeth bared as Payne remained limp in his arms.

The first and second skulls stood as still as statues, while the third stepped forward, his face empty, flames crawling up his legs as if he felt nothing. His exposed skin bubbled, blackening before bursting apart to reveal bright red muscle.

The paint on his forehead split, the flesh gone, melting as his natural bone emerged through.

There was a split second of nothing but the dance of flames before all three skulls moved in sync, as if they were one single mind. Sam tensed, but with his arms full he took a heavy hit to his side, expelling all the air from his lungs in the single blow. He fell forward, hold loosening on Payne as he caught the next kick, yanking the foot hard enough he heard the crack of bone. Another blow to his back, but he was already twisting, his claws slicing through flesh and muscle with an ease that turned his stomach. There was no cry, no recoil or shout of pain. The skull barely flinched as his skin fell away, moving forward to grip Sam in a damaging grasp.

"Enough," a smoky voice rumbled, deep against the crackles and pops.

The hold around Sam's arm dropped, and he let out a hiss as blood rushed back into the spot. He knew there would be a bruise, maybe even a fracture as he rolled his shoulder, ignoring the sharp pain that travelled all the way down to his fingertips.

A heavy whine, the ceiling cracking above them. Everyone tensed, and just as the centre beam groaned Sam threw himself over Payne, crouching over her body with his as the beam crashed down inches from her outstretched feet.

Dust, debris, and smoke choked him as he coughed, his lungs struggling as the flames came closer. They crept across the wood, circling around them in a deadly wall.

"Amazing, isn't it. Almost like being able to control such an obstinate element," the smoky voice said once more, a dark silhouette obscured by the smoke. "Imps have true talent in making such magic."

Sam concentrated on breathing, dropping his head lower as he sucked in great gasps. "Who are you?"

A chuckle, but the silhouette remained hidden. "Leave the Death-eater, the flames would take her as a meal."

Pressure at his back and sides, three sets of hands reaching to yank him to his feet. Sam hissed, but his arms were trapped, lungs burning as the smoke began to swallow him whole.

"Fuck yo –" A hand circled his throat, cutting off any remaining air.

The male cocked his head, red eyes assessing as his fingers tightened a fraction. He'd moved far faster than Sam could track, his sheer size eating up the space until he saw nothing but bare, slightly ashen skin.

"Your father's been keeping secrets," he said, mouth opening to reveal teeth sharpened to points. His horns curled, twisting down until the tips reached his jaw.

Sam tensed, unable to move as he became light-headed, and with his last remaining strength he pierced his claws into the Daemon's arm.

"But how the Fates have blessed us with you."

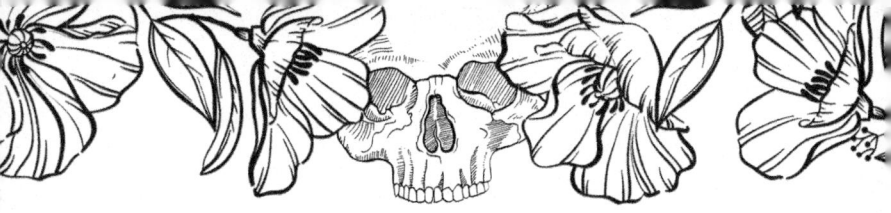

CHAPTER 24
AXEL

"This tea tastes like shit," Axel muttered, scowling into the cup.

"Stop whining and drink it," Titus said, wrapping his knuckles with fabric. "You're not even supposed to be here."

Axel glared at his cousin as he took another sip of the bitter liquid. "Kace said I couldn't help with the kids, he didn't say I couldn't watch. Besides, it's your turn to get the shit beaten out of you, and I wasn't going to miss that." He also didn't want to be alone, not that he would ever admit that out loud.

The tea was doing nothing to stop his violent cravings, brimstone dominating his thoughts. His skin still crawled with need, and nausea threatened at every movement.

"I'm going to tell Lǎolao you said her tea tasted like shit if you don't stop moaning."

"You wouldn't!" Axel's shout was louder than he realised as twenty sets of young eyes turned in his direction.

Kace pursed his lips, expression stern as he forced the kids' attention back to him.

"You're going to get me kicked out," Axel growled, keeping his voice low.

"You're not supposed to be here anyway," Titus chuckled, pulling his shirt off to leave him in bare skin.

The Guardians sometimes helped Kace and his associates train kids with poor living situations, all their fighting styles different. But the training wasn't about violence, it was about discipline. Kace taught them how to defend themselves, how to deal with their trauma, if any, and how to manage their emotions in a safe, confident way.

It was an unsanctioned class that closed down The Vault once a week, allowing the kids who didn't stay there permanently somewhere safe and warm for a few hours, a place where adults actually cared for them. They had the choice to join in, or simply watch. When Kace first started it, he barely had a few attend. Now there was a rotation of around twenty-five starting from as young as six, to around seventeen. There was no ageing out, once they were in, they were in.

Titus stood, stretching his arms over his head. It caused the tattoos on his chest to move, and he noticed a few of the kids' eyes widen at the skull and dragon. They were grey, but they stood out against the stark black and red lines of the glyphs that surrounded them.

"You're going to rip out your nipple," Axel said, laughing at the metal ring that glinted in the light. "That's gonna be interesting to watch heal."

Titus shot him the middle finger, but his eyes immediately dropped to the floor as his phone vibrated against the floor tiles. With a frown he crouched, touching the screen before he burst to his feet. "Fuck, get in the car!" he barked, concentrating on his phone. "Kace, we need to go!"

"Marshall's taking over here." Their brother appeared,

anger slicing across his face. "We're only a few districts over."

"What's happened?" Hunter asked, running over. "Is it Eva? Is she hurt?"

Kace gripped Hunter's shoulder. "Eva's fine, but right now we've got to go." He nodded to Titus, who was already heading out the door.

"Wait," panic gripped Hunter's voice. "Let me help, I can –"

"I need you to stay here and look after the younger ones," Kace said, his tone leaving no room for argument.

"Look…" Hunter pulled his hands out of his sleeves, claws piercing out his fingertips before retracting just as fast. "I've been shifting, just like you asked. I'm getting better."

"That –"

"Let the kid come," Axel said, and Kace's glare could have cut. "What could possibly –"

"Blood's been hit," Kace interrupted him. "So we need to go, and Hunter is going to stay here."

It took a second for the words to register. "Oh fuck! Sorry kid, we got to go!"

"Wait!"

Axel and Kace ran for the door, finding Titus standing by his car. "What the fuck took you both so long?"

Kace slid into the driver's seat while they climbed into the back. The tension rising as Titus continued to flick away on his phone.

"How bad?" Kace asked from the front, gunning the car far too fast down the busy streets.

"Bad," came Titus's tight reply.

"Why didn't I get a text?" Axel asked before he realised the answer. He wasn't a Guardian, so why would he have been notified? He dug his fingers into his thighs, body vibrating with energy. "Fuck, you think a Lord hit us?"

Neither answered, not until the orange glow of Blood Bar grew in the square just off Covent Road. With a sharp turn Kace parked the car on the pavement, barely missing the pedestrians who stood and watched as flames in the distance. A smaller crowd waited outside Blood Bar, many covered in soot and burns as paramedics parked a few buildings away.

"Fuck!" Kace cursed, the white-hot flames flicking between blue and red, the arms stretching out to lick at the adjoining buildings until they too were aflame. Charred wood, plastic and smoke drifted across the square, the smell choking as they watched helpless.

A fire engine was already there, firefighters gearing up the water while another barked orders.

The one in charge noticed them, storming over with a frown. "Get back right now, it's not –"

A crash as the door blew outwards, knocking several firefighters off their feet. The flames seemed to curl out of the gaping hole, pushing through the entrance to hold the crumbling brick.

"What the fuck is that?" Titus asked. "That's not normal, right?"

A snarl echoed above the crackle of flames, and two hounds stepped out from the entrance. Except they weren't hounds, their fur stripped back to mainly muscle and their bodies contorted into unusual shapes. Their heads were too small for their shoulders, paws closer to hands with the claws piercing through the first knuckle, leaving the rest of the human fingers limp beneath. They seemed to have more bones than needed, back legs longer than the front and slightly bowed.

It reminded Axel of the gory middle part of a shifter's change, where they were neither man nor animal.

He was wrong, they're not Shadow-Veyn. Yet his chi rippled with awareness that something dark was there, corrupt.

"That's definitely not normal," Titus said, looking back at the screaming crowd. "And really fucking public. Going to be a pain in the arse to erase any evidence of this."

"The Lessers aren't humans," Kace rumbled, body tense as the tattoos along his arms pulsed. "They're shifters."

Axel's heart raced, his attention drawn to the entrance to Blood. He hadn't seen Sam, waking up alone in a cold bed. He hadn't sought him out, and he was pretty sure Sam hadn't looked for him either. Axel didn't want to swap one addiction for another, even if Sam made everything better.

"Ti, who was working tonight?" His beast snarled at him to move, to find *him*. A growing pressure in his chest. "Ti!"

His cousin's mouth set in a firm line. "Sam clocked in."

"Go," Kace growled, barely able to keep himself under control. "We've got this."

Titus clenched his jaw, worry creasing his face before he split from his skin. His glyphs all glowed, so bright there was a flash before his beast stood in his place, three times the size of the man. Titus's beast was silver, the coarse fur just as metallic as his irises. His markings pulsed with light, a perfect echo of the tattooed glyphs from the man repeated in thin black lines. Their beasts were a mixture of wolf and lion, bodies built for speed with a canine shaped head and thick forearms. Their paws held serrated claws, teeth designed to tear and shred through the thickest hide. They were created to take down Shadow-Veyns, but the three that stood at the entrance were something else entirely.

Axel waited a second for Titus to howl, teeth bared as Kace remained as the man. The creatures responded, and as they both turned to the bigger threat, Axel ran straight into the blaze.

"Sam?!" he called through the smoke, lifting his arm across his face. Flames prickled against his skin, not advancing but not smothering either. The furniture had all been toppled, what wasn't charred broken as Axel picked out a few bodies lying amongst the debris. The fire flicked out, like an arm reaching as it caressed the top of the bar before pulling back with a snap. Liquid ignited, the flames seeming to ripple like water.

He had never witnessed fire like it, almost as if it was sentient.

Pops of glass, alcohol fuelling the flames as Axel crouched below the smoke, finding a blackened figure behind the bar. Blood thundering in his ears he moved closer, sinking to his knees with a hopelessness that stole his breath. Except it wasn't Sam, the blackened husk nothing but a vague shape, and yet he knew it wasn't him.

Find him, his beast whispered. *Mine.*

Panic seized Axel's lungs.

A grumble, the familiar sound of claws on wood. Axel felt the air shift a milli-second before he was hit, relaxing his body to roll with the impact. He dropped to the floor, flattening against the debris before slipping back beneath the creature. Its bones clicked as it scrambled to his feet, head deformed with a split down the centre as if the skin and muscle was ready to peel off the skull. Up closer he noticed that fur covered it in black patches, the texture and dark rosettes reminding him of a panther. Its head too was definitely feline, the body wider than expected for any of the larger cats known to be in the city.

"What the fuck are you?" Axel growled, keeping his body low as heat licked at his back. He slowly reached for the table that had toppled over, the leg already broken off with the edge scorched.

The creature snarled, unsteady on its feet while the entire room seemed to shift, the ceiling showering dust across them both. Smoke burned Axel's nose, grip tightening on the leg before he heard a moan beneath the crackles and pops.

The creature heard it too, head turning to the noise just as Axel lifted the table leg and stabbed it clean through its skull. There was no resistance, blood and matter squelching out as the end stuck into the floor, leaving it impaled.

Heavy footsteps, a hand landing on his shoulder and Axel almost broke it as he stood.

"Hey, what are you doing in here?"

Axel released the firefighter as quickly as he had struck, his skin beginning to redden from the heat, his back burning as fabric disintegrated.

"Get out!" the firefighter shouted through his mask. "The ceiling could collapse any moment."

"I heard something," Axel said, voice hoarse from the smoke. "Over there." He gestured to where a beam lay burning, his beast already sensing it wasn't Sam who had made the small noise.

Air stung his face as he was ushered outside, Riley approaching with a stern expression as a paramedic rushed over.

Riley ignored the paramedic, reaching over to grip Axel by the back of the neck before pulling him into a hug. Axel hissed out in pain, already knowing his back was a mess.

There were no other creatures when he pulled back, nor were Titus or Kace in sight.

'They're dealing with it,' Riley said mentally, not wanting to be overhead.

'*Sam's not there.*' Even mind to mind his voice shattered.

Riley's irises shifted to silver when he pulled back. '*We'll find him.*'

Axel nodded, allowing his beast to shape his words. "He's mine."

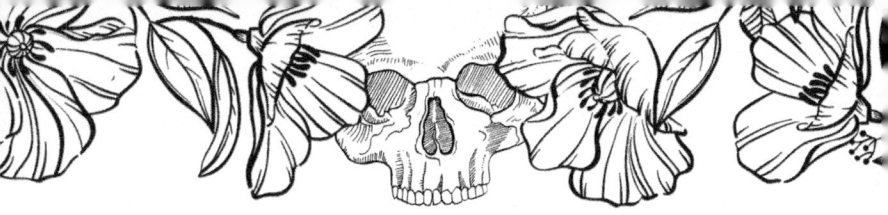

CHAPTER 25

SAM

Sam kept his breathing even, his body protesting at the stillness. His entire side burned, and opening his eyes to slits he understood why. He was in a cage, and from the pain he guessed it was made entirely of silver.

"I know you're awake," a familiar voice said. "Get up, you lazy fucker."

Sam hissed as every bone ached, sitting up in the centre of the cage. His head grazed the top, shoulders almost the same width as he tried to make himself smaller. His father sat on a wooden chair facing him, leaning forward with his hands clasped in his lap. Two men painted as skulls guarded behind, the one on the left familiar. They stood and stared, not one muscle twitching with an empty gaze.

Cinderblocks surrounded from what he could see, with concrete precariously poured onto the floor in uneven patches. A single bed, metal with a filthy mattress lay in the corner, marks clawed into the walls by the foot.

Sam composed himself, keeping his arms from touching the cage. There was no natural light, his ears picking up the artificial buzzing of the bulbs high above, placed randomly to create chunks of shadows. The scents were confusing, a mixture of dust, damp and... dirt.

Underground?

"You shouldn't have fought me before," his father continued, jumping up in a burst of violence to smack the cage with an open palm.

Sam controlled his flinch, barely.

"This was never supposed to happen. You're mine. My fucking son. My fucking Omega. Because of your disobedience I'm going to be punished." He struck the cage once more. "I'm –"

"You're going to be punished because you kept this from me."

Sam tensed at the voice, turning his head to watch a male he didn't recognise walk around his cage. He was one of the largest men he had ever seen, with wings arched high above his shoulders. They were black, leathery membranes stretched between surprisingly thin bones. Spikes dominated the upper curves, obsidian and sharp, while his horns curled down towards a boxy face, ending just shy of his jaw.

The Daemon crouched, and still he was taller than the cage, having to look down through the links, black hair long enough to brush the concrete. "An Omega, how fascinating. Tell me Conor, why you thought it was appropriate to expand your pack without my approval?"

Sam flicked his gaze to the man who made him, his face twisted with animosity.

"He's mine!" his father hissed. "What the fuck was Bishop doing going after my Omega, Gideon?"

The Daemon's head turned, his body facing forward as his neck twisted at an impossible angle.

"A deal is a deal," Connor said, pushing the words through clenched teeth. "My soul for a pack. *My* pack."

"Do you believe I haven't kept my half of the bargain?"

Gideon straightened, and Conor tensed, stepping closer to the skulls who remained like statues. "That I haven't provided you with capable packmates?"

"They're nothing but your puppets," Conor said in a clipped tone. "They don't see me as Alpha. They're weak, and all they care about is that bloody ga –"

The words stopped short when Gideon bolted forward, lifting him by his throat. Sam felt nothing as his father gasped for air, feet dangling freely as his hands shifted into claws.

"I think you're forgetting who you're speaking to." Gideon's features hardened. "Your lack of dominance isn't my problem. You sold *your* soul for a pack, which means you belong to me." He released his grip, and Conor fell to his knees, gasping for air. "I've provided you a pack, and a shelter and yet you sneak around as if you have any power here."

"My Lord," a familiar grumble from behind. The Daemon who had taken him from the bar entered through a crudely created gap in the cinderblocks, the space leading into nothing but pitch black. Auburn hair hung straight to his shoulders, emphasising the red in the irises when they grazed over to Sam.

"Perfect timing." Gideon lifted his hand, and the Daemon threw over a metal canister. "Go, before I listen to Bishop and kill you," Gideon said, dropping the canister onto Conor's head as he continued to cough on the floor. "Remember, you're replaceable. I don't need you to control my Lessers, I can get any shifter with a touch of dominance to keep them in line."

The skulls moved as one when Gideon stepped back, reaching down to help Conor to his feet, but he shook them off. Anger pulsed from his gaze, hardening into hatred when they met Sam's. Without another word he exited through the same gap Bishop had entered, the skulls following him obediently.

Gideon rolled his shoulders, clicking his neck as he crouched once more by the cage.

"What have the Fates brought me?" he said, voice deep enough it rattled Sam's bones. "Look at me."

Sam dragged his attention to the male, trying to keep himself calm as memories of being put in a cage as a small child rushed back. It was used as a punishment, the familiar burn of silver bringing a dread he didn't want to relive.

"You've been awfully quiet, I expected more of a fight."

"Release me and find out," Sam said with a hiss, able to feel the aggression of his leopard vibrate his voice. His body ached, muscles tight as he wrapped his arms around his legs, pulling them to his chest.

A dark chuckle, Gideon tapping the cage with a long fingernail. "What am I?"

Sam's lips thinned.

"I see it in your eyes, your fear a bitter layer on my tongue. You've met my kind before. So I'll ask you once more before I reach in there and tear the pretty amber from their sockets. What am I?"

Sam swallowed, ignoring the terror that had settled like a vice around his lungs. "A Daemon."

"Not many have met someone like me and lived." Gideon's smile sliced cruelly across his face, widening when he glanced at Bishop. "Who?"

"I don't know," Sam lied. "I only saw him in passing."

"Hmmm." Gideon cocked his head when he turned back, and Sam stilled, hoping his racing pulse didn't give him away. "You have no regard for your father. Why?"

"Fuck off."

Something flashed in his red eyes, but too fast for Sam to decipher. "It's interesting how you fear him."

"I don't fear him."

"A lie, but one I'll let slide for now." Gideon moved closer, pressing himself against the cage with Bishop stepping to the other side. "Such deep rooted terror, which makes me believe your father has always been a devious little cunt."

Another smile, one that made Sam's skin crawl.

"But he's weak, and weak men will do anything for a little bit of power. So we struck a bargain, his soul for a pack. And as you can see, I provided him with much more than he anticipated."

Sam swallowed, flicking his gaze between Gideon and Bishop. "The skulls."

"I thought it was fitting for them to look like death considering anyone I send their way ends up dead. He sold his soul, which means I own him. He's got what he wanted, and now he's once more an Alpha, just one who works for me."

"What did you do to them?" The skulls seemed like empty shells, unable to feel pain. One had walked through fire, his flesh melting off with every step and not once did he grimace.

"Nothing they didn't want. It wasn't difficult to release a gas, one designed to find those of fragile mind. Manipulate them until they would do everything for another hit."

"A drug?" Sam hissed, ignoring the prickling sensation against his back. Sweat coated his skin, and before long he'd start to blister.

"Crimson Mist is far superior to any drug. It's a catalyst, opening up capabilities beyond anything you could ever believe. Imagine being beyond pain, beyond physical form. But, as with many experiments there's a side effect, which brings me neatly back to you and the reason your father kept you his dirty little secret."

Sam recoiled as Gideon straightened to his full height. With a click the side of the cage fell, allowing Sam to scramble out until he hit a cold, slightly damp wall.

Bishop chuckled, but stayed where he was.

"An old acquaintance of ours once tried to ascend shifters," Gideon continued, a smile teasing his lips. "He believed your Breed would be strong enough to survive the magic, to create an army. He was wrong, and he lost himself in his beliefs before he met his demise. Shifters are nothing but feral animals."

"Then why the fuck am I here?"

"Because despite being a cunt, your father's right to have found you. Daemons are hard to generate, with the number of druids able to survive the transition almost at zero. Our old acquaintance, however, was able to leave us with some of his findings, giving us the knowledge to create an expendable, lesser version."

"Much lesser," Bishop added. "Nothing but obedient little shells, barely above the hounds."

"But men, none the less," Gideon said. "And we needed an Alpha to keep our new soldiers together. A pack you would say."

Gideon stepped closer, and Sam pressed himself against the wall, his body rigid.

"As I've already said, the drug has an... interesting side effect. The shifters that survive excessive exposure to the gas seem to slowly deteriorate, their minds unable to grow along with their new... abilities."

"They break, destroying themselves before we're done with them," Bishop said with a straight face. "Useless to us."

"They kill themselves," Sam said, voice dropping to a whisper.

"So we understand why your father wanted you, an Omega. Rare indeed. He wanted your aura to calm the

206

newer recruits, see if you could influence their minds from breaking."

Sam remained frozen, Gideon's breath like icicles against his face. "Recruits for what, exactly?"

Gideon's face was immobile as he leaned forward until their noses almost touched. His eyes glowed, a bright red with a pupil sliced down the centre. "For the Undead, of course. We plan to destroy the pretenders who believe they run this city, taking the Undercity Lords out one at a time until we have complete control."

With a snap his wings disappeared into his back. His horns curled up, disappearing into his jet black hair that was so long it brushed past his waist. After a few seconds he looked nothing like a Daemon, his eyes darkening to brown, and he even lost a few inches in height. With another click his clothes changed into an expensive suit, the tie blood red.

Bishop appeared at his side, staring down with his lips pressed into a thin line. He too had put on a glamour, both looking more human every passing second.

"For too long my people and I have been imprisoned below," Gideon continued, adjusting the cuffs at his wrists. "It's our time up here in the light."

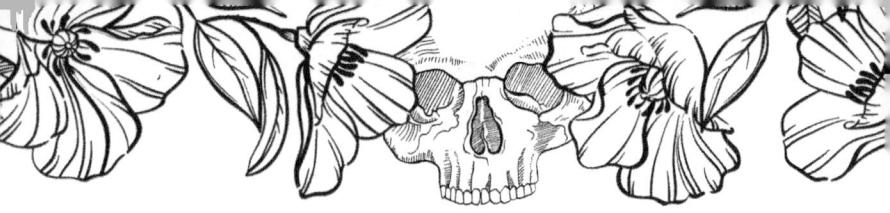

CHAPTER 26

AXEL

Axel stared at the man strapped naked to a chair, his ribs a burst of bruises in various stages of repair.

"I won't ask you again," he growled, but the man didn't flinch when his knuckles connected to his cheek with a sharp crack. Pain reverberated up Axel's arm, and he embraced it, concentrating on the feeling as he reared back his fist once more. "Where did they take him?" There was no response, no grunt or groan as his hit connected again and again.

"This is taking too long," Kace said, his presence heavy. "Let me deal with him."

Anger forced him to turn, his beast releasing a snarl that made even Kace hesitate. "Fuck off, he's mine."

"You need to calm right the fuck down, brother."

"Well, isn't that fucking funny coming from you?" Axel said, unable to stand still. "Has Sythe checked his face against all the registered packs yet?" They'd found a black stone wrapped in leather around the man's throat, and as soon as they'd snapped the thread the skull glamour fell away to reveal a worn, tired face.

"How the fuck am I supposed to know?" Kace said. "I'm stuck here making sure you don't accidentally kill him."

Axel tried to control his anger, his body vibrating with such concentrated rage he began to pace, his heart a rabbit in his chest. It had been five hours since they'd gotten the call Blood Bar had been hit, five hours since Sam had been taken. Titus and Kace had fought the two creatures, killing one while the other had shifted back to the man who currently sat bare arsed on a metal chair stolen from Jax's workshop.

"Oh, I'm so sorry that my interrogation skills are a bit rusty compared to yours," Axel said, each word dripping with sarcasm. "I'll make sure to practice –"

A knock, Sythe appearing in the corner. "His name's Lennon Cotter, registered missing three months ago by his probation officer."

The man lifted his head, but remained silent.

"Which pack?"

"He isn't," he said, face etched with anger. "According to the report he wasn't supposed to even be in the city. Was registered missing when he didn't turn up to his weekly offender meeting."

Lennon blinked slowly, eyes barely tracking.

"Riley wants an update." Shadows curled around Sythe's arm, his brother's ability unique amongst them. "That means everyone upstairs."

Dragging himself away from Lennon, Axel nodded, following both Sythe and Kace into the War room several floors above. Everyone else was already there, Titus in the corner in front of one of his many computers spotted around the estate. The screens that hung on the wall flickered, revealing the CCTV footage from the streets outside Blood Bar.

"Sam was spotted outside before the first sign of Hellfire was released," Riley said, his attention the screens. "Ti found him on the street's coverage running back towards the bar."

"Hellfire?" Sythe repeated, letting out a low whistle. "Where the fuck can you even get Hellfire now the doorway to the Fae realm has been sealed?"

"Why was he even outside?" Axel asked, watching as Titus rewound the tape, only to pause on the scene that turned his stomach. Sam, cornered by three men, including Lennon with skulls painted across their faces, and a fucking Daemon with his hand around his throat. Fire was a bright halo surrounding them, and even through the image Axel could feel the heat, the bar unrecognisable as it crumbled.

There was no fear in Sam's face, only determination before he disappeared in a burst of smoke, leaving behind the three skulls. Then nothing, the cameras melting against the scorching heat.

"Guess these are the faces of death that I've been hearing on the winds," Sythe continued in the background, watching the screen. "You would think they would choose something more inconspicuous."

"They're trying to make a statement," Riley said.

"Making a statement was hitting the fucking bar," Jax said. "The Lords know it's our place, and they know not to mess with us unless they want retaliation."

"The Lords don't see us as a threat, because unless they directly threaten us, we stay out of their way," Riley said.

"So it's a coincidence that there was a Daemon?" Sythe said. "Un-fucking likely."

"Unless you know where to look, we don't exist," Jax said. "So it's a possibility they weren't aware that the leader of The Guardians owned the place."

"Which brings us back to Sam," Axel said, body rigid

with anger. "These Undead specifically targeted him, the question is why?"

"What do we know about his father?" Riley said.

"That he was supposed to be dead," Lucifer said, leaning against the wall. "He was an Alpha over in Ireland, and from what I can remember his pack was made up of various predatory animals rather than just leopards."

Jax grunted. "How do you know so much?"

"Because we're friends you dickhead." Lucifer's voice was so cold it turned the room to ice. "I know that concept is strange to you."

"Mixed packs are unusual, but not unheard of," Titus said, trying to break the rising tension. "They're usually more volatile."

"Who gives a shit about his old pack," Lucifer growled. "Where the fuck's Alice? She should be here, she'll be able to help."

"Alice's busy right now," Riley said, the warning clear that it was the end of that conversation. "I'll be the one to deal with her."

Lucifer swore low beneath his breath. "She doesn't know, does she?" His laugh echoed around them, a gloomy cackle. "She's going to fucking explode."

Riley clenched his jaw. "I thought it was best if she found out from me."

"You're a dead man," Lucifer growled. "Did you really think keeping this information from her would help?"

"She's my mate!" Riley barked, crashing his fist hard enough onto the table the wood cracked. "She's out on a dangerous case. If I call her and tell her Sam's been taken, what do you think she'll do? Drop everything to rush back here and we have nothing to give her. Fucking nothing. Now, we need to figure out the connection between Sam's father and the Undead, that's what's important right now."

Axel ignored the migraine growing behind his eyes at an alarming speed. "Lucy, do you recognise the Daemon?"

Lucifer clenched his jaw, red eyes glowing when they met Axel's, only to shift over to the screen. "The CCTV's shit."

"You recognise him?" Riley said, standing from his chair.

Lucifer subtly stiffened. "Maybe. I can't be sure."

"You need to decide whether you're one of us or not," Xander said, crossing his arms as he remained in his seat. "You've made your point, not all Daemons are cruel, vindictive bastards. But he took one of ours."

"Do you recognise him?" Axel asked once more, stepping into his view as he glared at Xander. "What about a summon?"

Lucifer gently shook his head. "We don't share our true names, and it wasn't like I was part of the inner circle when I lived down there. I was an outcast, just trying to survive."

"Who. Is. He?" Axel prompted.

A heartbeat skipped before he answered. "He goes by Bishop, and he's one of the Originals."

"Originals?"

Lucifer laughed once more, the sound empty and hollow. "Surely you know the story? Of the first druids to accept the dark magic offered from the Fates? The nine that ascended called themselves the Originals. They're the most powerful, having had a millennia, if not longer to learn the magic."

"Nine?"

"Where do you think the nine circles of hell came from?" Lucifer said with a scowl. "Keep up, you should know this, it's our history."

Riley's features hardened to granite. "What happened to the nine?"

"What do you think? They were bound to The Nether, just like every fucking Daemon. There's always a cost for power. Three died at war with one another while four split into their own territories. Not sure what happened to them, and I don't care. Two stayed with that fucking fallen angel, learning from him."

"Hadriel?"

"He's a twat, but it's his power that keeps The Nether from crumbling, and also what created the fucking prison in the first place. I hope he's rotting alone down there in Hell."

"Lucy," Axel growled. "Who is he?"

Lucifer clenched his jaw. "I think that's Bishop, but it's not him we need to worry about. Wherever Bishop is, Gideon isn't far behind."

"Why would we be worried about Gideon?"

"Because while Hadriel reigned over The Nether as some sadistic god, it was Gideon who held control over the Daemons." Lucy's usual flamboyant personality dimmed beneath a flash of sorrow. "He was the fucking king. If Gideon has Sam..." He let his voice drift off.

"This is bullshit!" Axel said in a burst of frustration, his beast crawling at his insides. "I don't care who these fuckers are, we're getting Sam back. Where the fuck is your fight, batboy?"

Lucifer growled, his wings bursting from his back to knock Sythe to the side.

"I never said I was giving up! Sam's my friend too you little –"

"Enough!" Riley snarled. "Everyone take a breath. We'll get Sam back." His last sentence was aimed at Axel, who vibrated with excessive energy as he paced, unable to look at the CCTV footage any longer.

"What about Payne?" Titus said, his voice quiet and

controlled, a stark contrast to the rising tension in the room. "Has she woken up?"

"Yep, and she's pissed," Sythe said. "No lasting injuries, but she doesn't remember anything."

"She's lucky," Jax grunted. "Last I checked there's twenty-five dead and still counting. What about the guy downstairs?"

"Nothing from him," Kace added. "He's silent."

Axel scrubbed a hand down his face, panic and frustration strangling his lungs as he swallowed past the needles in his throat. He couldn't just stand there, discussing the situation so casually while every passing second Sam could be hurt. Or worse.

Slipping out of the room, Axel made his way back downstairs, Lennon barely acknowledging him as he approached. Axel reached down to grip his jaw, his mouth opening with a click.

"Fuck's sake."

There was no tongue, just a blackened muscle that had been crudely sliced.

"No wonder you haven't talked," Axel growled, releasing his hold. "Interesting way to keep your silence."

Lennon's head dropped, loose around his shoulders. With a frown Axel crouched down, moving closer. Lennon's mouth twisted, sweat coating his forehead. Hours Axel had beaten him and not even a flinch, and yet now he sat there squirming. Blood was a faint scent, and dropping his gaze Axel found Lennon's hands wet, his fingernails loose as he scratched them over and over again against the chair to leave red smears.

"You need a fix," he said matter of factly, recognising the signs as he reached to grip Lennon's jaw once more, his eyes not tracking. "Okay, we're going to make a deal. You've taken someone that's mine, so you're going to take me to exactly where they're holding him." Axel's grip tightened, hard enough he felt Lennon's bones groan. "If you don't, I'm going to peel every inch of your skin from your bones and watch as the drugs you crave slowly corrodes your mind. Understand?"

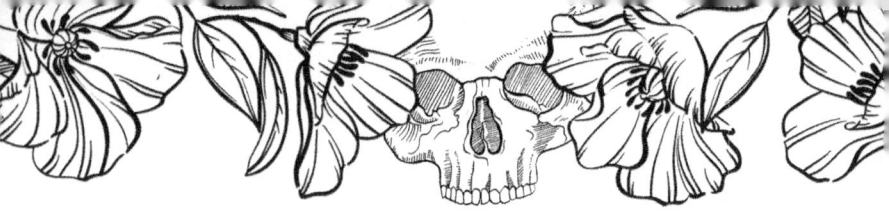

CHAPTER 27

SAM

S am closed his eyes, letting out a slow, unsteady breath.

The scents of dust, damp, and dirt.

The sounds of rapid heartbeats, cries of pain and inconsistent thunder as something rumbled high above.

It was too much.

Everything was too much.

"Do something, Samion!"

"You know I can't control it!" Sam hissed at his father, his hold loosening on the weeping man at his feet. The shifter wailed and shook, pupils blown as his fist gripped an empty canister and deflated balloon.

"Try harder, otherwise his death will be on your hands too."

Sam sank to his knees, the hard floor colder than the surrounding icy air as he pulled the man more into his lap. He didn't understand being an Omega, his influence something fluent and natural. There was no controlling it.

"Hey, I'm here," he whispered, allowing a purr to vibrate his chest. The man's spirit screamed for a release, his body far past what it could take as he twisted and turned.

Sweat, blood and a sickly yellow liquid coated his skin, seeping from his pores as his body shifted from one shape to another. Sam ignored the nausea, his stomach clenching at the sight as the man's limbs broke over and over. Fur burst through flesh before slowly returning to skin, only to repeat the painful process over and over.

Every click, crack and cry would forever haunt him.

"Why's he like this?" he asked as soon as the man finally went limp, eyes rolling into the back of his head. He was alive, barely. Sam now understood why some of the 'pack' killed themselves, he knew for himself how painful going through multiple shifts one after another could be. "What happened to his animal?"

"His animal's still there," his father said, reaching down to scruff the man, dragging him to the corner. "Just improved."

"Improved?" Sam wiped the liquid from his hands, his clothes coated in the sickly thick stuff. "How the fuck is that improved?" The man lay against the wall, left arm folded at the wrong angle beneath him, skin stripped to reveal muscle and bone. There was an extra joint, somewhere between wolf and man. At least, Sam assumed he was a wolf.

Conor turned with a snarl, storming over. "This is our evolution. What we were always meant to be."

"Evolution?" Sam climbed to his feet, the fabric of his shirt slick to his chest. "This is some sick joke, right? Look at him, look at the others. They're sick, broken because you're messing with nature."

"We have to break to truly evolve." Conor sneered towards the unconscious man. "We are the first Breed to walk this earth, our magic native to this land. Once I have a stronger pack we can rise up against those creatures and take our freedom."

"You're crazy if you believe you can walk away from this. You sold your soul for –"

"Shut the fuck up boyo! Do your job, just like you're supposed to," Conor snarled. "Just like you were always supposed to before your failings forced me to kill my entire pack."

"Supposed to? I was a fucking child, one beaten and molested to the point I barely survived myself. It wasn't my responsibility to keep the pack stable, Da. You always –"

The fist caught him on his jaw, Sam's head snapping to the side.

"It *was* your duty to look after the pack. It's the only reason you weren't killed at birth, you eejit. Your whore of a mother was an Omega, which was why she was chosen to bear my child." Conor pressed his finger into Sam's chest. "Three babes I killed before you came along, and look at you. This weak, little boy who still can't put up a fight. Pathetic." He spat.

Sam laughed, the sound on the edge of hysteria as he wiped the phlegm from his face. "You're a maniac. No wonder the pack was so unstable, your dominance is a –" He was prepared for the punch this time, moving at the last second so the knuckles only brushed his cheek. Using the momentum Sam twisted, rearing back his arm with all his strength. His fist connected, his father's nose collapsing with a satisfying crunch.

Conor staggered back, blood pouring down his face. A roar erupted from his throat, eyes reflecting his leopard with a ring of red when they met Sam's. "I'm going to enjoy showing you your place again," he said, words warbled through razor-sharp teeth. His body stretched, skin tearing as fur burst through with an audible rip. Crouching down, his back legs extended, the knees cracking as paws formed from his hands and feet, nails falling onto the concrete as claws pierced through. A snout stretched from his broken nose, healing far quicker than it should have as he transformed into a powerful leopard. The entire shift took less than five seconds. Which was supposed to be impossible for a shifter.

It was usually closer to a minute, with an Alpha being able to do it in half that time. Sam could do it in twenty seconds if he pushed himself, except the intense burn afterwards could be a life-threatening distraction. But even twenty seconds was still too long, leaving himself vulnerable to an attack.

Sam steadied his legs when his father returned his attention, tail whipping around angrily. His once orange fur was tinged with grey, rosettes that were almost identical to Sam's, darker than they should have been. Small spikes protruded from his spine, creating a wave of movement with every step as he prowled forward. The amber eyes of his leopard had bled entirely to red, reminding Sam of the hound from the alley.

Sharp pain seared across his chest, already beginning to ache as his father launched forward, claws catching. Arching backwards, the leopard flew over his head hard enough to hit the solid cinderblock wall with a thump, causing a few of them to wobble and fall. It gave Sam a second to reach for the metal bed, pulling up the mattress as a barrier as his father attacked once more, his powerful claws slicing the fabric and stuffing to shreds.

Shifting the mattress against his shoulder, Sam kicked out at the metal frame, the cheap furniture creaking. Another kick, the screws loosening as part of the bed collapsed to scrape against the concrete. More claws grazed his skin, blood hot as it dripped down his arm as the mattress finally ripped in two. With one last shove Sam bolted to the side, reaching down for the broken frame just as a heavy weight landed on his back.

Teeth at his throat, but there was no instinct to submit as he immediately ripped the leopard over his shoulder, and in the same movement swung the metal pole. It connected with his father's head, and even though the first hit knocked him unconscious, Sam felt himself lift the pole above his head once more. With a cry he held it, arms wavering as blood pooled below his father, so dark it was almost black.

Sam's hands clenched, fingers cramping as his father transformed back into the man, slower than his original transition but still far faster than he should be able to. Fur disappeared beneath ashen skin, bones clicking back into place. His chest moved rhythmically up and down, entire body relaxed.

"Fuck," he whispered, knowing he couldn't kill his father. Not when he was the one keeping Sam alive right then. Lowering the pole he released it, flinching at the clink it made when it connected to the concrete.

"Well, isn't this interesting."

Sam snapped his head to the side, not having sensed Bishop, who casually leaned in the doorway, the only exit open behind him. A grin split his angular face, auburn hair so straight it seemed to shimmer as he moved.

"Seems you're smarter than your father believes." His crimson eyes flicked to the blood dripping down Sam's throat, then to his father in question. "Pity you didn't finish the job."

Warmth dripped down Sam's fingers, droplets pattering onto the floor as he stood there, calming his racing heart. His throat throbbed, but he knew it wasn't a life-threatening injury. His father hadn't wanted to kill him, just force him to submit to his dominance.

Sam was way beyond submitting to his father, or to anyone else who believed they could force him.

"Can't kill him," Sam said calmly despite the pressure wrapping around his lungs. "He's the Alpha." The word tasted sour in his mouth, but he also needed to remain alive to be able to escape.

"We both know there's no pack dynamic, no connections. It's why Conor panicked, thinking you could fix it." Bishop straightened, and Sam stiffened as a darkened figure emerged from behind him. The hound sniffed at the air, growling low as it moved forward into the room.

The hound was more horrifying than he remembered, the harsh artificial lighting above showing every angle and strange feature. It was smaller than the one he'd faced in the alley, with a gaping hole at the end of its snout, the bottom jaw missing to leave a row of sharp teeth and a floppy tongue. Vapour wafted out, curling to drift around its side where it danced between the exposed ribs, a flash of white against blackened fur. The hound flickered, disappearing into the shadows before re-appearing closer.

The lights above sputtered, seeming to whine before going out one by one, allowing the hound to pass between the spots of darkness. Each step Sam felt his lungs tighten until hot breath brushed against his arm. He knew the hound was there, yet his eyes saw nothing but empty space.

"Amazing, isn't it?" Bishop said, watching intently as he remained in the single remaining stream of light. "But they're nothing but feral animals, barely able to follow basic instructions."

Sam let out a hiss as he felt a tongue lick against his skin, lapping at the blood only to leave a dull burn. Carrion and death, that's what its breath smelt like, so heavy it was suffocating.

"They were gifted to us," Bishop said with a shrug.

"Creatures spliced together by Hadriel back when he had the power. He's a god in his realm, but now the fallen angel is stuck down in Hell, while we're up here no longer imprisoned."

Sam kept his voice placid. "I don't know who Hadriel is."

"Sure you do," Bishop chuckled. "The fallen angel who cursed the Guardians? The same one who created the fucking Nether, also known as Hell where my kind have been kept chained for millennia. Ring any bells?"

Sam swallowed his panic. "I haven't heard of any Guardians." He slowly lifted his arm, blood dripping down to his elbow before a phantom tongue struck that too. "How will I help the pack if you let him eat me?" he asked, trying to change the subject.

Fuck. What had Axel and his brothers got to do with this?

"We've been through this, they're not a pack." Bishop let out a low whistle, and the tongue stopped, but the hound never reappeared. "And we both know you're aware of the fucking pricks who have been a thorn in my Breed's side for years. You work for their leader, after all."

"Leader?" Sam frowned, hoping his face mirrored disbelief. "Look, I'm just a bartender."

Bishop took a step forward. "If that were true, I would have killed you already. So you're really going to want to be more than just the bartender." Reaching into his back pocket he pulled out a single metal canister, rolling it between his fingers.

Sam stared at the drug, jaw taut.

"Don't worry," Bishop said with an amused smile. "You're going to enjoy this."

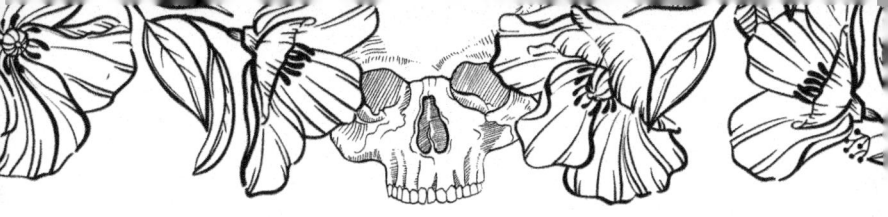

CHAPTER 28
AXEL

"You could have said we were going to the market," Axel said as he walked past the obscured, unkept graves. "Do you even have a token?"

Lennon shot him a frown over his shoulder, lips opening to reveal his blackened chunk of tongue.

"Yeah, yeah," Axel grunted. "Speaking isn't the only way to communicate, you know."

Lennon snapped his mouth closed, bouncing from one foot to the other. His eyes ping-ponged around the surrounding tombs, never settling on a single object for too long. With a meaty finger he pointed to a large headstone with three concentric circles, but Axel shook his head.

The Troll Market was an underground bazaar frequented by the meaner dredges of the Undercity, a place to buy anything from illegal charms, specialised weapons, organs to trafficking of all kinds. Humans, Fae, shifters, whatever you wanted you could buy with the right amount of money. Only those with tokens had access, and the tokens themselves were difficult to come by. There was a certain amount available at one time, and the only exceptions were those that held stalls, or if you offered up certain services to the two Fae Lords who ran the market.

Axel didn't have a token, only ever visiting when on Guardian duty. Without a token he couldn't gain access, not without going through the Gatekeeper.

As they stepped closer to the gates, Lennon made a sound from the back of his throat. His fingers trembled when he pointed once again at the other entrance, stamping his foot when Axel shrugged.

"We don't have a fucking coin token. What else do you want me to do?"

The stone mausoleum was just beyond the tall, sharp fence, the metal oxidised as he reached over to rattle the locked gate.

"Run, and I'll hunt you down," Axel warned before he turned his back. "Gatekeeper!" he called through the gaps, ignoring the flickers of white in his peripheral. Cemeteries were the one place some of the stronger spooks could become corporal, but only if you acknowledged them for more than a few seconds. "I need entrance."

Lennon crouched behind a large grave, knuckles white as sweat glistened off his forehead. Mewling sounds echoed from his open mouth, but Axel ignored him as he waited.

"Ya lost?" a strange, detached voice echoed. "Or you out 'ere taking the Mick?"

Axel felt fingers brushing his shoulder, followed by pins and needles as he spun, only to find nothing but empty air.

"I need entrance," he repeated. "To the market."

"Ya have to be careful around 'ere mate, especially in dis area," the voice continued. "Ya don't know what you'll find." The air rippled before a man stood only a foot away, his figure slowly solidifying as he gained attention. "Ya don't 'ave a coin. No coin. No entrance."

The ghost was dressed in a double breasted suit with a

chain pinned across the lapels. A newsboy peaked cap topped his head, the colours dark, opaque as the cemetery appeared through his flickering body.

"What do we 'ave 'ere then?" The Gatekeeper tipped his head to Lennon, who kept his gaze pointedly to the earth.

Axel stepped closer, blocking the ghost's view. "I'll pay for a coin. Name it."

"Ya think you 'ave the bees?"

Axel frowned, trying to calm his temper. "Look, how much for a coin?"

"Settle down, ya ain't answered the bleedin' riddles yet."

"Riddles?" Axel growled. "Look, I haven't got the ti –"

He held up three ghostly fingers. "Answer three riddles, pay the charge an' I'll open da door, easy peasy."

Axel dragged a hand down his face. "Fine."

The Gatekeeper grinned, tugging at his lapels before clearing his throat. "If you have me, you will want to share me. If you share me, you will no longer have me. What am I?" he said in a clear accent void of the earlier cockney twang.

Axel took a second to think, his voice edged with irritation when he finally answered. "A secret."

"What goes all around the world, but stays in a corner?"

"A... stamp."

The Gatekeeper clapped excitedly. "Last one," he began once again without his accent. "What has a head, a tail, is brown but no legs?"

Axel stilled, mind racing through possibilities.

Fuck. Fuck. Fuck. Why did it have to be riddles?

A sharp whistle, and Axel turned to find Lennon with two blades of grass between his lips. He pointed to the earth, where he had spelled out the answer.

"A penny!"

The Gatekeeper pouted, widening his stance to place his hands on his hips. "'here's no coins left."

"What?" Axel almost burst from his skin. "Then why the fucking riddles?"

The Gatekeeper shrugged, a smile cracking his lips. "See you la'er."

"No," Axel barked as the Gatekeeper flickered, "I'll pay in Ravyns."

The Gatekeeper reappeared, head cocked as Axel waited with little patience. "Cost a dragon."

"A dragon?" Axel repeated, his voice loud enough to echo against the tombstones. "You've got to be shitting me?" He knew it would be expensive, but not that expensive.

"No coin. No entrance," the Gatekeeper said with a grin, rocking back on his heels. "A single dragon gets ya lifetime access. I shouldn't even be doing this deal." He held out his ghostly hand.

Ravyns were the currency used in the Undercity, including the market. They were small polished onyx coins, each with their own image depicting their worth. An imp was one-hundred, a sphinx one-hundred-thousand while a dragon was around one million. Axel had no idea how much money he had left from his inheritance, but he would use every last penny if he had to.

"Deal." Axel clutched the Gatekeeper's hand, ignoring the pins and needles that rattled down his arm. A small burn started from the centre of his palm, and when he pulled it back there was a black mark.

With a chuckle the Gatekeeper disappeared, and the door to the mausoleum opened silently. Wiping his palm against his jeans, Axel gestured for Lennon to follow him as he stepped forward, noticing the pale, shimmery veil that covered the double doors. Once you owned a token it would forever follow you, appearing only hours after leaving the market. Convenient really, as long as Axel remembered to make the payment.

No metal was allowed, the material an allergen to the Fae as Axel double checked his knives, leaving them hidden behind a headstone closest to the entrance. "Move," he demanded, making sure Lennon went through first.

Pulling his sleeves down to hide his glyphs he stepped through, the glamour trying desperately to push him back before it finally released with a small pop. The noise was the first thing that assaulted Axel as he waited on top of the stone steps, then quickly it was the scents. The market was an attack on the senses, hundreds of wooden stalls with even more shopkeepers screeching for a sale. There was so much going on, each stall a burst of colour and textures that drew your attention.

Reaching over, he gripped Lennon's collar, holding him back. The walls were painted with anti-violence wards along every available space in the cavernous room. Each mark would constantly pulsate, the patterns darkening when they absorbed any violence whether it was magical or physical. It was a deterrent, one that worked to an extent. With the amount of people at the market, a single punch or two wouldn't flare up the wards, but if there was a full-blown fight the wards would kick in and neutralise both parties until they could be removed. The guards didn't care who you were, or what happened, they followed their orders so as not to draw attention to the doorways that were the Undercity's best kept secret.

Lennon pulled out of his grip as they descended the stairs, moving quickly through the crowd. Axel pushed through, cursing beneath his breath as Lennon scurried far quicker than expected. They passed tables selling crystals, exotic fruits, as well as black spelling items that could only be found there.

High-pitched squeaking came from above, and Axel stopped himself from looking up at the hundreds of cages that hung from the ceiling, the pixies trapped weeping as they waited to be sold.

The thought was sickening, their cries loud amongst the general cacophony of voices, but Axel continued to chase Lennon. He brushed up against a troll, the Fae large without the usual glamour as he growled in warning, his meaty arm covering the bowl of grey sludge he had been consuming. He swung on his stool, eyeing Axel with distaste before returning to the small pop-up restaurant.

There was no glamour, the Fae that attended stripped to their original features. It was a place for them to be who they were meant to be, and not what they projected through magic to fit in.

Another turned to eye him warily, purple eyes flicking down to study the glyphs on his hands. Axel quickly tugged on his sleeves, not wanting to reveal what he was even if he looked just like any other druid. The Guardians were a shadowed rumour amongst the Undercity, a band of barbarians who even the Lords stayed away from in most situations.

They wanted to remain a rumour, not needing any consideration that could interfere with their duty.

The woman stood, a frown marring her pretty face. Her entire body was wrapped in black leather, an insignia stamped in the centre of her breasts indicating she was an assassin.

Of course she fucking was.

Axel quickly looked away.

He really hated the market.

The entire place made no sense. One stall sold questionable meats, and another hand embroidered squares that could either be framed, or used as doilies. One stated, '*Sugar and spice and everything nice!*' and another said, '*Leave before 9pm, or I'll fucking eat you!*'

Axel managed to manoeuvre through a particularly rowdy crowd who were all betting for a shiny black orb and grabbed onto Lennon's shoulder. His fingers dug in, hard enough he felt the skin beneath his nails give as he hauled the shifter back.

"Come here," he growled, pulling Lennon with him towards the corner. "Show me where I can find the leopard you took from the bar."

Lennon's skin was damp with sweat, his eyes barely able to hold as they flicked everywhere but Axel. He had been picking at his lips, the edges red raw as he gestured to another stall only a few feet away.

As Axel turned, Lennon shoved his elbow into his stomach hard enough it expelled all the air from his lungs. Axel grunted, but didn't release his hold as he dug his fingers in harder.

"You fucking..." A flare of awareness across his chi, and as he released Lennon a shadow passed over him. The Daemon from the CCTV stood there, auburn hair tied neatly on the top of his head. He had no horns, nor wings but his eyes burned red, and Axel's instincts screamed at him to attack. "Bishop."

The Daemon's mouth quipped into a smirk. "So, you've heard of me, yet I have no idea who you are."

Axel clenched his fists, widening his stance before Bishop gestured to the anti-violence wards that seemed to pulsate harder since they'd been standing there.

"There's a reason we're meeting in such a public place," Bishop said. "We seem to have something you want." He barely looked towards Lennon, the shifter not keeping his interest.

"Give me Sam back, or else."

"Or else what?" Bishop said with an arrogance that set Axel on edge. "You have no idea where we're keeping him, or if he's even still alive."

A roar erupted from Axel's throat, and he ignored the glares from those passing by. "Fuck you! If you've hurt him I'll –"

"What will you do for the leopard's freedom?" Bishop interrupted. "What will you give us, Guardian?"

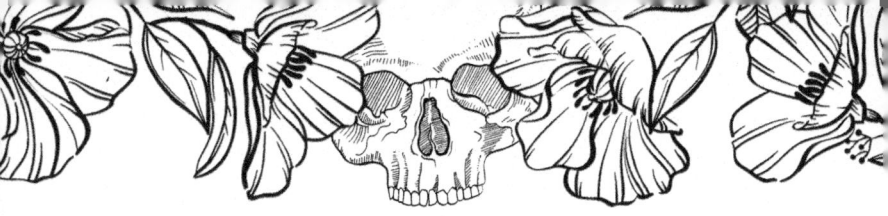

CHAPTER 29
AXEL

The house was cold, quiet when Axel returned. Which was exactly what he wanted as he took the stairs two at a time. He needed the space, his chest heavy as he walked the darkened corridor towards his bedroom.

He didn't have time to think. He had to act, before any of his brothers figured out what he was about to do. The thought of a world without Sam's happiness, his sunshine and light was something Axel couldn't comprehend. He was fooling himself believing that he hadn't fallen for Sam almost immediately after meeting him, his smile infectious. That was all it had taken, their eyes meeting from across the room and boom.

"You're back."

Axel halted outside his door, shoulders hunched as he turned his head. "Alice... I'm just grabbing something. Where's everyone?"

"Out hunting, but I'm sure you already guessed that," she answered, sitting in the groove of the window, Poe her cat sleeping silently by her feet. Moonlight sliced through the window, casting her features in shadows. "Where have you been?"

"Out."

"Was it your idea to let the shifter go?"

Fuck.

"He wasn't going to help us, he was just expendable to them."

"Expendable to who?"

Axel swallowed, finally turning his entire body, only to press his back against the door as if it would swallow him whole. "I'm going to get Sam back. I promise."

Alice tilted her head, the moonlight moving to highlight the tears that glistened down her cheeks. "My job is to find people," she said, voice breaking. "And yet you let our only clue walk free. What the fuck is wrong with you?"

Guilt wrapped itself around his lungs, constricting every breath. "You need to trust me."

"Trust you?" Alice snapped, electricity shooting up her arm from her palms. It was a shock against the encroaching darkness, disappearing as quickly as it came. "He's my best friend and –"

"And he's my mate!" Axel barked, the realisation punching him like a jackhammer, so hard he swore something cracked. "He's my mate." It was the truth, a fact he had suppressed for so long because of his own issues. Sam was his mate, and even if he could never commit to just him, for Axel he was it.

Mine, his beast growled, and Axel could only agree.

Alice blinked past her tears. "Mate?"

"Fuck," Axel whispered, yanking at his hair hard enough his scalp stung. "Please, you need to trust me."

"Did you say mate?" The tears fell harder, and Axel stopped himself from crushing Alice to his chest, to comfort her when she stood so alone. But he needed to keep the distance, to get her away as time ticked down.

One hour.

"Please, you need to trust me," he said, desperation edging his tone. "I'll get him back."

"Trust you?" Alice was quiet for a moment before she gave him a wary frown. "Sam's impulsive," she said, her words coming fast. "He's the most impulsive person I know. He has this addictive personality, and takes everything to the extreme. It's like he finds something he likes and then goes crazy for it. Alcohol. Smoking. Sex." She barely stopped to take a breath. "Do you know he has over thirty novelty t-shirts? All because he saw one once that made him laugh, so now it's this whole thing between us –"

"Alice... what are –"

"He hates the hospital," she continued as if she hadn't heard him. "More than hate, he's terrified. You can't take him there unless it's an emergency. Oh, and he adores movies, but has terrible taste. He'll drop everything to help someone else, but he never expects anyone else to do that for him."

"Alice, I don't... why are you telling me this?"

"Because you need to know him like I do," she said, swallowing hard as grief lined her face. "I need you to love him like I do, no, even more so. Because he believes he doesn't deserve it."

"That's ridiculous, how can he believe he doesn't deserve love?"

"Because he's an idiot who's haunted by his childhood." Alice reached to the crystal around her throat, twisting it around her fingers. "Axel, you're asking me to trust you, yet you let our only clue go."

"I –"

Alice held up her hand, sparks dancing between her

233

fingertips as her power brushed his chi. "You called him your mate, but do you love him?"

Images of Sam flashed across his mind, every smile, every laugh loosening the pressure in his chest. "He believes he doesn't deserve love, but it's me who doesn't deserve his." Emotions clogged his throat, but Axel pushed through as Alice waited. "But I don't care, because he's mine and nothing will stop me from getting him back."

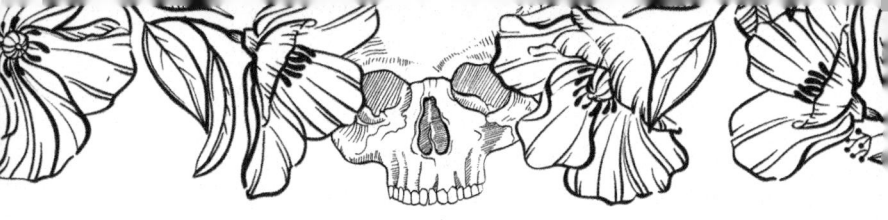

CHAPTER 30

SAM

Cold air teased Sam's bare feet, so sharp it was as if icicles caressed his skin. It had hardened the sickly yellow liquid against his shirt, flaking off with every movement. He wasn't sure how much time had passed, waking up in a daze to find his father and the man who had passed out gone, only for a woman to stand in the entrance, large eyes staring.

He tried his best to not make any sudden movements, sensing her fear. Yet she stood there as still as a statue as he slowly moved around the room, pulling apart the bed until it was nothing but a bunch of metal poles. He'd already shoved the remains of the mattress into the corner, finding nothing inside that could be of any help. The room was essentially bare, the walls made from a mixture of concrete and dirt with cinderblocks stacked for support. There were no windows, nothing but the single doorway in which the woman watched.

Taking a second, he closed his eyes, the sudden dizziness almost forcing him to his knees as he reached for the wall to steady himself.

"Is there a bathroom?" he asked, voice rough, as if he'd

spent the last few hours screaming. "I need to –" Hands touched his forehead, the sudden warmth helping with the nausea. Sam tried to relax his body, the woman trembling from being so close. "Thank you," he said quietly, meeting her gaze for the briefest second before her eyes skirted away. She was dominant, strong. She shouldn't have had the need to look away.

Her hands pulled back, and with her head she gestured to the doorway.

"Through there?" he asked, going first while she remained where she was. The lights above buzzed, the wires crudely attached to the ceiling in what must have been an electrician's nightmare. The concrete beneath his feet gave way to sodden earth, squelching with every step. He quickly found a set of rickety wooden stairs, the door above open to reveal a slash of light. Taking each step slowly, he carefully pushed the door open, and three sets of eyes stopped what they were doing to turn.

Sam hesitated at the top, the man on the left standing frozen besides a large pot of boiling stew, while the other two held knives in tight fists, one cutting potatoes and another carrots.

"Bathroom?" Sam asked, and after a beat the man by the pot pointed to the right.

Nodding his thanks, Sam continued, the floor turning to creaky rotten wood and a mixture of overlapping threadbare rugs. He passed several closed doors, the windows outside pitch black and covered in a silver mesh. The double front door was locked from the inside, a large chunk of wood closing it tight.

The woman carefully passed him, conscious to not touch as she stopped at the bathroom, the door removed with only the broken hinges remaining.

Avocado green tiles covered the entire room from floor

to ceiling, a matching bathtub full of black sludge sat to the left with a shower-head dripping from above. The sink was just as dirty, but the water clean when Sam turned the tap, the mirror above shattered. Pulling the shirt from his chest, the hardened yellow liquid cracked, and Sam yanked the entire thing off to hold beneath the freezing water. Cold rattled his spine, the ends of his fingers blue as he wrung out the fabric.

Sam sensed his father seconds before he felt the grip at the back of his neck, his face forced into the mirror with a crash. Pressure on his shoulders, enough weight to be more than one person as he fought the hold. But his movements were weak, sluggish.

"Enough!" Lips against his ear, a rush of heat that prickled against his skin. "The only reason you're not dead right now is because I need you," his father growled, adding pressure until blood dripped from Sam's sliced cheek. "Remember who's Alpha, or you'll go straight back in that cage."

The mention of the cage stopped all of Sam's fight. He opened his mouth slightly, his breaths coming in short pants as he tasted the surrounding aggression, his leopard close to the surface. He'd closed his eyes on impact, protecting them from the sharp shards as he slowly peeled open the one that wasn't crushed to the mirror.

His father had pulled back enough that Sam could see his smirk, the other set of arms gone from his shoulders. With a last push Conor stepped back, and Sam slowly followed. "Clean yourself up and meet me in the living room in five."

Sam waited a beat, his father disappearing around the corner before he reached up and pulled the shards from his skin, placing each one carefully on the side of the sink.

A tap on his shoulder, gentle compared to the heavy

pressure before. Having already scented one of the men from the kitchen, Sam turned, only to find a piece of paper pushed towards his face.

'It takes few times to get used to,' it read. *'The first time the worst, then it ~~euphoric~~ feel good. Make you strong. You'll like it here, like us. Food, mist, and a roof.'*

Sam remembered the mist, the pain in his lungs before his leopard exploded violently from his skin. Dropping his t-shirt, he touched where he was bitten before brushing his fingertips down his chest and arms. Each wound had healed entirely, not even a red mark remaining. He hadn't shifted just the once, but past the first initial pain he remembered nothing.

Thwack... Thwack... Thwack.

The man flinched, blinking several times before he turned to the doorway where the woman appeared with a t-shirt. Flipping the page on his notepad he scribbled another note.

'It cold. Need new ~~tee~~ top or may freeze. We huddle for warmth.' The man frowned, pulling the paper back before adding more. *'I Travis.'* He tapped beneath his name several times with his pen before continuing. *'That Rachael.'*

Thwack... Thwack... Thwack, the sounds echoing down the corridor.

Both Rachael and Travis winced once more, eyes widening as they nervously moved from one foot to the other.

Accepting the t-shirt, Sam slipped it on quickly. It was thin, with holes down the side, but it was better than his old wet one that had fallen to the tiles in the scuffle.

"Hi Travis," he said before acknowledging the woman. "Racheal. I'm Sam."

'Meet Alpha before he get angry.' Travis underlined 'angry' several times. *'Go now or won't get mist.'*

It didn't take Sam long to find the living room, ignoring the L-shaped stairs that curled into high ceilings. More rugs lined the wooden floors, the walls papered in yellow and beige stripes, the paintings depicting fox hunts with hounds. Except the foxes were larger than normal, shifters running for their lives from horse mounted humans with shotguns.

Thwack... Thwack... Thwack.

Conor kneeled in the centre, fist covered in blood as he rhythmically reared back his arm to punch forward.

Thwack... Thwack... Thwack.

Each hit sent a sickening pulse through the group who watched by the wall, both Rachael and Travis taking a seat each on the worn fabric sofa.

"That's enough," Sam's voice was sharp, his own fists clenching by his side as he waited for his father to finish beating the unconscious man. He remembered all too well his father's punishments. "You're going to kill him."

Thwack... Thwack... Conor stopped with his arm raised, head snapping to the side. "Careful boyo," he said, rage lining his face. "Did you want to finish Lennon's punishment?" At Sam's silence Conor released his fist, the last punch the hardest. It sent the man named Lennon across the floor, his face broken, the skin that wasn't covered in blood black and blue.

Conor stood to his full height, which, Sam realised for the first time, was a few inches shorter than himself. He looked wired, agitated as he reached for a bowl that had been placed on a side table. With a growl he tossed the contents at Sam, who barely controlled his flinch as pain erupted across the side of his face.

Salt. His father had thrown salt.

"That's for interrupting Lennon's punishment," his father barked, stalking forward until they were toe to toe.

Sam straightened, knowing that if any grains had gotten

into his cuts they would scar. Salt was used often after a beating, and not even shifting could help the damage.

"And for knocking me," his father continued, voice dropping to barely a whisper. "Do that again, and I'll make sure your childhood looked like a fucking fantasy compared to what I'll do to you. You're not too old to be locked in a cage, Son." He moved even closer. "Or tied to a mattress."

Rage roared to the surface, so hot it blurred his father's face as Sam forced himself to remain rigid, to not react. There was a touch of fear, the child he once was unable to stop the memories.

"This is our Omega," Conor said brashly, spittle hitting Sam's face. "He's new to our pack, and we must introduce him to your animals before we allow free skin privileges."

Sam flinched then, unable to stop the reaction as nausea settled like a lump of coal in his gut. Skin to skin contact, it was how shifters calmed their animals, and the reason his father pushed more than just a casual caress.

There were six shifters, three sitting on the sofa with two standing each side. Not one had moved the entire time, not even a single twitch as they watched the beating, and then the salt. Lennon alone rolled onto his back, ignored by the others.

"How many are there in your pack?" Sam asked, studying each shifter slowly. Not one kept eye contact, each gaze skirting away as soon as he met them. There was some severe dominance in the room, and most of them were high tier, with the single woman the highest, barely below his father. A Beta, at least.

"This is it," Conor replied. "There was ten, but there's been a few... accidents." With a click of his fingers he pointed to Travis, who immediately stood, and then started to strip. Nudity was nothing for shifters, embarrassment of the naked body something not developed in a Breed who

240

had to be naked to shift from their human shape to their animal.

Sam could feel the disjuncture between all the pack, the hesitancy and aggression as Travis completed his shift into a wolf. Bishop was right, there was no connection between them, no loyalty. To become a pack was to submit dominance to the Alpha, offering them your throat where they bit down until blood coated their tongue. In return they then bit the wrist of the Alpha, creating the blood bond and threads of life that entwined them as a group. It was natural magic found from the earth. A way for the pack to connect on a spiritual level.

Sam remembered the feeling, like a warmth from an open fire. Except his experience as a true pack was anything but warm. There was no blood bond between anyone in the room, and his father would know that being the Alpha.

This wasn't a pack, just a group of dysfunctional, individual shifters.

"Here," Conor demanded, and Travis stepped closer until his nose was buried in Sam's stomach. He was large for a wolf, twice the average size, with his back paws deformed. Human fingers were still attached, seeming to hang by a single bone. His eyes seemed sunken, swallowed by his sockets, enough to interfere with his sight, and there were sharp spines spotted throughout his fur.

Sam remained where he was, allowing the wolf to become familiar with his scent.

"They're mostly wolves," Conor said, upper lip curled in disgust. "They dominate this fucking city. Not many cats except for Nick, but he never returned." With another click of his fingers Travis stepped back, only for Rachael to begin shifting.

"White Dawn own the surrounding territory, you need permission to be here or else they have the right to kill you."

Shifter law was old and barbaric. White Dawn was one of the largest packs in Europe. They controlled most of the southern part of England, allowing other smaller packs to have their own sections if they pledged fealty. The only person above the Alpha of White Dawn was Xavier, the councilman. He stood for the shifters on the Council of Breeds, and was their judge, jury, and executioner.

Conor grunted, unbothered. "We're careful about territorial lines with White Dawn. We can't take them on until we're stronger."

"What do you mean take them on?" Sam held his hand out for Rachael, who had warily approached. Her nose was cold in his palm, the bottom of her jaw crooked to reveal that her tongue was missing. "Their pack has hundreds of members, and you have seven."

Conor tensed, knuckles white. "Careful boyo," he warned. "You're part of this pack now, I've already taken your blood. We'll complete the union after I've introduced you to everyone."

Terror trembled down his spine, leaving trails of ice. "Touch me again, and I'll kill you," Sam growled, meeting Conor's angry eyes without recoiling. The blood wasn't permanent, a shifter able to move packs easily enough if the ritual was repeated. But Sam couldn't think of anything worse than being connected to his father once more, to be able to feel him spiritually. It would be too much, too close to the nightmares he had buried beneath years of fucking therapy.

If it was between completing the union, and death.

Sam knew what he would choose.

Conor's enraged smile widened, his teeth sharpening as Rachael moaned low in her throat. Without looking away Conor swiped her to the side, his hand grazing her head.

"You're going to regret everything." His voice could cut glass.

Thick claws an inch long speared through his fingertips as he reared back his arm. Sam was ready for it, knowing that he wasn't really a fighter, but knew that he when he went down, he would take his abuser with him.

With a snarl Sam moved towards the swiping claws, bending to tackle his father around the waist. They both fell in a clash of claws and teeth, Sam unable to shift anything but his hands as Conor turned his head, and bit down on his forearm.

Sam ignored the pain and hands on his shoulders, adrenaline racing through his blood. His claws pierced into Conor's face, not enough to kill but enough for his concentration to break. With an angered grumble he turned, shifting faster than Sam could slice.

A grip on his throat, tight enough Sam had to release his own hold as he was forced to the side by one of the others, only to find a dark leopard snarling in his face with two deformed wolves flanking him. Sam couldn't help but laugh as claws tore through his body, his father's rage the one thing that would be his end.

Without Sam he didn't have a pack, and Gideon would surely destroy him.

A comforting thought in his last moments.

"That's enough." A voice sliced through the air like a whip, but Sam was unable to turn as darkness touched the edges of his vision. He was no longer cold, a heavy heat radiating from his chest as the weight lifted, only for his lungs to burn seconds later, just as he fell into nothing.

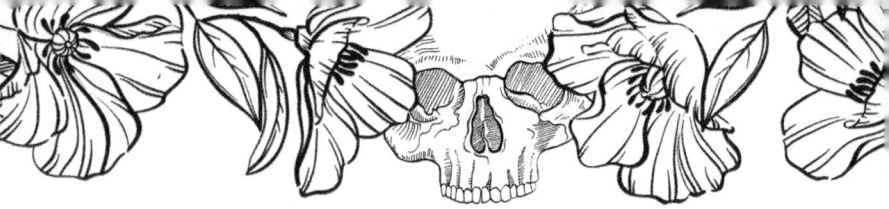

CHAPTER 31

AXEL

Debris crunched beneath Axel's boots, crumbling to dust as he broke open the chains locking the back entrance to Blood Bar. The inside was unrecognisable, destroyed, with every surface covered in grime. The once vibrant place, full of light and laughter, had been devastated, the natural wood turned to blackened rubble while everything else had disintegrated into various shades of grey.

Police markers littered the floor, footprints still visible in the ash as splashes of yellow tape brought the only colour. The ceiling had collapsed, exposing holes in the roof where rain drizzled through in a pitter patter against an exposed metal beam. Riley's glass office had shattered, the only part remaining the reinforced ledge where the door had once been. The stairs had collapsed, the wall separating the staff room, bathrooms and closets gone to reveal everything gutted.

He could have spent hours going over every inch, but Axel knew he didn't have long, awareness spreading as he opened his phone and pressed send.

'Thank you for everything you've done over the years, for all the shit you've protected me from. Even as kids you were always there for me, and I took advantage of that. You're more than just my cousin, Ti. More than just my brother. I'm sorry.'

He ignored his phone's vibration as he shoved it quickly into his pocket. A bag rustled, hand shaking as he brushed his fingertips against the packet of three pills. *Just in case,* he had thought. Three pills, each with a different coloured smiley face to take the edge off his panic. To help with the dread that had been biting at him with such sharp fangs he'd thought it would swallow him whole, more painful than anything he'd ever experienced.

The need to drown himself in a high, to knock himself out until there was nothing but peaceful obscurity, was almost overwhelming. Almost.

He was weak to buy the pills, but he hadn't brought himself to take them. He had to stay focused, stay alert.

Because this wasn't about him, regardless of how loud his addiction howled. How the whispers scoured across his brain, doubt, hate.

It was about Sam.

"Wasn't sure you would show," the familiar voice cut in, deep and edged with a dark undercurrent that immediately set Axel on alert.

He had sensed Bishop lurking in the shadows, like prickles against his chi. "Where is he?"

Bishop's smile was full of poison as the air pressure dropped, and another Daemon appeared. He wasn't as tall, head void of hair and dominated by thick horns that were more squarer than curved, angled towards his shoulders. His wings were held tightly to his back, thin membrane pulled tightly between the bones with only the primary feathers remaining at the edge. His fingers were long and thin, black nails broken as he gripped Sam's arms hard enough his skin mottled in bruises.

"Sam?" Axel stepped forward, only for Sam's head to be wretched back by his hair, throat exposed and a blade kissing his skin.

He had barely made a noise, eyes rolling in the back of his head as he remained limp. Small slices decorated the side of his face, the flesh angry while larger wounds bled down his chest. He was alive, but barely.

"You said he wouldn't be harmed," Axel said, voice a ragged rage that echoed in the broken room.

"And he wasn't. At least, he wasn't harmed by us." Bishop gave a wicked slant of his lips. "You need to be more specific in your communication."

Axel widened his stance, fingers itching to touch the blade hidden at his back as he calmed his temper down to a simmer. He had stolen it from Jax, the handle holding crystals to make the metal charged with a little bit of arcane.

But he had to wait, unable to do anything until Sam wasn't blocking Baldy. He only had the one chance, and needed to wait for the best moment.

Axel couldn't drift, the ability to break down your molecules to move one place to another in a blink of an eye, a rare ability amongst all Breed. But Daemons could, their magic evolving over millennia for them to drift through the veil separating the realms. So it took everything for Axel to remain where he was, to not burst from his skin and let his beast annihilate the Daemons who had taken his mate.

"Drop him," Axel growled at Baldy, who just smirked with disdain in response.

"Not yet," Bishop answered. "This was your choice, remember?"

Axel ignored the slight buzz at the back of his head. His

body ached, his muscles so tightly wound he was as solid as granite. Everything seemed to be in hyper focus, every glint of dust that drifted in the air to every drop of the rain that glistened from the broken roof.

It was if everything was more acute, his senses jacked.

"I remember." Axel licked at his lips, blood a thunder in his ears. "I'll give you my soul, but in return you have to release his." A growl across his mind, his beast pressing for freedom. "Safely, and without further harm," he added before his words could be twisted in the contract.

"Do you believe your soul's worthy?" Baldy chuckled, grip loosening enough that Sam sagged against the floor.

Axel needed to get closer.

"Do you have any idea what I am? What I'm capable of?" Axel allowed his beast to shape his words, the tell-tale tingling of his irises shifting to liquid silver. "My sole purpose, the reason for my existence is to destroy your kind." He took a confident step forward, concealing his chi as he felt Baldy spread out his own, dark tendrils searching for a weakness. Testing his strength.

Baldy's grip loosened further, his chi an acidic taste at the back of Axel's palette as he flicked his gaze towards Bishop, who watched with a quiet amusement.

"And I've destroyed many over my lifetime."

Come. On, he thought. *Just a little more.*

Bishop's laugh cut through the tension, a sharp cackle that sent tremors down Axel's spine. "How amusing, but I think we should come to our conclusion." The floor cracked beneath his feet, the small debris, dust, and ash sinking into the markings that opened up around them in a perfect circle. Axel recognised some of the glyphs, but many were old, ancient, and far beyond his knowledge.

Shit.

He only had the one chance. He was going to have to take it. He just hoped it was enough.

Please don't be fucking late.

"My soul for his," Axel said once more. "Do we have a deal?" He stood only inches away.

Bishop tilted his head, cool eyes assessing before he held out his hand. "Your soul for – "

A pop. Loud enough they both jerked in surprise, followed by two more. Baldy groaned, a hole appearing in the centre of his forehead as blood oozed slowly down his pale skin before he collapsed. It was seconds, a few heart-beats before Axel finally reacted, pulling the knife from his back, and launching himself towards Bishop.

His blade sliced through Bishop's chest with little resis-tance as he forced the arcane to coat the metal, a heavy thud vibrating behind him. The only way to kill a Daemon was to burn them with magic from the inside out. Something rather difficult when they wouldn't remain stationary for very long.

"Lucifer!" Axel snarled over his shoulder, only to be caught by a heavy wing knocking him back, his hold loos-ening on his blade as it clattered to the ground. One of the horns pierced his arm, hooking into the flesh before he ripped himself free with a tug. "Get Sam out of here!"

Bishop turned, distracted with a new enemy as red arcane burned his palms, so hot it seared against Axel's chi. His own body reacted, his tattoos blazing to life as he concentrated his own magic, feeling the power beneath his skin as he dropped to his knees and reached for Sam.

Baldy blinked blindly at the ceiling, his face a sea of red. It looked like he had been shot, twice in the chest with a bullet seeming lodged against bone and one in his forehead. The holes had already started to reduce, and it wouldn't be long until he had recovered enough to attack. One Daemon was difficult enough. Two was suicide.

"Sam?" he called, pulling him away as Baldy's hand twitched. "Hey kitty, you there?"

Sam's head rolled loose on his shoulders, his breathing laboured as his face twisted into a frown. Weakly he raised his hand, brushing his fingers featherlight against his jaw. "I must be dead," he breathed.

His attention shifted to over his shoulder, eyes widening as Axel turned. Bishop held a red sphere with a heart of grey between both his hands. With an angered sneer he launched the arcane, the sphere soaring with such power it licked at Axel's chi, burning even from the distance. He knew he would be too slow, the possible injuries catastrophic as he remained by Sam's side.

A flash of black leather and blonde hair.

Axel watched as the arcane hit Titus dead in the centre of his back, the magic eating away at his armour and then flesh as it launched him across the room. He landed against a beam, bending at a painful angle as he sagged to the dirt. The entire structure of the building groaned, rubble falling down to kick up the ash.

"Ti!" Axel screamed, jumping to his feet, but Bishop was already there. Reaching down he gripped Titus, and with a smirk they disappeared in a burst of smoke. "Wait! Fuck!"

A sharp pain sliced into his back, a blade piercing through his chest just shy of his heart. Dropping to his knees with a gasp he turned, only to come face-to-face with Baldy. With a wink he reached forward, and Axel's last thought before disappearing with a static pop was of Sam.

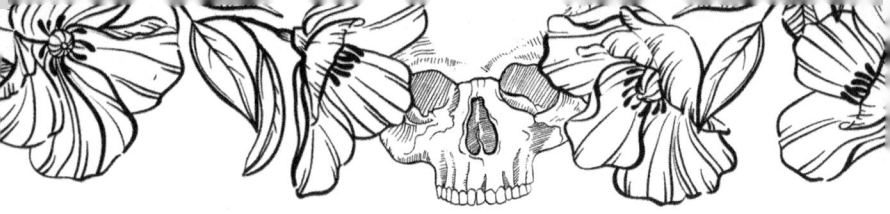

CHAPTER 32

SAM

S am felt like he was falling, his entire body jolting forward before he recognised the familiar burn of silver. His entire body was on fire, from the tips of his toes to his nose, every single inch of skin burned.

With a shout he pulled off the weight on his lap, the fabric softer than he expected before hands tried to pin him down. Sam released his claws, trying to shred anything and anyone who touched him.

"Sam!" a feminine cry, one he recognised in the back of his mind. "Stop, you're going to hurt yourself!"

Safe. He realised. Her voice was safe. With a groan he settled back, reaching up to wipe the liquid from his eyes. Everything was blurry, each movement agonising as he blinked until he saw the rough outline of a woman.

"Baby girl?"

Alice came closer, more into focus. She had been crying, eyes red and bruised. Sam's arm shook as he reached for her cheek, blood coating his claws as he stopped at the last second.

"Did I cut you?" Ice sunk in his stomach, his movements too slow to see whether he had hurt her. His nose wasn't working, the lack of scents alarming. "Alice?"

She lifted her arm, and thin lines of red dripped. "I'm fine, it's just a scratch."

"I'm so..." Sam tried to reach for her, his skin glistening metallic beneath the lights.

"You're sweating silver," she explained, carefully wiping across his skin with a cloth. "We weren't sure if you would wake up." He heard the tears in her voice.

Sam took a second to reply, screaming inside his head at the pain of the soft caress. "Silver?" He didn't remember, nothing other than death. He should be dead, so why wasn't he?

"The doctor thinks you were injected with something, so your body's working it out of your system anyway it can. Your eyes are no longer red, through."

Sam stiffened at the word doctor, panic rising once more as he tried to focus on the room. He expected white walls and an antiseptic stench, but instead it was natural woods and fine art. The sheets covering his hips were pale, but not exactly white as he tried to swing his legs off the side of the bed.

"What do you think you're doing?" asked Alice in a chiding tone. "Samion Murphy, you stay in this bed right now!"

His muscles shook, feet barely able to take his weight as he slipped off entirely. Alice hovered, arms out ready but not touching. Her face had curved into a scowl, and Sam realised she had lost weight. "What happened?"

Alice gestured to the bed, and with a reluctant grunt Sam rested back. His legs had stopped shaking, his body bare but slick with the metallic moisture. Grabbing the sheet, he pulled it against himself, trying to wipe some of the metal off his skin. Alice removed the fabric from his hands, lips set in a straight line as she carefully began to wipe.

"Alice?" he asked, voice a harsh rasp as he tried to hide his wince. "What happened? Where's Axel?"

Alice was silent a few minutes longer, concentrating on removing the metal. The burning slowly subsided, his thoughts no longer as sluggish as he finally lost patience.

"Alice?"

"Axel was taken," she said, finally explaining what had happened. "Titus too."

"Taken?"

A shadow, Lucifer appearing in the doorway. "He sold his soul in replacement for yours." He leaned against the frame, chest bare with bandages wrapped around his shoulder. Smaller wounds sliced up his face, lips split as his red eyes met Sam's. "Technically the plan went well, you know, except Titus." A shrug.

"Axel did *what?*" Sam pushed up from the bed, taking a few steps closer to Lucy, his muscles steady. "Why... why would he do that?"

Why would he risk himself for me?

Lucifer exchanged looks with Alice, straightening from his lean. "Why wouldn't he?"

"We have to get him back." Sam's voice broke, a pressure on his chest at the thought of anything happening to him. "We... we..." He couldn't breathe, his lungs struggling to gain air.

"Give him a minute," Lucifer said when Alice went to grab him.

Sam crouched, dropping his head low as he concentrated on sucking in oxygen. The pressure hadn't lessened, a dull ache just above his heart.

"He shouldn't have done that," he said, forcing the words out. "He shouldn't have sacrificed himself for me."

Axel, despite his vices had one of the best hearts Sam had ever known.

"It was a stupid plan," Lucifer said, brows snapping together. "I told him this and yet here we are. Don't ever let me get mated."

Sam's head snapped up, eyes widening. "We're not... we're not mated."

Lucifer shrugged, seeming not to care despite his eyes flicking to Alice. Sam wanted to snap back that he would never mate, but he couldn't seem to get the words past his tongue. Not when all his energy needed to be on finding Axel.

Fuck!

"How long have I been out?" The marks on his arm looked days old, yet the memory of his father's claws was fresh. "When can I shift?"

"Two days," Lucy said when Alice hesitated. "You can't shift until the metal's out your system according to the man in the white coat."

Alice shot Lucifer a glare.

"What?" he said with a frown. "Look at him? He's going to do something stupid and honestly, I'm here for it."

"Two days? They've been gone for two fucking days?" Sam was steady when he moved, brushing past Alice to find the bathroom.

"Sam, you're supposed to rest." Alice followed, but he ignored her as he turned on the shower and stepped inside.

He didn't give a shit about his nudity, and neither did Alice as he swallowed his pained growl. The water cascaded over him, but he couldn't tell whether it was hot or cold as his entire body rejected the sensation.

"Jax said he's working on finding them, we just have to wait."

"Yeah, because we can trust Jax," Lucifer said, and Sam

looked up from between the wet strands of his hair to find him standing beside Alice. "Hurry up and heal, and we'll go get him."

"I swear Luce, if you carry on, I'm going to fucking bind you to a circle and leave you there." She pointed towards his chest, his height dwarfing hers and yet Sam would put money on her every single time.

"Don't tease me with a good time, *Little War*," Lucifer grinned, but it didn't reach his eyes. "Jax is taking too long, we need to get them before it's too late."

Before it's too late. Sam ignored the pain as he wiped down his entire body, the water as his feet like oil.

"Do you even know where they are, *Xahenort?*" Alice said, using his summoning name, the one no one was supposed to know. "Or are you just reacting because your plan with Axel failed?"

Anger burned through Lucifer, his horns piercing through his hair as he snarled. "It didn't fail. The goal was to rescue Sam, as you can see Sam is currently very much fucking rescued."

"Yes, because Axel and Titus being taken was exactly what was supposed to happen!"

"It wasn't my fault I was attacked by three fucking hellhounds! Do you know how hard it is to get unhallowed blood out of leather? Besides, I didn't know Ti was going to shoot up the place. He wasn't even supposed to be there!"

"Enough," Sam grunted, barely heard above the water.

"If you want someone to blame, blame him," Lucy continued, crossing his arms like a petulant child.

"This is exactly why you're supposed to tell someone else about your stupid fucking plan!" Alice said, sparks dancing between her fingers. "You and Axel are both morons."

Ignoring them arguing Sam began to shift, the familiar ache a comfort as he concentrated on the change.

"This is the thanks I get for saving —"

Alice's shout hurt his enhanced hearing. "Sam! Really?"

Sam rolled his shoulders, feeling every bone click into their new position. His fur was the correct colour as he stretched, claws extending out before retracting into his paws. Tail swishing, he turned to check the rest of his body, relaxing for the first time since he'd woken. He looked exactly as he should.

Alice reached into the shower to turn off the water. "What a surprise, you're pushing yourself."

A knock, Sam's ear twitching as Riley called through. "He up?"

Alice frowned, tiredness lining her face. "In here."

Riley appeared seconds later, looking between Sam and Lucy before landing on Alice, dark brow raised. "We're heading out in an hour."

You've found them? Sam shouted, suddenly frustrated that he couldn't speak as a leopard. Luckily, Alice was on the same wavelength.

"So, you know where they are?" she asked, and Sam pawed at the floor.

"We're narrowing it down, but Ti was the computer guy. Head to the war room, Jax and Sythe are figuring it out while we weapon up."

Sam didn't even let Riley finish before he tore through the house, sliding across the wood as he raced down the stairs. The war room was essentially a large dining table surrounded by screens, boards, and weapons. Jax frowned when Sam entered, but turned back to the computer screen where Sythe sat.

"Oooo who's a pretty kitty," Sythe said, lifting his hand as if to pet.

"I wouldn't," Jax said in his usual monotone. "Sam will likely bite your fingers off." Sam growled low in his chest, and Jax's upper lip twitched. He had once tried to stroke Sam when he was sunbathing, and in return had met with his claws. It had only been a little scratch, and Sam still remembered the shocked expression as he had returned to his nap.

"I see you're feeling better," Sythe muttered. "J, are you sure you've given me the right details?"

Jax glowered behind him, having to bend to see the screen over Sythe's shoulder. "Yes. I told you the trackers were experimental. Ti wasn't even supposed to use the fucking bullets without testing them first. They could have exploded straight from the gun."

"What bullets?" Alice asked as she came in, having changed her wet shirt to something closer to what the Guardians were wearing. Sam always assumed it was leather, but he scented something else as it moulded to her body perfectly. The sheath she kept tight to her spine held her unique sword, newly added crystals hanging from the pommel.

Jax stepped away from Sythe, who was quietly swearing beneath his breath. "Ti and I have been experimenting with the idea of trackers."

"Genius actually," Sythe added, frowning at the screen. "So if we came across a Daemon we could tag them, at least for a short distance. It would work if Jax knew the fucking software."

"Ti's the compute guy. I'm the weapon guy," Jax growled. "Look, just move and I'll do it." He yanked at the chair, and Sythe punched him in the arm.

"What's the progress?" Riley asked as he entered, wearing the same armour as Alice. He had knives strapped down his chest, and a gun at his hip. Lucifer, Kace and

Xander followed behind, all matching except for Lucy, who had a bright pink bum bag strapped diagonally.

"Look, red dots." Sythe pressed his finger hard into the screen. "Those are the trackers, right?"

Jax frowned. "I have no fucking idea."

Sythe pushed away from the computer, throwing up his hands in frustration. "You're as helpful as a chocolate fucking teapot!"

Xander moved towards the screen. "The trackers are popping in and out, but it looks like they're still in the city."

"You think we can strengthen the signal?" Riley asked.

"What part of experimental does no one understand?" Jax growled. "If Ti was here, then probably."

"I can pull someone from my team," Sythe began, "but I'm not sure if they can work with Ti's software."

"Leave it, we don't have the time," Riley said, turning to the others. "We have a rough area, that will have to do."

"Let's do this!" Lucifer hollered, clapping his hands together. "Can't you guys sense them or some shit?"

"If they're conscious," Xander muttered. "We ready to head out?"

Sam hissed, drawing their attention before he began to shift back. It took longer than he would like, his body still recovering. "I'm coming," he said when he had human vocal cords. "I need to be there."

"That was assumed," Riley said before Alice could protest. "But you're a liability."

Sam let a growl vibrate his chest.

"He'll stay out the way," Alice said, turning to face Sam. *We'll do this together,* her face read, and as Sam nodded something hit his chest.

Lucifer shook his head, gesturing to the towel that Sam had caught. "Your cock's fucking out, mate."

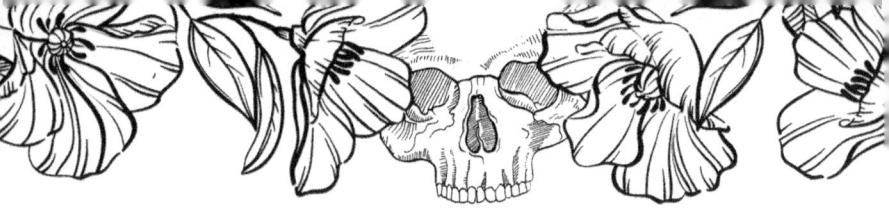

CHAPTER 33

AXEL

A painful wave rolled through Axel's body, his muscles rigid as he gritted his teeth. It pulled at the chain around his ankle, his skin splitting each time another wave hit.

Eight. Seven. Six.

A chuckle, but Axel ignored it as he continued to count in his head.

Three. Two. One.

The magic released, his body sagging in respite. He'd lost count how many times the cuff around his ankle had shocked him, the hours blending together as he carefully leaned his left side against the wall. The knife through his chest ached, his body trying to heal around the wound.

"Go on," Baldy spurred. "Remove it, see what happens." He kicked at a rock, and Axel shifted to the side seconds before it could hit, the blade sinking closer to his heart.

"Where is he?" Axel asked for what must have been the thousandth time. He could feel Titus, knowing he was close, but he couldn't seem to connect. Every time he stretched out his awareness, he heard nothing but white noise, and then the cuff ignited and cut him off.

Dust rained down in intervals, the ceiling vibrating as something heavy passed above. There was nothing on the three walls that surrounded him, nothing but endless grey and some paler lines that looked like metal had been scraped against the surface. The room he faced was much larger, with movement for the first time in hours. The light was limited, and even with his enhanced eyesight, they strained to make out the shapes in the darkness.

Baldy stretched out his wings, the black feathers and membrane blocking his view for a second before snapping closed. The hole in his head had closed, leaving only a shadowed mark. He had been hit twice more, and Axel had taken great pleasure in knowing one of the bullets had lodged against one of his ribs. He hoped it fucking hurt.

"I need a piss."

Baldy just rustled his wings in reply.

"Fine," Axel muttered as he glanced down at the cuff, the silver covered in markings that burned a deep red as if embers consumed the metal. "Don't moan if I get bored and piss on you." It wasn't druid magic, the runes harsher in shape as it began to tighten. Axel braced himself as his tattoos brightened with the wave, his muscles forced to tense. Ten seconds, that was how long it lasted.

His body slumped, but he caught himself before he fell on the knife that protruded an inch from his chest. Each breath was agonising, and he knew that if he pulled it out, he may nick his heart, the magic in the blade temperamental.

"Piss anywhere near me and I'll cut it off," Baldy said as he cocked his head, the sight amusing as his horns caught the fabric of his shirt.

Axel couldn't help his strained laugh, especially as

Baldy had to rip the tip of his horn free to leave a tear. "You're new at this, aren't you?"

Without a word he turned towards the room, and Axel glared at the two Daemons who stood by the centre, illuminated in a harsh light.

"I'm going to enjoy this," Baldy chuckled, walking out of the three walls. "Almost as much as I'm going to enjoy destroying that cat. I've never taken an Omega before, I wonder if he'll squeal different?"

Axel snarled, shoving forward until he reached the end of his chain. Bishop watched him from a distance, but it was the other Daemon that caught Axel's attention. He was huge, not counting the wings that must have been at least twenty-five feet when spread. He stood with the confidence of never being denied and when his gaze settled on Axel's he froze, beast silent. His gaze was ancient, old enough Axel felt it in his bones.

"It must be a decade or so since I first heard of these druids hunting us down," he said, his voice a deep rumble that carried across the distance with ease. "Guardians trained to kill my kind."

Axel tensed, muscles stiffening as the wave started once more. Baldy appeared in his peripheral, a chain rattling over his shoulder as he dragged something heavy behind. It took a second for Axel to realise what it was, his jaw clenched so tight as he waited for the wave to end and release him.

"Ti!" he shouted, except it came out more of a whispered puff, his arm weakly reaching out.

Titus was dragged behind, leaving a red smear from the open wound on his back. His eyes were open, liquid silver glazed over as he remained limp.

"This Guardian has been interesting to learn," the greater Daemon said as Baldy yanked Titus violently. "His body's able to withstand more magic than I thought possible for someone that hasn't ascended. He hasn't screamed once. Fascinating really."

"Stay the fuck away from him!" Axel shouted, louder this time as he yanked at the cuff around his ankle. The heavy metal bit into his skin, but he didn't care. "You've got me, do what you want with me!"

"You?" the Daemon appeared before him, drifting the distance in a second. "Why would we choose *you*?" The packet of three pills appeared in his hand, and with a chuckle he dropped them just out of reach. "I must say, my kind have feared you for so long, but you, you're a disappointment." He crouched, a slow smile curving his lips. "I bet you would've screamed for me, and even if you didn't, I wonder how long we can tease you with whatever poison you're addicted to before you break?"

With a click he appeared back over with Bishop, the floor beneath their feet breaking open.

"Please!" Axel shouted, "use me. Let him go!"

Baldy finally reached the centre, unhooking the cuff around Titus's ankle. The floor around him continued to open, the cracks rumbling as Axel climbed to his feet.

Steadying himself on the wall, he called to his cousin. "Ti, get up! Fight this!"

Titus groaned, rolling onto his side. It showed his back, the skin stripped to muscle with the edges seared, flesh blackened. Slices had been made along his shoulders, shapes and marks that continued to bleed down his skin. Some of the wounds should have started to heal, but most looked fresh, raw.

The greater Daemon gestured to Titus, who was trying to settle his weight on his palms. "I wonder what will happen if he ascends?"

Axel snarled, the cracks on the floor brightening until red light poured out. Titus had been placed in the centre of two concentric circles, runes Axel recognised appearing in the gap in between. He had been shoved into a summoning circle, one used for calling, and trapping Daemons.

"This wasn't the fucking deal, Bishop! My soul! You're supposed to use my soul!"

Bishop pulled his auburn hair up into a ponytail, a small smile curving his lips. "Don't worry, we have your soul too." He disappeared in a puff of smoke, only to reappear a moment later holding a young woman, her body shaking as she silently cried. She held a book to her chest, lips trembling as she spoke quietly beneath her breath.

"Your fellow Guardian has already passed several tests, so we're going to skip a few steps for his ascension," the greater Daemon said, holding his hand out to the woman. "I'm sure he'll be able to take it, he's taken everything else I've given."

The woman took a step forward, unable to release the book as the Daemon yanked her closer. With a long fingernail he stroked down her cheek, catching the tears that flowed freely.

"This is for our freedom?" she said, voice a quiver that barely carried. "For the greater good?"

Bishop smiled, stepping closer to touch her shoulder. He looked almost human, the sharpness to his features softening and his body covered in a band t-shirt and jeans rather than armour. His horns were hidden, as were his wings, and his eyes had transformed into a warm brown. "Let the light guide you."

Her face glowed, effervescence radiating from her smile before the greater Daemon reached over and slit her throat. There was no change in her expression, her blood a violent stain that soaked the front of her white dress. It wasn't a simple trickle, the spray wide as it landed on the circle, only to sizzle and hiss at the contact.

She fell just as another wave scored through Axel's body, forcing him to his knees as he groaned through the shock. Titus had finally settled himself on all fours, head hung low between his arms as his shoulders trembled to hold his weight.

The blood soaked into the runes, brightening the already vivid light that emitted from the cracks.

The greater Daemon turned his head, meeting Axel's eyes for the briefest second before his lips moved, and Titus screamed.

"Ti!" Axel tried to reach forward, but nothing could stop as Titus twisted into a painful angle, back bowing until he made a perfect arch. Every glyph along his body glowed, seeming to pulsate along with his cries. "No!"

Rage burned like fire in the pit of Axel's stomach, growing as he thrashed against his chain. His beast roared, and Axel vibrated with energy as he turned to his ankle, the skin slick with blood. With all his strength he hit down, his bone groaning, but didn't break.

Wings in his vision. "What the fuck do you –"

On his second hit his ankle shattered, his foot twisting enough along with the blood lubrication to slip out of the cuff seconds before it began its next wave. He immediately changed into his beast, allowing the magic to course through his veins as he turned to Baldy, his large jaws snapping straight around the Daemon's throat.

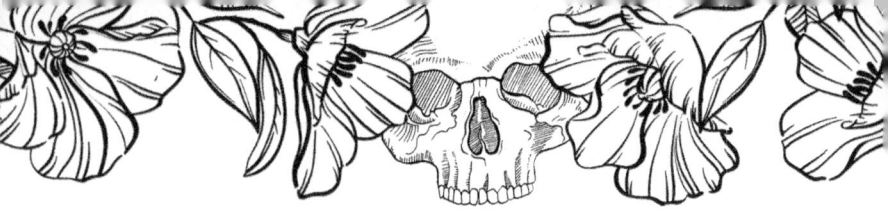

SAM

Fuck, he ached, the dull pain something he tried not to focus on. So instead Sam concentrated on the silence, anxiety a pressure at the back of his mind as he walked behind Riley and Alice, with Lucy by his side. Lucy wasn't one to remain quiet for so long, making Sam's nerves one hundred times worse. It was uncharacteristic, especially considering Lucifer didn't even growl at the man who had rudely thrust a leaflet into his face. Sam expected a burst of violence, not a sharp glare and slight grumble.

Fuck. Calm down, he thought, absently brushing his fingers over the cool metal of the gun strapped to his chest like some cop wannabe.

"Are we any closer?" he finally asked, unable to bear the silence between them any longer. He was going to burst, the tension so tight he was surprised he hadn't already. He was in sensory overload, the train station a chaos to his nose and ears as they walked through the crowd, trying not to draw attention. Well, as much as a group of people dressed in black and covered in weapons could be discreet. Sam was surprised no one had called the transport police already.

Riley had tracked Axel and Titus down in the underground, the signal tentative as they took the stairs down to the platform, a train just leaving as it whipped up a gust of air.

Alice looked over at Riley, who cocked his head as if listening to something Sam couldn't hear.

"Do you know," Sam continued as if he had verbal diarrhoea, which was entirely possible. "I think it's super creepy that the Guardians can communicate in their minds like some dysfunctional superpower."

Riley turned to look over his shoulder, blue eyes piercing. "Xee said their signal is failing, so they're circling back towards us."

"I didn't say it wasn't helpful." Sam bit his lip, flicking his eyes over the commuters who quickly looked away, quickening their pace. "Costume party."

Lucy snorted, the first reaction since they had entered the station. "We're going as sexy assassins."

Riley held up his arm, indicating for them to stop. They had come to the end of the platform, the track empty as he peered into the darkened tunnel to the right. Glancing up at the time board he jumped down, turning to pick Alice up around the waist.

"I could have done that myself, you know," she muttered, shaking his hands off.

His smile was private, and after a second she responded.

"Hey, you can't do that!" someone on the platform shouted. "There's a train coming!"

"Don't worry," Lucifer said with a wave of his hand, stepping down. "We're professionals."

Sam joined them, conscious not to step on the tracks as he met the others at the mouth of the tunnel. It was an endless void, not a spec of light as Alice held out her hand, a ball of light appearing in her palm.

"Lux pila." The ball floated higher, giving them a little illumination in the otherwise pitch black space. "This doesn't look friendly."

"Do you know what," Riley said as he led them single file into the tunnel, Alice's light guiding the way. "I think it's super creepy your eyes reflect the light."

Sam couldn't help the laughter that burst, breaking through the nerves that was eating him slowly. "Touché."

Pulling out his torch, he flicked on the switch, Lucy reaching up to turn on the circular light attached to his head. He turned to Sam with a grin.

"You look ridiculous," Sam said, hitting the side of his torch when it dimmed. "But also genius. Why didn't I think of that?"

"It's handsfree," he said, punching the air.

Riley whistled. "Guys!"

The wind whipped up violently, lights appearing in the distance.

"Incoming," Alice called as they all pressed their backs to the wall. The train passed in a bright blur, the rattle of metal a thunder of sound that vibrated the air far closer than was comfortable.

Lucifer growled, rats scattering from between their feet. "There's Veyn down here, I can sense the fuckers."

"We need to keep moving," Riley said, moving faster than before. "I don't trust the signal not to drop out, plus the authorities are probably going to start sending people to get us." The tracks split into two, and after a second hesitation Riley chose left. "Luce, can you puff further up and see if there's any doors or exits?"

"Puff?" Lucifer said, insulted. "Fucking puff?"

The pressure dropped, and Lucifer jumped from

behind the group to further along the tunnel, his little light bobbing with every step.

Squinting into the darkness, Sam was careful where he walked, keeping to the left as Lucy disappeared, continuing to search further ahead. Sam wasn't sure how long they walked, long enough he felt himself becoming agitated once more. "Alice, what's it like to be mated?" He had asked her that question before, but this time it was different. The idea of being stuck with one person had always been horrifying, to be bound to someone forever. Logically he knew it wasn't forever, but Sam valued his independence so strongly that it was all he could concentrate on.

Alice shrugged. "That's hard to answer, all of our mating bonds are unusual."

"Our beasts seem to react differently per couple," Riley added. "It's not a typical mating, the soul bond unique to each individual. If you ask Kace he would probably say he had no control, his beast bonding to Eva without either of them realising it, which makes us believe there's more magic involved than we initially realised."

"Shifters mate, but it's a bond similar to a pack," Sam said. "We don't call it magic."

"Humans marry." Alice shrugged. "They have no magic, but they don't believe their joining is any less. It's not about the magic, it's about sharing burdens and supporting each other through anything."

"It's a partnership," Riley said, the tattoos along his arms glowing gently. He pressed his back against the wall, Alice and Sam following as another train shot past.

Sam kicked at a rat that tried to nibble his boots, the critter almost the size of his foot. "How do you know if they're the one? That it's real and not just some chemicals in your brain telling you they're just attractive?"

"I knew," Riley answered, stopping to turn. "I knew a

lot quicker than Alice did, that's for sure. Maybe because of my beast? I don't know, I just knew she was it for me, attitude and all."

"Careful," Alice warned with a quiet smile. She brushed her hand against his chest, and his eyes teased silver at the edges. "I won't forget the attitude comment."

"Xander was similar," Riley continued. "His beast attached itself to Kyra long before Xee could see past his prejudice."

"And Kace was... Kace," Alice said with a chuckle. "Everyone deserves to have their own person." Her last words were aimed at him, but Sam dropped his gaze.

"Aye, may –" An high-pitched screech, the hairs on the back of his neck reacting to the sharp sound.

"Fucking prick!" Lucifer's voice boomed from the distance, a single dot of light. "Why can't you just fucking die?"

Running further down they found Lucifer on his back, what looked like a hellhound snapping at his face. Except it didn't have a canine face, the snout split into eight to reveal several circular rows of razor-sharp teeth. Its ribs were spread out like novelty wings, pale white compared to the black of the scales.

"What the fuck is that?" Sam asked, hand automatically going towards his pistol. It looked like an obscene flower, with each piece of snout a scary petal.

Alice grabbed her sword, but before she could swing Lucifer pushed it off, the creature catching itself against the opposite wall and landing perfectly on its feet. It definitely wasn't a hound, it's body much skinnier with an uncomfortably long neck. Its legs were almost feline, the paws covered in fur like a pair of fluffy socks.

"Shadow-Veyn," Riley said calmly, as if he was

discussing the weather rather than something from a nightmare. "Classification C."

"You say that like I'm supposed to know the significance," Sam said as the evil flower hissed, swinging its grotesque head from side to side. There were no eyes, the face stripped back to reveal empty sockets. "Is Classification C bad?"

"They're all bad."

"Oi," Lucifer bated, swinging his arms. "You ugly fucker!"

The Shadow-Veyn pounced without hesitation, following Lucifer's voice as he braced for the impact. His arms burst into dark red flames, mouth opening in a vicious grin as he caught the creature. It landed heavily, the weight sending him staggering back and knocking into Sam, who caught his foot on the tracks.

"Shit." Bending down so the Veyn's strike struck the wall rather than his head, he yanked, and as he pulled free the space beneath his feet gave way.

Landing with a grunt he crouched, the surrounding darkness a void as he tried desperately to keep calm. His entire body complained, each bone rattling as if he was over a century rather than late twenties. He could hear footsteps, the scuttering of creatures that were invisible in the dark. Releasing a growl, he heard them all scramble, except a single pair of red eyes in the distance that remained.

A train rustled above, sending stones and debris raining down.

"Sam?" Alice called, but he couldn't look away from the eyes, a mixture of fear and frustration freezing his body. "You okay?"

Reaching down slowly Sam searched for his torch, releasing a breath when he felt the familiar plastic. It flicked on with a whine, the light not as strong as he swung it towards the eyes, only to find nothing but empty space. Dirt surrounded him on all sides, wooden beams keeping the structure from crumbling.

Alice called down once more. "Sam?"

"There's a tunnel beneath the underground!" he shouted back, moving the torch to where Alice's head appeared overhead. "Fuck!" He must have fallen several stories, the fluttering of wings as bats escaped through the newly made gap.

"Mother fucker!" Lucifer dropped down beside him, his little light on his forehead broken. He pulled it from his head, a disgruntled curse before he began to shake it violently. "Bloody... fucking."

"Give it here," Sam said, grabbing the small torch. The batteries rattled inside, loose as he opened the top. "Here." He handed Lucy the light, and he quickly placed it back on his head.

"Cheers." His front was covered in a green slime, a few cuts along his jaw that bled down his neck. "The train," he said with a grin, and Sam didn't need the visual of the evil flower thing being crushed beneath.

A thump, Riley landing beside them. He looked towards Lucifer, who disappeared before returning seconds later with Alice.

"That's quite some distance," Riley said, peering up. "These could be anything. Old mining shafts or evacuation tunnels from the war."

"There's tracks," Alice pointed out.

Riley frowned. "There must be –"

A deep scream reverberated from the darkness, one full of such pain Sam felt it within his chest. "Is that...?" he began as Riley rushed forward. "Hey, wait!"

The light bobbed as he chased after him, the tunnel

becoming tighter before it opened out into a large room that split into three routes. Tracks went in every direction, the metal old and warped. Boxes lay forgotten, empty on the side with some of the wooden panels broken and splintered.

Riley didn't stop his stride, head whipping around before he transformed into an amazing white beast. He shot down the centre shaft, following the red light that glowed in the distance before Alice slid to a halt.

"Fuck," she muttered, holding her sword in both hands. Two hounds emerged, one from the left and another from the right. They were much larger than the ugly flower, with green gunk seeping from between their teeth, sizzling as soon as it hit the dirt. They stepped over the tracks with ease, nails scraping against the metal.

"Go, get Axel and Ti!" Lucifer growled, drifting over to the first hound and punching it in square the head, the move so unexpected and fast Sam wasn't sure it even happened. "Go!" He threw a ball of arcane at the second, burning down its side as Alice grabbed Sam's arm, launching them towards the centre tunnel.

Red light illuminated the way, sickening thuds echoing behind as the tunnel opened out into a large room. Alice didn't hesitate, taking the situation in one quick sweep as she called arcane to her hands.

Sam didn't care, not as Riley fought Bishop, the Daemon teasing as he drifted from one space to another. He threw balls of fiery red, each one missing Riley who jumped out the way surprisingly elegantly for his sheer size.

Titus lay contorted in the middle, his scream harrowing as the circle surrounding him pulsed a violent red. A lady lay dead beside, her eyes open and palms clutching a book with blood a halo around her head.

Sam looked around, panic building as he searched for Axel, finding nothing but another corpse in the corner, torn in two with its head a few feet away. It made his heart stop, a cry escaping his throat until he stepped closer, Alice's warning a muffled shout.

Horns, the head had horns.

So where the fuck was Axel?

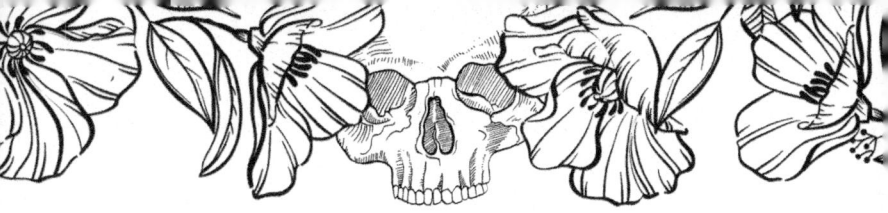

CHAPTER 35

SAM

He wasn't sure what he expected, the feeling of such panic a weight he never knew he could experience. He ignored the danger to step closer, Alice pulling him to the side to dodge any over-shot arcane. His skin burned as the magic dissipated, but as soon as it had gone, he shrugged out of her hold, searching in every little nook built into the walls, chains glinting in each one.

"Sam, we got to..."

They seemed to be open cells, and a rock settled in Sam's gut, so cold it numbed when he realised Axel wasn't in any of them.

Where could he be? Sam scanned the rest of the room, unable to see any other exit or entrance.

"Sam?"

His ears buzzed, the idea that he wasn't there, that he was already gone was enough to bring Sam to his knees, and it was only Alice that kept him steady as chaos surrounded them in a blur.

Alice's voice drifting in and out. "Sam, I need to help Ti..."

"He's not here." He couldn't sense him, blood, piss and one hundred different scents confusing his nose. "Alice, he's not..."

Sam grabbed Alice just as the hound revealed itself, teeth so close they brushed against her arm. It stunk of carrion and death, its stench giving him a second warning as she turned, and grabbing Sam's gun, shot the hound in the head. She shoved the weapon back into Sam's hand, grabbing her sword just as the hound shook the bullet free.

"Get it together," she said, eyes glistening. "We'll find him, but not if you get yourself killed."

Sam lifted the gun, the metal surprisingly heavy in his hand, and pulled the trigger. He had never used one before, but being so close, the three bullets sank into the hound with little aim. Not one stopped its advance as Alice tried to push it back with strikes of her sword and magic. Fire and lightning poured from her hands, and as Sam aimed once more something wrapped around his waist, pulling back hard enough it expelled the air from his lungs.

Reaching for the knife strapped to his thigh Sam went to cut, but was released just before the blade slit the rope of fur. Gun lifted he turned, only to face one of the most beautiful beings he had ever seen.

Sam had never seen Axel as his beast, but he knew it was him, without a doubt as he looked into the familiar silver eyes. He was both beautiful and terrifying, body built for power as well as stealth. He stood tall, far larger than any shifter with his head reaching Sam's chest. His fur was a multitude of greys, split with lines of black that were identical markings to the tattoos that Sam had traced on the man. It was a tail that had grabbed him, one of seven that moved like whips towards the hound.

Blood coated his snout, much darker than the blood on his side which revealed large lacerations so deep muscle was a shock of red. Burns scorched his chest while his back leg was twisted, the ankle broken as he stepped around Sam to attack. There was no competition, the Veyn falling beneath his powerful jaws within seconds, his body expelling the green poison from every swipe of the hound's claws.

Sam stood frozen, the relief so powerful his heart beat a powerful ache.

"Get down!" Alice threw her arms around him as she knocked them both to the ground, a burst of heat soaring above. The arcane hit the wall, exploding as he quickly rolled until Alice was beneath, gritting his teeth as the sparks rained down against his back. The little licks of magic seared against his skin, eating away as a howl rocked the room, a commanding bay that drowned out the squelch of Axel shredding the hound.

Riley took a hit to the chest, but Bishop looked worse, the wings from his back torn clean off while gashes sliced his face almost in half. He no longer held a smile, his arm held tightly to his chest. With a look of pure abhorrence he disappeared, not returning as Riley howled once more.

Alice shoved against him, pulling herself free while he jumped to his feet, chest tight and hands shaking. The hound's head plopped by their feet, a sickening thud as Axel tore a leg.

"Get back!" Alice said, yanking Sam's shoulder. "They're not always –"

Axel whipped round with a growl, leg still held in his jaws. He dropped low, ears flattening as he flicked his attention between Alice and Sam. His claws kneaded the ground, eyes settling on Alice before Sam stepped forward.

"Hey big guy, remember me?" Sam kept his voice soft. "Aye, of course you do," he mused, wanting to wrap himself in the beast's warmth. To stroke down his fur with his own until Axel wore his scent. "You've had your hand down my joggers."

Beast blinked, dropping the mangled leg at Sam's feet. It rolled towards his boots, the fur stripped to the bone. Black vapour coated the entire thing, dancing around the wound as if it were trying to heal. Beast cocked his head, tongue lapping at the blood around his snout before he flicked his head back and returned Riley's howl. More calls joined, echoing from the tunnels as Beast burst into a white light, the man standing there seconds later.

Sam caught Axel as he sagged, a knife protruding from his chest. "Fuck!" It was so close to his heart. "I've got you."

"Ti?" Axel swayed, and Sam tightened his grip. "T... Ti?"

The screaming had stopped, and Sam turned to find Alice beside Titus, the circle no longer glowing. "Aye, we've got him, it's going to be okay." Tears burned down his face, a featherlight touch brushing along his cheek.

"You're so fucking beautiful," Axel murmured, his eyes glazed, fading as his hand fell away.

"Hey, stay with me!"

Axel convulsed, forcing them both to their knees. His chest rattled, the skin around the knife darkening to grey.

"Axel, please!" Sam didn't have any healing ability, and with every passing second Axel's breaths slowed. "You can't leave me now, not after making me fall for you!"

"What happened?" Lucifer dropped beside them. His hand touched the knife, only to snap back as an electrical spark shot from the end. "Fucking hell, it's pierced his heart."

"Help him!" Sam snarled, leaning down to press his forehead to Axel's. Touch centred shifters, calmed their animals as Sam called on a purr, the vibration light. Axel wasn't a shifter, but that didn't matter, because he was *his*.

276

"I'm sorry," Axel said, voice barely above a whisper. "Love you."

The tears came hot and fast, the kiss wet when Sam brushed his lips to Axel's.

"Brace yourself, this is going to fucking hurt." Lucifer reached for the dagger, sparks trying to push him away before he pulled out the blade in one, clean movement. Blood pumped like a fountain from the wound, and Axel gasped, eyes drifting closed.

"Axel?!"

Lucifer pressed against the hole, his palms glowing as he clenched his jaw. Alice appeared over his shoulder, eyes wide as she called for Riley.

"Fuck, he's stopped breathing." Lucifer began to pump Axel's chest, Alice trying to pull Sam away.

He refused to let go, needing to let Axel know he was there, for him to feel his bare skin as if the simple connection would be enough. A flicker of heat had settled in his chest, a determination that blazed hotter than any fire.

"You can't do this! You're fucking mine!" Sam reached for the flicker, instincts driving him to open his heart, to allow the connection he never truly understood and had never wanted.

Until now.

Sam gasped as something deep inside snapped taut.

"You're mine Axel, do you hear me? In life, soul and everything that comes after."

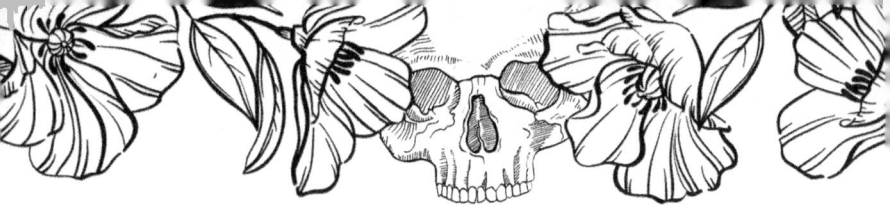

CHAPTER 36
EPILOGUE

SAM
SIX WEEKS LATER

"I don't think I've ever seen you nervous," Axel said, squeezing Sam's hand as they stood outside the door to his grandmother's home. "It's fine, she's gonna love you!"

"Maybe," Sam muttered, pushing his hair behind his ears. He'd never had to meet the family. "But... what if she doesn't?"

Axel laughed, rolling his eyes as he pressed the doorbell. "Then she's a fool, but I know she's –"

The door whipped open, revealing a tiny woman with pure white hair and dark eyes that glistened with mischief. "Who's a fool?"

"Errr, not you Lǎolao!" Axel said quickly, bending down to kiss her on the cheek, but she was already pushing past him to peer up at Sam.

"There he is," she said with such a warm smile, it was like being welcomed home, rather than meeting a stranger. "Come, come. My Axel's told me so much about the cat who wouldn't give him a chance."

Sam shot Axel a pointed look, but he only shrugged in reply, a laugh shaking his chest.

Guided by the tiny woman, Sam followed her up the flight of stairs into a warm and welcoming flat. It was hard to envision both Axel and Titus growing up there, the rooms small but cosy, decorated with so many photographs of the two of them laughing. Spices and meat scented the air, along with so many teas they lined one of the back walls.

"Thank you Mrs Liu," Sam said as he was ushered down into a chair. "You have such a beautiful home."

Titus smirked from the seat opposite, hidden in the corner by the wall.

"Please, call me Lǎolao." She placed a large bowl in the centre of the table before moving towards the connected kitchen.

Sam couldn't help his smile. "Lǎolao," he repeated, saying it with her pronunciation rather than Axel's.

"Hmmm, something smells –" Axel froze when he noticed his cousin. Sam knew there was still so much left unsaid between them, Titus's recovery taking far longer than Axel's. But they had done it together, refusing to leave each other's side despite it.

"All my boys together," Lǎolao said with delight, squeezing her hand over Sam's before placing another, smaller bowl in front of Titus. "Don't worry, Ti, it'll be your turn next to find someone special. Actually, my friend Susan's granddaughter's just come –"

"We're making dumplings," Titus interrupted his grand-mother's attempt at matchmaking, shuffling awkwardly in his chair. Axel sat to Sam's left, the table dwarfed by the two men, while Lǎolao took the remaining seat to his right.

"We must teach Sam how to make the perfect dumpling," she said. "My Axel loves his dumplings." Her grin was infectious, as was her enthusiasm as she explained every step in making the filling, and then the dough.

"Like this?" he said after a while, staring at his pathetic attempt at closing the wrapper.

"No, no," she chuckled. "Like this. Pinch, pinch, pinch." Lǎolao carefully demonstrated how to fold the dumpling with more patience than he had, both Axel and Titus sniggering with their perfectly prepared ones.

Sam's brows came together in concentration. "Aye, just you wait," he said to them. "This time next year, I'll be a master."

Lǎolao chuckled, supervising as she carefully moved them into the steamers. She'd asked him about his life, about his work and his parents. Axel had tried to redirect the conversation, talking about the legal proceedings regarding his old landlord but Sam had decided to be honest about his upbringing.

He didn't have a home full of love with his parents, didn't have an entire childhood where he could look back and have happy memories. And that was okay, because without everything he had suffered, he wouldn't be the strong leopard he had grown to be. He wouldn't have met his best friend, and he wouldn't have met Axel.

He had no idea if his father still lived or not, and he'd decided pretty quickly as he watched over Axel's recovery, that he didn't care.

He wasn't a fighter, and unless his da threatened someone he loved, Sam wouldn't give the man that had sired him another second thought. He was nothing but the past, and Sam only looked towards the future.

A future with his mate.

Mate.

Sam smiled, turning to find Axel watching with an effervescence that radiated from within.

I love you. Sam may have not gained any cool telepathic superpowers when they mated, but Axel knew, Sam made sure he showed it often.

Axel smiled, and Sam couldn't believe he was lucky enough to have someone to call his own.

The table jolted, Lăolao scolding Titus who had 'accidentally' kicked Axel. "What you looking at, Pretty Boy? Cat got your tongue?"

"Your face beneath my boot in a minute," Axel growled, forcing Sam to laugh as he returned to his lesson.

He hadn't only gained a partner when they'd mated, but also a pack, a family. For years it had just been him and Alice, connected on a spiritual level through trauma. Now when he looked at the threads of life, he was tied to them all, the Guardians more than just brothers in word, but in spiritual magic too.

For the first time that Sam could remember, he was whole. He didn't feel trapped, or have the need to add others to his bed. Not even when Axel had said he was open, that he would never stop Sam from what he wanted. That he would love him regardless.

It had taken Sam too long to realise love wasn't simple, it wasn't about opening your soul and making yourself vulnerable. It was an equal partnership, about sharing your life, and sharing theirs in return.

And Sam was more than ready to finally share everything with his mate.

It was as if he and Axel were always meant to be, and Sam had just been too stubborn to see it sooner. It was something he would never repeat, because Axel was his, and he wasn't letting go.

AXEL

Axel watched Sam laugh along with his grandmother, both facing the steamer as she told him every embarrassing story from his childhood that she could remember. He drank the foul-tasting tea, Lǎolao none the wiser for the reason he'd asked for the specific one. He wasn't sure if it helped with the cravings, the intrusive thoughts still there, just quieter. Some days were better than others, but his mate was there to support him.

'How's the withdrawal?' Ti asked, linking their minds as Sam continued to win their grandmother over with his charm. Not that he needed to even try, she was smitten from his first smile.

'Manageable.' Many times he'd caught himself losing his temper over little things, his body aching for a substance he refused to give. *'Sam's helping.'*

'Helping? That's what we're calling it now?'

Axel smiled, elbowing Titus in the arm while taking another sip of his tea. He tried to hide his grimace, the liquid somehow both sour and sweet at the same time.

He'd been hurt, the blade piercing his heart to the point they weren't sure he was going to survive. Lucifer, out of everyone, was the one who reacted, using his arcane to cauterize the wound closed until he was strong enough to heal on his own.

Axel remembered floating, the feeling of weightlessness in the dark and then an intense pull, one he couldn't ignore. The next thing he knew he had woken up in a very white bed, an exhausted leopard asleep tightly to his side.

'How you feeling?' he asked, knowing that since the underground, Titus had become reclusive, locking himself up in his room for longer periods of time or disappearing to their apartment. *'What did Lǎolao think of the eyes?'*

Titus had changed since the underground, even if he wouldn't admit anything was wrong. He was still the same cocky arsehole who had stolen all the sheets from his bedroom only the other day, replacing them with bright pink ones covered in kittens. But there was a difference, something in his aura that had darkened. Then there were his eyes, no longer bourbon but a deep burgundy as unique as Sam's amber.

Titus touched the freshly pierced silver ring that went through the centre of his bottom lip, matching the one in his left nostril. *'If she noticed, she didn't comment. She's too distracted with Sam to even notice your limp.'*

Guilt sat heavily on his chest. *'Ti... I –'*

'There's nothing to say,' he interrupted, upper lift lifting into a curve. *'Nothing to forgive.'*

Axel felt dryness prickle his eyes, but he quickly blinked it away. *'Yeah, well I haven't forgiven* you *yet. Pink sheets with kittens, really?'* At Titus's chuckle he continued. *'Sam thinks it's hilarious, he won't let me throw them away.'*

'Who says your mate wasn't involved in picking the sheets?'

Axel watched his cousin through the corner of his eye. *'I swear, if you bring him into our war...'* He let the threat settle.

Ti's smirk was wide, and Axel groaned at what was to come. Looked like he was going to be buying more glitter.

'Hey, what did you do with that information I sent you?' Titus asked, suddenly serious.

'I did what had to be done.' Titus had found Sam's father, and his so-called pack. It hadn't taken Axel long to report them to White Dawn, causing the pack to be permanently disbanded per shifter law. Axel himself had dealt with Sam's father, needing to know he could never harm his mate again.

'You think that's what Sam would've wanted?'

'My mate isn't like us,' he replied. 'He's pure hearted, and that's okay, because he has me to protect him.'

'One less concern for us, I suppose.' Titus leaned back, head cocked in thought. 'Leaves us with those two Daemons —'

'Bishop and Gideon.' Axel had made sure to commit their names to memory, knowing that when they found them, which they would, he'd personally take them to final death.

For Sam, and for Titus.

'They've already sunk their fucking teeth into the Undercity, we need to weed them out before it goes too far,' Axel continued.

Titus grunted in agreement.

Sam's laughter filled up the entire room, such life in the sound that Axel couldn't help but smile.

'I'm so happy for you,' Titus said, voice softer even though the mental connection. 'That you've found someone who loves you the way he does.'

Axel turned to watch his mate, wondering how he'd ever convinced someone so carefree to settle for someone like him. 'I never thought it would happen, and now I can't imagine it any different.' He knew he was lucky that he'd found the other half of his heart, and for once he looked forward to the future, one without pain. A future with a certain cat that made even the roughest storms seem tranquil.

Sam must have felt the attention, his leopard prowling behind his amber irises, darkening with desire when they steadied on Axel.

Titus dramatically gagged, Lǎolao frowning from the kitchen before calling them all back to the table to taste their hard work. Sam sat back in his spot, hand resting on Axel's thigh as he waited like an over-excited child.

Before he could grab a dumpling, Axel reached over and stole one Sam had made, shoving the entire thing in his mouth in one. It burned, the mixture uneven and the wrapper somehow doughy.

Axel swallowed, reaching for another of the terribly formed dumplings. "Delicious."

Sam chuckled, his smile brightening his face. "Liar." Flour marked the tip of his nose, as well as a few streaks across his cheek that Axel gently brushed away. He had new scars there, tiny ones that would fade in time.

They told his story, one Axel was now honoured to be a part of.

Heart of Crimson

He'll do anything to stop her... and she'll do anything to survive.
Preorder Titus & Rae's story
https://mybook.to/HeartofCrimson

Want more of Sam & Axel?

Sign up for my newsletter and get a bonus (sexy) epilogue!
Download!
https://BookHip.com/DBQVSXH

Thank you for reading Whisper of Fate, the third in The Curse of the Guardians series. If you enjoyed this book and would love to see more, I would be forever in your debt if you could leave a review on the platform(s) of your choice!

Reviews are super important and help other readers discover this series.

Much love,
Taylor

P.S. Want a fun, safe place to chat about my books with others? Join my exclusive reader group, Taylor's Supernatural Society!

Keep in touch with Taylor Aston White

Instagram
@tayastonwhite
TikTok
@taylorastonwhite
Facebook
/taylorastonwhite
Website
www.taylorastonwhite.com
Bookbub
www.bookbub.com/profile/taylor-aston-white
Goodreads
www.goodreads.com/taylorastonwhite

Sign up for Taylor's newsletter mailing list to receive updates, exclusive content, giveaways, early excerpts and much more.
Plus there's a free short story!
www.taylorastonwhite.com

About the Author

Taylor Aston White loves to explore mythology and European faerie tales to create her own, modern magic world. She collects crystals, house plants and dark lipstick, and has two young children who like to 'help' with her writing by slamming their hands across the keyboard.

After working several uncreative jobs and one super creative one, she decided to become a full-time author and now spends the majority of her time between her children and writing the weird and wonderful stories that pop into her head.

Printed in Great Britain
by Amazon